MW01539711

". . . a rich view of a unique period in our nation's history."

—BLUE INK REVIEW

"A Poignant, rich story of one family's struggle to survive in postwar America."

—KIRKUS REVIEW

LIGHT IN WINTER

To Cindy

Bless you

[signature]

10/9/14

Copyright © 2013 by O. Henderson Jr.

Library of Congress Control Number:		2013921380
ISBN:	Hardcover	978-1-4931-4418-1
	Softcover	978-1-4931-4417-4
	eBook	978-1-4931-4419-8

All rights reserved. No part of this book may be reproduced or transmitted in any form or by any means, electronic or mechanical, including photocopying, recording, or by any information storage and retrieval system, without permission in writing from the copyright owner.

This is a work of fiction. Names, characters, places and incidents either are the product of the author's imagination or are used fictitiously, and any resemblance to any actual persons, living or dead, events, or locales is entirely coincidental.

Printed in the United States of America by BookMasters, Inc
Ashland OH
September 2014

Scripture taken from the King James Version of the Bible.

Rev. date: 08/28/2014

To order additional copies of this book, contact:
Xlibris LLC
1-888-795-4274
www.Xlibris.com
Orders@Xlibris.com
540837

LIGHT IN WINTER

(A Mama's Prayer)

O. Henderson Jr.

To JH

"She is a tree of life . . ." (Proverbs 3:18)

They still tell the story in Missouri country:

Johna was a slave, but unbowed. When provoked, he refused to work, and his back became a mosaic of scars. Each time he escaped, it took longer to bring him back, and his recovery was astonishing. Old Martin could see that a source of Johna's strength came from Lilja, so he brought her up to the big house. The women tried protecting her, but he accused her of sassing and stealing.

He would flog her himself and in the main yard and in front of everybody. There she hung from the great oak. He put down his cane and picked up the cat-o'-nine-tails, which cracked, hushing the crowd as he tried to produce a scream. But none came.

"Call me master!" He glared at Johna. "Master!"

Men grimaced; women and children cried. Old Martin was sweating and covered with dust when his whip broke. So he grabbed his cane. Suddenly Johna seized his throat, and the overseers battered Johna until he let go.

"NOOO!" Lilja screamed for the first time.

Both men died, and that oak became legendary. The plantation was added to the Jeffersons' acreage.

George's ancestors worked the plantation and took on the Jefferson name. Word was his grandmother was smart and a saint. Which meant she was wise, God answered her prayers, or both. Her sayings and deeds were passed down. As for the Almighty, George reasoned he was the most important relationship a body could have, or an inevitable illusion.

The country had changed more than he realized and much more than his children imagined. There were red and yellow faces before the pale faces wrote the histories, masses rebelling reaching for space. Defeated Indians and whites and black slaves, and with freedom, the blacks migrated North. Asians flooded from east to west as English, Irish, Italians, and Jews kept coming, reaching, jostling, sweating and spitting, mixing . . . in spite of themselves.

George tried to delve deeper into his heritage and to know what these united states meant, what his grandmother meant, and indeed what he meant.

And . . .

Chapter 1

The wind blew from the Mississippi, rushing the hills. In the darkness trees leaned, and the whistling threatened like it didn't care; and whatever was harmed was harmed. A crashing tree echoed from the forest onto the farmland unto the slope cluttered with shanties, where it was reduced to a clap. The shanties blinked as the inhabitants looked out and returned to what they were doing.

The whistling ceased, and a single light was on. Cloth sacks covered the windows. Inside, a kerosene lamp flickered, and three young women packed. They had tended the house and helped in the field. And they had buried their papa yesterday.

Jean had been bossy since her mother died. She was sixteen and a woman. "We have to leave. Old Sam won't let this farm out to no gals." Dark eyes and a narrow face made you study her.

"Where we gonna go?" Mary was skinny like Jean and continued packing. Her braids dangled as she leaned over the faded carpetbag. As the youngest, she was accustomed to taking orders and didn't mind as long as it was fair. She finished and grabbed the broom.

"We gotta stick together." Ruth usually thought before speaking; everyone called her Babe-Ruth. She was eight when their mother died. Her mother's brother and her papa were the only male kinfolk she could recall. She was fourteen, with strong arms and ankles, suggesting that what couldn't be seen was well formed.

With high cheekbones, brown eyes, and thick hair, it was difficult to tell which came first: her mind, which was nurtured by the talk of old folks, or her chin, which seemed forever poised in dignity. Perhaps each fed upon the other; she seemed a creature of a higher order. She finished packing and put biscuits in a tin and her papa's pipes in the sack with the baseball gloves.

Mary began to cry.

"Hush! We need a man. One a' us gotta get married!" Babe-Ruth looked at Jean, who was at the window, folding their papa's overalls.

"I'm sixteen."

"Mama was sixteen when she married Pa . . ."

Babe-Ruth had said enough.

The moonlight shone through the cracks with the sound of beetles; cots squeaked, and they wriggled in and out of dreams.

They were up early and on the road and in single file. Word of mouth carried the news, and they couldn't read. Lilbourn was fifteen miles away. Their pa said to contact Mr. Bull if anything happened. An occasional wagon and truck passed. It got warmer, and they passed the water bottle. Hours went by, and they opened the tin of biscuits and rested under a tree.

"I never walked this far." Mary slipped out of her shoes and wiggled her toes.

"We more than halfway there." Jean passed the bottle, and Mary moistened her feet. "Don't waste that water, girl!"

That evening, they arrived in Lilbourn, a junction not on the map, where trains picked up crops and farmers came to buy hardware and gasoline. Storage bins and oaks formed the skyline. Cape Girardeau (*Cape Jarrod*) was fifty miles away. They stood in front of the General Store under the sun. The porch sagged, and paint peeled from the tobacco sign. Red snuffboxes lined the dust-covered countertop. Mary stayed with the bags. Their pa always brought Mr. Bull something.

"Be there in a minute." Simon was a puffy, red-faced colored missing some lower teeth. He leaned on the counter; an apron hung from his belly as he grinned and spat into a Maxwell House coffee can and wiped his mouth. He ran the place, but he acted like he owned it. "Y'all the Kitchen gals? Well? . . ."

"A bar of that shavin' soap." Babe-Ruth put a nickel down. She remembered that her pa didn't like him. Their pa hadn't said so, but they could tell.

"Sorry, about your pa." Babe-Ruth took the package and pulled Jean. "Don't be in such a hurry." He spat again. "How you gonna support yourselves. Got people around here I don't know about? Stay . . . Y'all can help me run things?"

"'Fraid not." Babe-Ruth didn't look up as the door squeaked shut behind them.

"What you gonna do? I gotta good business." Tobacco juice ran from his mouth as he followed them out.

"No!" She nudged Mary, who tightened her grip on her bag.

"Is you the boss? Can't your sisters speak for themselves!"

"She said it right." Jean skipped, and they broke into a trot.

"Y'all always thought you were something." His voice trailed off, and they couldn't hear him. "Coming roun' with your noses up in the air and that big butt of yours. Gal, you ain't nothin'!" He coughed, spitting tobacco. "Y'all po es dirt!"

A half hour passed, and Mr. Bull's cabin appeared between the trees. He was in the field and put down his pail. They ran at him, and Mary hugged him first.

"Howdy, Mr. Bull."

"Howdy back at ya. Well, y'all made it." He wiped bobbing his hat. "Sorry about your pa . . . a good man . . . all of that."

He put his hat back on and pawed the dirt. He wasn't at the funeral and had his own ways. He didn't like all the crying and carrying on and figured that once a body was dead, there was nothing more to do than keep on doing what you should. He spent a lot of time in the fields with the sun beating down, grasshoppers jumping around his boots, and his sweat soaking into the ground. He figured only the Almighty could bring rain and make the crops grow, and he was the main one he listened to. Most viewed him as an old hermit, but their papa trusted him.

Strange soul that he was, the girls felt comfortable with him, and about every three months they would visit. He usually gave them candy, and they stretched while he and their pa talked. They hadn't thought about it at the time, but the talks were serious. Mr. Bull was a widower, tall, silvery haired, with a flat overpowering nose and bearing like a soldier. The cabin had a large porch, with a well and pump, and an outhouse in back. They followed him in. There was a bedroom and a wide kitchen.

"Y'all sleep in there. I'll use the hammock on the porch."

"Papa said we should come see you."

"We discussed it some."

Jean and Mary took a short nap, and Babe-Ruth played with the dogs while Mr. Bull finished cooking.

The dining table contained two chairs and a stove, and he went to the bedroom and returned with another chair and set the table. He bowed quickly, scratched, and left again and returned with a sack. Babe-Ruth dished the beans, and Mary cut the corn bread. Jean slid him the package of soap, thinking he had delicate hands for a farmer. He nodded.

"Yo papa told me to give y'all this when that day come." He handed Jean the sack. "I was his bank." He passed the onions, but there were no takers. "They started calling you Babe-Ruth . . . 1927. Said you had a knack for baseball."

He chuckled, pushing the onion in his mouth with a spoonful of beans, meaning it was more than playing baseball that made her papa give Ruth that nickname.

Jean put her spoon down. "We're looking to marry somebody who'll let the other two stay with them awhile."

"You won't find nobody like that in no town!"

They had him thinking, and he didn't look up again until he was finished. The moon was out, and he stood in front of the screen door a long time. Crickets chimed as they snuggled in the feather bed. He squirmed in the hammock.

Morning came, and at first they didn't remember where they were.

"Time to get up. We got business and it don't wait for nobody."

They eased out, ate leftover corn bread and jam, and washed. He was still thoughtful when he appeared in the doorway and as they boarded the wagon.

"I know a young man, works for his pa' cropping. Done some works for me too, hardworking, don't drink . . . chews. Daddy's the head sharecropper for Jefferson plantation."

They squinted in the sun on the dusty road. Ten miles farther was Colonel Jefferson's big house

Mr. Bull's wagon swayed. They were enjoying the morning and passed rows of coloreds in bandanas and straw hats picking cotton and loading wagons. Finally he stopped the wagon and got down.

"Ephraim, is ya working or socializing? I bet that farm of yourn can run itself."

Mr. Bull didn't laugh. He got down, and the two men moved out of earshot. The talk went on several minutes with frequent glances over at the girls.

Finally Mr. Bull returned mumbling. "Missy Sarah will have her say, then we'll see. Ol' Jesop's hard. Says he needs extra workers. 'Spects y'all to pull your weight. Y'all live yonder for now." He pointed to a cluster of shanties.

After a while, Jesop returned with his son.

"This is Mr. Jesop and son Caleb." Mr. Bull helped them down and said their names. Caleb was dark, the size of a grown man, and seventeen. He had a gap between his upper teeth that was distinctive.

"I knew your pa . . . Mr. Kitchen was a good man." Caleb pulled on his overalls strap and paused. "Everybody 'spected him. I remember when y'all was small." He wiggled the straw in his mouth and stared at Mary, who tried acting older.

"Caleb, take the bags. Then go and fetch Missy Sarah." Jesop turned to Mr. Bull, and they headed toward the shanties.

"The daddy and mama was straight up. Ain't no better way to tell." Mr. Bull paused. "Missy Sarah will approve. If anybody gets cold feet, I expect 'em back like I brought 'em."

They shook hands.

"Hear about that Joe Louis Barrow?" Jesop was carrying the news. "Knocked out by Schmellin'." Mr. Bull shook his head in disgust and got up in his wagon and rode off.

Over the next few months, the girls settled in and worked the fields. The days were hot, and they drank plenty of water. August was even hotter; the rains brought relief in September.

Monarchs blanketed the meadow in early October. The mist was thick, and Jesop couldn't see very far. A caterpillar moved on his sleeve, and the sun reflected in his eyes. He put the pail down and leaned against the ancient tree. He was thinking about his daddy, who he had never known but had been a slave; their stories occurred in his dreams with tales of runaways, ghosts, and talking critters.

Jesop headed up to his shanty, poured water into a basin, and grabbed a towel. "You beat me up this mornin'."

Caleb grinned. "Couldn't sleep. Got up . . . Did me some thinking." He broke corn bread into mush.

"Pour yo'self some coffee and me some too." Caleb put strips of jowl into the frying pan and poured. "Which one is you done chose?"

Caleb paused. "Jean's pretty . . . Babe-Ruth got a way about her."

"I know what you mean."

"When I'm sure, I'll tell Missy Sarah. Then Mr. Bull can fetch the preacher."

Jesop's gray hair was combed back. His face descended to Caleb with the same eyes and jaw and gap between his upper front teeth. His first wife died, and their three boys were spread all over the country. His daughter, Mildred, lived up in New Jersey and was fifteen years older than Caleb. His second marriage was childless, and one day she disappeared. Caleb was his third wife's child, and she died a few months after Caleb was born. Jesop was the plantation boss, and all the sharecroppers dealt with him. Only Missy Sarah dared contradict him.

The oak was more than six stories high, with wide leaves, acorns, squirrels, birds, and a trunk that frowned. Steffers Jefferson immigrated to the New World from England. He was tall and bony with a red neck and couldn't hold a tan. He begot six sons and three daughters. Spurn and brother Cliff widened the farm when cotton was good. Cliff begot Standard, who begot Sheth, who expanded and bought slaves. Sheth begot Lem, who begot Jonathan, who became a gentleman farmer. Jonathan's son, Samual, went to military college and became a colonel; his son became an officer too.

The big house's pillars ran up to the roof, with a porch upstairs and downstairs and eight bedrooms, a winding staircase, and a chandelier.

Upstairs, the colonel looked in the mirror while Jim, his manservant, shaved him. The blue-and-white porcelain chamber pot in the corner matched the face bowl and tub. After that, the colonel put his shirt on and went down to breakfast.

"Sarah, you make the finest biscuits in the world. In the world, I'm tellin' ya!" He peered through the curtains. "It's gonna be a nice one."

"It will if you haven't eaten all of Sarah's biscuits." His son John was beside him. "Sun makes a body feel good."

It was Jefferson land before the Civil War, and Sarah's kin worked the big house. Sarah was as old as the colonel and was there when his wife died giving birth. Sarah wasn't the midwife, and they handed John over to her; she was the only mama he ever knew. She brought in a girl who was about to wean her own child to do the nursing. When that was done, she took over.

Neither father nor son could hold a tan. Both were medium sized, with the same blue eyes, pointed jaw, and long face. Gray hair, bald spot, and the stoop set them apart.

"You shoulda seen that filly run, Pa. You'd a been proud."

"You're good with her, John. The boy and me couldn't get her to run. Wasn't payin' her feed."

The stables were in the rear just off the servants' quarters and the family graveyard.

Later that afternoon, Sarah was baking, and Mr. John stood by the window nibbling an apple. Hanging around the kitchen was something he had done since he was a boy. He liked the sweet smell of baked bread and fruits, and he would often get a taste of what she was cooking, but mainly it was peaceful.

He had been married but divorced, and his wife left him with the child. He put the boy, Tom, in a Northern boarding school. The colonel and John teased Tom, calling him a Yankee. On weekends, John's girlfriend, Loretta, came from Cape Jarrod. She had yellow hair, and Missy Sarah called her a *fluzzie*, but she never explained what that meant. The colonel acted like she wasn't there. Loretta thought of herself as a city girl; Cape Girardeau was twenty miles away and not a city. She talked a lot. It wasn't a problem, and nobody listened.

Chapter 2

F ive miles southward, farmer Jamison let his pasture out for the camp meeting each fall. Blankets speckled the meadow. There were tools to sell or trade and quilts to sell and show. Women brought pies to purchase and for pie-eating competitions. Just east of the big tent, traders and peddlers set up for business until the meeting started.

Jamison had the Birmingham Black Barons down for an exhibition, a masterstroke, and thereafter it was difficult to know if it was a camp meeting or a prayer service sandwiched around the baseball game. Crowds came; the preachers and traders were paying. And with a better field, a controlled spectator area, and an improved tent so as not to be overshadowed by the game, Jamison made some real cash.

Babe-Ruth was excited about the game. Caleb loaded the wagon and got up beside Jesop. Jean and Mary didn't care to come. Two of Jesop's workers, Leslie Hocum and James Bradford, stayed put too.

"Last year Gibson hit a ball I think is still going." Jesop chuckled.

"Coloreds can play as good as anybody." Caleb had seen them play and was relishing the opportunity.

The visiting team, the Cuban Giants, was as black as the Pittsburgh Crawfords, who were making their third exhibition. By being called Cuban, they could play against more white teams. Black ballplayers barnstormed for years and spent their winters in South America, where they were lionized.

Whites sat on benches, and the hills around the diamond were fenced. Red, white, and blue banners lined the fences with the number

400 emblazoned in dead center field. The preacher threw out the first pitch, and everything had the blessing of God.

The revival tent appeared majestic behind center field. The sun beamed on Paige; the word was he was on loan from the Elite Giants. Paige was tall, with a narrow face, perpetually jabbering and slinging his arm like a rubber hose. A roar erupted after a strikeout. The opposing team had the great Josh Gibson and the lightning fast Cool Papa Bell. Vendors sold sweet potato pie, lemonade, and caramel popcorn.

Babe-Ruth had never seen such a show, and it was the largest gathering she had ever seen. She noticed the women and children and especially the vendors. It was the last inning. The game was tied—Cool Papa stole home! After the game, Caleb drove, and Jesop puffed on his pipe. The tent meeting had been earlier and was gearing up again. Jesop was suspicious of preachers and anybody who didn't work the fields.

In the days that followed, the spectacle of the game stayed in Babe-Ruth's mind. On Tuesday, Missy Sarah came by. Babe-Ruth put corn into a basket and watched her finish a slice of melon.

"Watermelon is sweet."

"I'll have Caleb bring you one tonight."

"Well, is he done decided?"

"Decided what?" Babe-Ruth smiled.

"You knows what I'm ferrin' to, child. Don't play foxy with me. You don't think I done come down here just for corn did ya?"

Babe-Ruth wiped her hands and sat.

"Missy Sarah, how long you and Mr. Jim been married?"

"More'n you been born." Missy Sarah's gray braids complemented her black skin. Her sparkle and contentment seemed indifferent to circumstances. She had most of her teeth, and it was hard to tell her age. She searched Babe-Ruth's eyes. "You the one!"

"Missy Sarah, is ya happy? Is bein' married been good to ya?"

"You don't know a thing 'til ya tried, yes, I'd say the married life been good. Jim is regula. I knew he'd be kind. Couldn't have chillun, but I raised Mr. John."

"Caleb works hard, I don't feel a lot. Don't feel a lot against." Babe-Ruth unfolded her arms.

"He ain't never gave Jesop no trouble . . . I knew you was the one."

Babe-Ruth was feeling lazy, but she grabbed her scrub board and pail and headed for the well. She washed everybody's things, including Jesop's and Caleb's, then carried water in for cooking and drinking.

By evening, she had done a full day's work, which included bringing Jesop, Caleb, and her sisters lunch in the field. It was just hot corn bread with butter and a little syrup in the middle, with onions for the men, but that and the cool water and the way she served the corn bread, in a basket covered with a blue gingham cloth with the clay bowl of butter and jar of syrup made it seem special. She worked the field, but she was the main housekeeper and only in the fields on Tuesday and Thursday.

Caleb and Jesop came to dinner often. At times she brought it to them. Caleb loved catfish; it had Jesop remembering dishes. He would describe a dish, and she would make it.

After a few weeks, it was time for Mr. Bull to mount his wagon and check on the girls. So what if it set him back a day. He walked and swung his arms like he owned something, and he did, one of the few coloreds that did. It was just sixty acres, but it was his. A lot of folks worked the land and died on it the same as he would. You ask what's the difference? Owning was just a piece of paper, and perhaps owners lived better, but not all. To Mr. Bull, it seemed worthwhile.

He learned to read as a boy and had been taught in secret; it wasn't sure that he would have been hung or shot, but it was frowned upon. He read the Bible and taught his boy to read. When his wife died, it was just him and the boy;, and in the winter, he sent him twenty miles away to the small Methodist school.

As a boy, Mr. Bull assisted a carpenter and learned his trade; and when the man died, Mr. Bull still got plenty of work if he was willing to travel. He saved and bought his sixty acres from a farmer that was moving North. He read the deed himself, and the preparers had to change it several times because of problems in the language. They thought he had a lawyer or a preacher, but he had a knack for books, and he didn't see any reason to let them know. Outside of old newspapers and letters from his son, he read the Bible daily.

His son, Jeremiah, was a high school principal in Gary, Indiana. Mr. Bull didn't talk about him because it would have been bragging. His wife hadn't taken to books, but he read to her from the Bible, and she wore him out with requests. Her favorite book was Esther, and he would find her the appropriate Psalms as he saw the need.

He reached for his jug of water and put a piece of candy in his mouth. He would be at Jesop's place in an hour. It was peaceful seeing the sights. He tipped his hat, feeling the fruits of society; being around and seeing people was a rarity he almost forgot he needed.

Jesop was having lunch and offered him some, but he declined. He filled Mr. Bull's water bottle and told him where to find Caleb.

Napping was tradition after lunch, and Caleb fidgeted under a tree with a bandana over his face. It was no shame awaking a man from a frightful nap, and Mr. Bull nudged his shoulder, and Caleb sat up.

"What's wrong?"

"Don't know . . . Had a bad dream." Caleb brushed off and stood up.

"Got some news for me?" Mr. Bull tilted back his hat.

"We ain't told nobody but Missy Sarah. Babe-Ruth done agreed. You can bring the preacher the third Saturday of next month."

Mr. Bull extended his hand. "The sisters gonna live with y'all?" Caleb nodded, and they shook. "You a goodun. Y'all 'ill have somethin'."

He studied Caleb, then walked back to the wagon, thinking about his promise to a dead man; he put the water jug on his shoulder and took a swig, directing the mules and unwrapping a candy.

A month went by, and the wedding was a week away. Babe-Ruth was fourteen and had never been with a man. It was early evening, and Jean and Mary were picking vegetables. Babe-Ruth put the dishrag down; she could see Caleb coming. Nobody walked like him.

They eat like pigs. It must be their way. He works real hard and respects his pa and seemed all right on the inside. Dark men are better than the light ones that expect you to take care of them. We'll be sleepin' in the same bed. He need to take a bath more.

It wouldn't be a common-law marriage. Papa said it wasn't decent . . . He got the making of a good man.

"Hey, Babe." He stood in the doorway. "You know the marriage is in seven days."

Her expression didn't change. He was welcome, of course, but a choosing her was not a marriage.

"Just be nice." He bobbed the bandana in his fist. She turned away, and he held her by the waist and pulled her around. "There you go."

She was at peace and laid her head on his chest, spying the marrying tree. It brought good luck. Everyone knew the story.

They made their vows under Johna's tree on the third Saturday of the month, and Mr. Bull was there, and he brought them a Bible and had the preacher write in it. It was a short service, and they served turnip greens, spiced cake, and fried chicken.

Babe-Ruth realized there were more differences between man and woman than she thought. Caleb had a strong, bitter smell that was there even after a bath (it wasn't dirt but him). She thought it had something to do with being a young man because her pa didn't have that smell. Caleb, she thought, was harder and seemingly unconscious of most bumps and discomforts. Men had a kind of dumbness. It was their secret. They couldn't smell very well and had little revulsion to dirt and disorder; he washed up in the morning and took a full bath weekly, but she wondered if he appreciated wearing clean underwear. Females were more civilized. She never said it that way, but it was her conclusion.

There were three women living under Caleb's roof, a bigger shanty with two rooms, a large kitchen area, and a garden. He studied Jean and Mary and tried to be the boss. Mary and Jean went along, but Babe-Ruth wasn't sure it was leadership; to her it was bullying.

Jesop chuckled; he was thinking of grandchildren. He probably had some with his other boys, but they were in other places. He thought they would have let him know if they cared enough or knew how to write.

It was their usual snowless winter. Babe-Ruth had hardly vomited in her life and had never had a temper. Now she couldn't trust her impulses and had to restrain herself from crowning Caleb with a pot when he chewed with his mouth open. Food sloshing in his open mouth made her feel like she was on a boat. She hated being a woman for the first time. Her ankles swelled, then her hands and face, and then kicking and cramps began as the vomiting waned. Missy Sarah seemed to understand everything.

"Now you gotta eat some crackers in the mornin'. It'll help settle your stomach, and then later, eat lightly, a little at a time."

The cramping worsened, and backaches caused her to stretch and nap at midday.

"Take these leaves and boil you some tea. It'll relieve the cramps, but you can't lift what you did befo'. You ain't the same."

The time came to have the baby, and it was Babe-Ruth and Missy Sarah, who would be the midwife; Jean and Mary fetched. Jim and Leslie kept Caleb and Jesop company and stayed out of the way. The baby was big, with fat cheeks and soft skin, and they named her Jessica. Nobody knew where Babe-Ruth got the name, but everyone was proud. It was like Jessica had three mamas.

Babe-Ruth was fifteen and looked her age. The days were hot; a cool wind came with the darkness, and they slept at times without blankets. Her emotions settled, and she felt like herself again. Summer passed, and days were filled with harvesting, eating, and sleeping.

She was in the kitchen bathing Jessica in the sunlight. She dried her off and put her down, then looked into the pot of beans. She had lunch ready to take to the fields and had forgotten what day it was.

Jesop and the men were a sight: the sun glared down, drying their sweat, leaving a veneer of salt on their foreheads and cheeks. After they ate, she dowsed their foreheads, and the saltiness ran onto their tongues. She had to check the baby, finish cleaning, and prepare supper. She hoped there would be time for checkers after dinner.

There was dreaminess about harvesttime. Evenings tumbled into days, with occasional rain. Sleep was deep and hard, and they would be up at the crack of dawn.

"These gals have been real good for the place. Everything's better for them being here, but I ain't been seeing Babe-Ruth in the fields since she had that child." Jesop waited for an answer.

"She figures she's done working the fields." Caleb put a plug in his mouth.

"Well, she ain't!"

"Daddy, you tell her. I tried, but she's stubborn."

"Son, you gotta let her know who wears the pants." He shook his head. "It's the last time I straighten her out for you."

I like that gal, he thought as he made his way through the garden and up the porch. He thought about Jessica as he opened the screen door. He liked kissing her fat cheeks and watching her holler. He never got enough, and nobody complained.

"How ya, Babe?" The sweet smell of butter roll was inviting, and the vanilla walls glowed. Jessica sucked a breast, and Babe-Ruth worked with her free arm. He took off his hat and dusted.

"Sit down and let me give you something." She poured a cup of coffee and sliced the steaming butter roll. "Jess, your grandpa is here, girl."

He relaxed, with the sun warming his scalp.

"Now, Babe-Ruth . . ." He paused, recalling. "Your baby is three months old, and we still needs you a few days a week in the fields. Y'all some good workers."

She poured him more coffee.

"Pa Jefferson, I gotta baby now. I ain't gonna carry Jessica to no fields with those snakes and bugs."

"I ain't gonna argue. That's it!"

"Well, I'm sorry." She stared back. "We got a different notion 'bout what a woman is. I can't be like those women that work for you, totin' their babies to the fields and wearing men's boots 'cause they last longer. What kinda woman is that?"

"I guess you're better'n yo sisters! I see my boy buying you fancy curtains. You will work the fields!"

"Pa Jefferson, I'm Caleb's wife—I won't!" He wasn't sure, not just if he heard her words, but also her looking right into his eyes and she not a quarter of his age? "Now, you been good to me and my sisters, and I love you for it . . ." He shook his head, turning away. Something hurt inside, and it wasn't a simple thing. "You don't know nothin' about no woman."

He retreated to the window, where she and the big-jawed baby crowded him. The sun felt good, and he caught their reflection in the glass and blew his nose.

"Babe, you're right. And you is one. My Loretta died fo' Caleb could walk. She was strong . . . good too. And life was good . . . We'll do it your way." She knocked him back with kisses. "Don't drop that baby, woman!"

The rest of the day seemed timeless. She laid out clean towels, and the sun was setting. Footsteps and laughter approached. Caleb had Mary and Jean listening to his tales.

"Ha ha ha! I gotta a hundred more."

"Welcome. Wipe your feet and wash up.

The table was set as they dried off.

"Girl, that cotton is bad on the hands." Jean held bruised hands up, rubbing them together.

"Umm!" Mary's eyes widened, but no one looked up. "Girl, you did it up right tonight."

"Papa came by."

"Did? What'd he want?" Caleb feigned surprise and looked up.

"He decided it was all right for me to stay home and take care of y'all." There was real surprise on his face, and she put more corn on his plate. "In a few years we oughta go North. There's factory jobs and nine months of school. I think we could do better."

"I guess you know all there is to know about the North! Been there?"

He finished eating and slammed the door on the way out. It was an hour before sunset. A breeze patted his forehead as he took tobacco from his bib and bit down.

Chapter 3

In the months that followed, Babe-Ruth and Caleb argued over trifles. The first time he slapped her, she chased him with a butcher knife. Then she calmed down and realized she could have killed him, her temper could have landed her in the penitentiary, and Jessica would have been without a mother.

A few weeks later, there was some racket in their room; the sisters came in and broke it up. Nobody saw him slap her, but it had happened. He thought things were settled, but he woke up with her beating him with a skillet, and the sisters had to intervene again. He was sore all over and swollen the next day and couldn't see the black and blue bruises, but they were there.

Babe-Ruth fought back, and Caleb realized hitting and slapping was only causing resentment. He had heard of men being killed while they slept, and Jesop confirmed it and said he knew of one personally. Caleb would remember it.

The country and the world were changing, and they were not aware when FDR was reelected, Hitler and Mussolini made a pact, and there was a conviction for the kidnapping of the Lindbergh child. They knew that a lot of people were moving North. Over the next four years, Babe-Ruth had two more children. The second was Ann, and the third, they called Junior. Caleb spent the day mending fences with Leslie Hocum and James Bradford. He thought about Jean and Mary. He knew James and Leslie had been thinking about them too and seemed to be moving slowly.

It was in the fall and after supper, and Caleb took down the over and under; he had been hunting since he could keep up and got a gun when he was twelve. He was a good shot and loved hunting.

Jesop was ready, and three dogs pulled him. Tramp was his favorite; the others, Rascal and Tree, were coon dogs, mongrels that knew what they were after. On a dry night, they would bring them back with fresh meat. Jesop had the kerosene lamp in one hand and Tramp's leash on the other. He hadn't trusted Caleb with the lamp when Caleb was young, and carrying it had become a habit. Jesop's shotgun was broken down and hung over his arm, and Tramp pulled him to the action.

Rascal and Tree were off.

"Get that sunovagun!" Caleb was breathing hard. The critter was treed.

"He's up there and he's yourn." Jesop tied up Tramp. The lantern blazed in the creature's eyes.

"There!" Caleb's shot brought him down. Jesop's bag was tied, and they were off.

They treed another, then a third. Another fat one guaranteed they would be eating coon for days. They would catch a few for Missy Sarah. Coon was tasty when cooked properly, and when the yearning came, they were on the hunt. Missy Sarah was the expert at cooking it, and they paid tribute.

Jesop was still a good shot. They bagged six and went home sweating and laughing. If drunken whites thought they wanted to scare some niggers, they thought twice because he and Caleb might shoot back.

They put the dogs away and took the coon to the backyard. The musk glands and fat were removed, and the pelts would be sold. They soaked the pelts in a concoction of saltwater and baking soda, which would be drained and refilled in the morning. The body, minus the entrails, was hung out to drain, then dumped into kettles of saltwater, and the pelts were scraped and stretched. Caleb and Jesop did the cooking. Everybody didn't know how to cook coon, and the women had no interest at first.

"Go ahead, take another piece." Caleb motioned to Babe-Ruth. Papa Kitchen wasn't a hunter, and it was their first taste of coon. Babe-Ruth took a second piece. She nodded; Caleb and Jesop grinned. "Now you been to heaven!"

Caleb brought Missy Sarah's share skinned and soaked.

Coon was cooked outside and kept high to drain away the grease. Carrots and onions were put in the body cavity, and it was turned slowly about three hours. Salt, pepper, and garlic were added, and toward the end, a little molasses. They worked in shifts, and it was a time for sharing and telling stories. "Rabbit is some good eatin', so is squirrel and possum, but you can't beat coon for eatin' in the wild." Jesop licked his fingers and took some scraps to the dogs. Sunday they would have stew that he would cook himself.

The women were tired of all the bragging, and Babe-Ruth thought she could improve upon the recipe. When they went hunting again, she had her chance. She salted and peppered her stuffing, a mix of cornmeal and a little flour, then added celery, peppers, and onions. She started with an open fire, then stuffed the mixture in the large roasting pan with a few onions and garlic, pouring away fat and seasoning with hard cider.

Jesop's eyes sparkled with his first bite. "Caleb, this is the best you done." Caleb looked down as Babe-Ruth chuckled. "I knowed you had Missy Sarah help. This was done by a cook." His eyes sparkled at Babe-Ruth.

That evening, she visited Missy Sarah to learn more.

"You can do anything with the coon you have a mind to. You have to clean it right, drain it good, and if it's big, you gotta scorch it for ten minutes. You don't have to be so smart if the critter's small. I've seen them weighing forty pounds—only half of a biggun is meat if you cut the head off and prepare it right.

You can barbecue it. Cook it outside on a grate with good dry wood. After a couple of hours it will get tender and you can start puttin' on the garlic and then get your sauce ready. If you pierce it, it'll be tastier. The colonel won't eat no coon—hear me! Shucks, I been feeding him coon for years and he swears it's possum!"

Everyone on the plantation worked too hard to be fat, but they loved eating and talking about food. Missy Sarah told Babe-Ruth about spices, vinegar, and hard cider. Delight flooded from their eyes.

The sun highlighted red and golden-brown leaves and acorns on the grass. Jesop ran the comb through his hair. He couldn't read, but he knew his numbers and make his mark. He knew how and when to plant and knew seed grade. He grew cotton, supervised others, picked it, and got it to market for top dollar. The colonel left him alone. Jesop thought about the ten acres of mostly forest. There was a meadow with a stone where he buried Caleb's mother. The colonel hardly knew it was there. Nobody used it but Jesop and his kinsfolk (going in at night and coming out with some coon and rabbits). He had thought about the land for a long time and even dreamed about it.

Jesop shaved and wore his best overalls. He made his way to the back door, knocked, and waited for the servant Jim, who opened, nodded, and fetched the colonel, then led him in to the sunporch. Jesop liked the colonel, a fair man with a fine place who Jesop reasoned wasn't taking his wealth with him to the grave.

"How ya doin', Jesop?"

"Fine, Colonel, fine." Jesop, hat in hand, wiped his forehead; the colonel beckoned him to sit. "Boss, you got the finest place around." Jesop grinned, thinking about Johna's tree.

"Well, boy, you done it again." The colonel took the ledger. "You're maintaining profits in spite of the times . . . I'm gonna give you a bonus like last year. I hope your workers get their share?"

"Yes, sir. A lot is kin. I do by them same as you do by me."

The colonel didn't own a store, and his workers could buy wherever they chose. They shared in the orchard and had their own gardens. Sometimes pigs were distributed and shared by families after the main lot was shipped.

The colonel wrote out a note, and Jesop tucked it in his bib (it was unusual for sharecroppers to get a little cash, but the incentive was good for everybody).

"I love working this farm. We made it pay. You know, sir . . ." Jesop paused with a sigh. "I been savin'. We've never farmed those ten acres on the north quarter. It's full of woods, we hunts there, and my wife is buried there. I been wantin' to buy 'em from ya."

The colonel stood like he had been slapped. "What? . . . Ever know a nigga to own a piece of a farm like this, boy? Think those bastards woulda given the fair price if I wasn't there? Shit! You can't even read—get the hell out!"

Jesop rose but stood his ground.

"Damn you!" The colonel groped for his cane to strike, then leaned back, clutching his arm. "Damn you!" Sweat filled his brow, and he eased unto the daybed. "Jim!" Jim put a pillow under him and hurried to fetch his medicine. "Can you beat that?" The colonel's color returned as Jim

31

wiped his forehead, and Jim went to the window and watched Jesop disappear into the fields.

Caleb never saw Jesop stand up to the colonel, but old Jim told them, and Jesop said it was time. There was a lot Caleb didn't know about Jesop. And if Caleb was wondering if Jesop had killed a man, he had. Caleb was the second to hear it from Jesop's mouth.

The big house was quieter. Young John was present when the next crop was sold, and it was different. Jesop didn't like him looking over his shoulder and took it as a slight.

"Sarah, you leaving these chairs all over the place!" The colonel looked down at the broken water glass and stumbled; she rushed to get a broom. "I guess you ain't listenin' anymore." He went to the porch, squeezing his hand, assuring himself of its strength. Maybe it was his glasses; he had had them checked. "Bring me some cold water."

"Here I come." Sarah made haste.

"Can't nobody hear?" He didn't hear her coming and hollered, insisting, afraid, knowing his ears were failing. Mr. John and Missy Sarah just looked at one another.

The day was cloudless. The wind caressed the necks and brows of the field-workers. The sky was bright, eternal, and made you stare. Babe-Ruth welcomed the silence. She liked the way the kitchen felt in the mornings when she pulled the curtains down, opening the doors, letting in the coolness, then closing the doors and capturing the morning air. It was nap time for Jessica and Ann, and she looked at Louis sucking her breast. He was two months old, and it had been a difficult delivery.

Her body had changed through the years, and she became keenly aware of it after Louis's birth. She had recovered fast after the first three, but this time was slower, and the weakness and aching lingered. The outward changes were subtle. Her face was leaner, firmer, and there was hardness in her arms. Old Jim had died. Missy Sarah was grieving, and Namie Baker, one of Jesop's kinfolk, assisted in Louis's birth. It wasn't the same.

Louis was a different child. He was medium sized at birth, but a vigorous eater. There was a peace about him. He didn't cry much and seemed older in ways she couldn't put her finger on.

She thumbed through a magazine while breast-feeding. She didn't understand the writing. It was over a year old and the only reading material in the house except for the marriage Bible. She loved the pictures of women dressed in fancy clothes and the dishes of food.

She had seen mostly poor white women up close except for the lady who visited Mr. John some weekends and one sent by the government to inspect the farm. The government woman dressed in a suit and had authority like a man. Everyone was concerned that she be given a good impression. Babe-Ruth noted the texture of her skin, teeth, nails, blue eyes, and delicate movements and got close enough to smell her perfume. She continued thumbing through the magazine; she thought the government lady was classier than the women in the pictures.

The recipes were a mystery. The pictures were delightful, and she experimented trying to produce a similar product. Cakes and pies were her specialty, and she imagined hers were as good as theirs. She made pound cake using the best sugar, flour, eggs, and spices she could muster and added her special flavoring with a precise number of strokes. Good cake making wasn't for the trifling; the extra strokes weeded them out.

She changed Louis to the other breast and thought about the one-room schoolhouse ten miles away, then about the rumored lynching, and closed the magazine.

Caleb drank some water, then lifted the bundles of cotton into the wagon and looked over the fields. Now they were six; he and Jesop added a room for Jean and Mary as a temporary measure.

"How is old Jesop these days? He been leaving when the sun gets hot . . . How old is he anyway?" Mary handed Caleb the last bundle and rested her hands on her hips.

"He looks thinner to me." Jean was admiring the load.

"He'll go on forever . . . Don't really know his age . . . Not sure he does . . . Slowin' a bit, though." Caleb looked at the sky. It would be a good night for hunting coon.

Chapter 4

Caleb reverted to his bullying ways. She didn't mind him being the man, but she wouldn't take it. They squabbled, and she threatened him with the steel poker. He seemed to forget about it in the morning. She took lunch to the fields with the kids tagging along, holding on to her dress, with Louis swaddled on her chest. They stopped to see Missy Sarah, then it was back to prepare supper and clean and wash.

They played checkers after dinner, but Babe-Ruth didn't. She put the kids to bed and swaddled Louis in his crib. His forehead seemed cool, and he wouldn't suck. Caleb came in laughing and stopped.

"Everything all right?"

She didn't answer. She was still mad, and he was acting like their squabble hadn't happened. She studied Louis; he was peaceful, but she wanted him closer and moved the cradle into their room. The night was cool, and she checked on him every few hours. She remembered the night her papa woke her up and said her mama had gone to be with the Lord. She was only seven and didn't realize what that meant at first. Understanding eased in. Her papa had never talked about his own ailments, but he seemed slower. He wasn't and old man… not in the way Mr. Bull was. It was difficult to get to sleep and she dozed in an out of thoughts and dreams.

The day was different. Why was she worrying so? It was a tendency, and she remembered nights with other children when she got up and listened to their chests; it was a part of motherhood, and she reassured herself.

Morning came, and she squinted as she pulled up the shades. Louis felt cool and flopped in her arms. She screamed.

Caleb jumped up, and Jean and Anne rushed in, unsure if they were dreaming. Louis was dead! It was written all over Babe-Ruth's face.

Jean and Caleb fetched Jesop and Missy Sarah. When they arrived, they washed him, then bundled and put him in a cradle on the porch.

"Let me hold him." Jesop took a turn, then Caleb. They put a rocking chair out and took turns beside him all day and all night. Caleb didn't say a word and put his arm on Babe-Ruth's shoulder whenever she was beside him. Visitors showed their respects, looking into the cradle and silently praying and embracing Babe-Ruth. She took the last shift, and she imagined him as a grown-up; her reverie lasted until the sun came out. They buried him in the meadow and moved a large stone over the gravesite and used cement for a headstone that said his name and the year of his life. Jim Bradford did the writing.

Everyone had his or her own thoughts, and nobody talked. They bowed their heads, but nobody prayed aloud.

That first week, Babe-Ruth would wake up sweating, dreaming she smothered Louis while they slept. It reoccurred nightly. Missy Sarah forced her to drink soup and tea because she hardly ate and was losing weight. After a fortnight, she was eating more. She thought a lot about her mama and papa. She knew Louis's death wasn't her fault and crib death wasn't understood.

The leaves changed colors, and there was a peacefulness, with no news and the outside world far away. She was gaining weight and in the kitchen cooking and could hear Leslie and James on the porch.

"Tell me again about that Joe Louis rematch with Schmelling in 1938."

"It was in New York, Yankee Stadium. The place was packed." Leslie leaned closer. "The German threw a right to Louis's head and missed. Then Louis hit him with a left jab to the midsection. Schmelling dropped his guard, and Louis went to his jaw—he was down. He got up twice more, but the boy put him down twice more."

This was the shortened version that James Bradford told. The longer one lasted three to four minutes. The real fight hadn't lasted that long, but depending on the occasion, he would draw it out. It was like James was ringside. The truth was he had never been out of the South. His mama had lived in the North as a girl and had taught him to read. He left Leslie laughing on the porch and went inside where Babe-Ruth was cooking.

"Where's Jean?" He peeped into the pot of collard greens, smiling as steam covered his face.

"She'll be back soon. Pickin' more greens. When you gonna teach me to read?"

He tore a brown sack into quarters, took a short pencil out of his bib, and wrote the alphabet, then proceeded to go over the letters. She took a piping hot piece of corn bread, sandwiched it with butter, and poured honey over the top and handed him a spoon, which he used as a pointer.

"Practice it. When you know it by heart, we'll do more." He finished and headed out to find Jean.

Babe-Ruth had wanted to read as long as she could remember. She had never spent a day in school, but she knew she was as good as anybody. Reading, she sensed, was sacred. She put the papers and pencil stub away. Each evening, she would write those letters for James Bradford.

Caleb felt like a big brother keeping an eye on James and Leslie. He especially liked James, who was dark, over six feet, with sharp features and a narrow nose like some whites. His eyes sparkled, and he appeared endowed with special powers. Babe-Ruth lit up around him. Caleb chuckled watching them working on the writing.

First she learned the alphabet. Jim (people his own age called him that) made her recite it backward and forward, an exercise he believed brought mastery. Learning the vowels and consonants was difficult, and she wrestled until they were hers. It was difficult to understand how r and wr made the same sounds, and she was furious when he told her "kitchen" was spelled with a k and "cake" with a c. She spelled everything in the house. Learning flavored her chores and reflected in her eyes.

"You ain't listenin', woman!"

When Jim grew impatient or had an attitude, she tried harder. It won him over, and he'd get his second wind. She thought if he was going to be marrying Jean, he was going to need patience, and she was breaking him in. He had a basic respect for women, which was hard to change if it wasn't already there, and she thought he was good looking and meek for knowing so much.

"Babe-Ruth gets real humble when she's learnin'." Caleb chuckled, relating the events to Jesop.

Jim and Caleb related formally, and Jim understood.

"Howdy, Jim, you off a little early . . . Courtin' cuts into the work some?" Jim nodded.

Jim worked at several farms and during the off-season worked in a mill. He was the first colored man his own age that Caleb knew who could read, and Caleb wasn't about to let him act like he was better. Secretly Caleb thought he might be.

"I expect he got a place big enough for a small family." Caleb bent over the chair he was fixing, eyeing Babe-Ruth. "Ain't been there in a while, but he worked on it some." With the family growing, Caleb needed the space. "When Jim marries that gal, he oughta take her North. He's a smart 'un. Never figured him for a farmer. He good at it though."

It was just people, animals, and land. Away from the plantation, there were lynchings and race riots up North in a world of newspapers, magazines, radios, and picture shows. He supposed most coloreds up North could read; Jim said they were fighting in Europe.

"You don't seem to be laughin' at my jokes." Leslie paused as Caleb and Jesop loaded the wagon. Leslie was the nearest thing to being fat on the plantation, with his round face and protruding belly. He was tall and muscular, but his "feedbag" was displayed like an ostentatious jewel; after a meal, he'd stick it out like he was with child. He laughed when work was hard; it was his way of saying that it wasn't. "Jesop, tell one of them animal tales."

Jesop knew people. Leslie had been an orphan and was light skinned and had the good sense to attach to good people and hold on. Around them, he was as clear as glass.

They continued loading wood taken from the forest. Leslie had left, and Jesop was bent over.

"Son, I'm old. I can still run this place, hire extra workers when we needs them. They ain't no future for you here. I just wanted those acres to have one of us put a little house on it and have our own burial place. He 'spects you to stay and work for his son and it to go on forever. He ain't the only man. Now you got kids, and I see Leslie and James gonna marry her sisters. Y'all' do good up North."

Caleb knew Jesop and Babe-Ruth hadn't talked. He would think about it; he might get James Bradford to write his sister, Mildred, up in New Jersey. Then he would see.

Jean's and Mary's marriages were a month apart. The ceremonies were performed under Johna's tree with the preacher and special meals. Caleb welcomed the space. He began shaving. It wasn't necessary, but he felt it was time, and the more he did, the more he needed to. The wooden box containing his instruments was off-limits, as if there was something special about an old clay cup, a brush, some soap, and a razor.

Manhood was an idea that came from watching Jesop, Mr. Bull, and older men and listening. Sure they said "yessuh" and "nosuh" to the whites, but with everything that had to do with being men, they were as good as anybody. He met a few Northern boys, and they talked different. He reasoned they were the same as him and were showing off. He thought that Babe-Ruth might teach him to read, but it wasn't the time.

Jesop had said Caleb's mama died shortly after giving birth. It was a good story for a child's mind, but he pumped Missy Sarah, and she finally told him. Caleb was four months old and not weaned when it happened. Jesop came in from the fields and found a white man pulling up his pants and standing over his wife's body. Jesop strangled him with his bare hands and buried the body. He had to be a stranger because nobody came looking for him. It was the first time Missy Sarah had uttered a word about it, and she told Caleb so. She said God put a little meanness in every man, and that was the reason why.

That Sunday, they had just come in from the ball field and were drinking lemonade. Caleb was smarting from the baseball game; Jesop had been the umpire, and they took turns watching the children.

"Keep it low—they can't hit ya!" Jim patted his glove.

"Ain't no men hittin' offa me today. I'll let up on the women 'cause they can't hit my easy stuff. I'm strikin' out Babe-Ruth." Caleb always bragged.

Babe-Ruth came up. "Come on. Bring it on!" And she walloped the first pitch and ran the bases with the women screaming. Caleb threw up his glove.

Everybody gathered for dinner later on. Mr. John says, "Boy, you 'speck you can run this farm for me someday?" Caleb laughed at his own imitation.

"Listen, the colonel's son couldn't run this farm if it was ten acres. The man can't do nothin' that I can see."

"Well, he owns the land. It'll be his anyway when the colonel dies." Babe-Ruth avoided Caleb's eyes.

"Pass the chicken." James Bradford was greasy mouthed and grinning.

"Me too." Leslie handed her his plate.

"Leslie, you could eat a full course meal before they hang ya." Mary filled the plate.

"I suspect I could. I'd have no taste for dessert though. The thought of dying would wipe out my sweet tooth."

James laughed until he was on the floor. Even the children laughed.

"Me and Babe and the kids is movin' North." Caleb thought it was as good a time as any to tell them. "Gotta make a move. They lynched a man a few months ago just to show who's boss. Jim Bradford wrote Mildred. We can stay with them awhile. There's work in the lumberyards. A man can make thirty-five dollars a week. If the war heats up, it'll be more."

He surprised Babe-Ruth too. She had suggested it before Jesop, and it made him feel better.

"Y'all gonna be stayin' for dessert?" Leslie asked, but nobody laughed.

Caleb hadn't said when they were going. Maybe he was just talking. Babe-Ruth avoided her sister's eyes. They'd probably wait until after harvest. If things worked out, maybe Jean and Mary would follow.

Jesop lit his pipe. He had never dwelled much on the future; it was his secret. He remembered running like a jackrabbit from drunken whites shooting at him for sport. The colonel gave them all kinds of hell and reported them to the sheriff. Jesop chuckled at the thought; he bought rifles after that.

Chapter 5

"I have said, ye are gods; and all of you are children of the most High. But ye shall die like men, and fall like one of the princes." (Psalm 82:6-7)

The Migration

A million Americans voted Socialist. Some hoped for a great proletarian revolt. But the government was building dams and bridges, paying not to sow, plowing under cotton, slaughtering baby pigs, and buying and storing grain. It was the New Deal.

People migrated like locusts. The pot was melting, but mostly churning: South to North, East to West, jostling.

Dutch Reformed, Polish Catholic, and Jews settled in the Midwestern City. Then Southerners, Latvians, and Italians, and they kept coming.

Mr. Deyoung emigrated from Holland and had prospered in his furniture business. Some countrymen followed, and he employed them. Business expanded, and he was more than well off. His son, Douglas, was curious and smart. Maybe he would run the business someday. But perhaps he would be a doctor or a lawyer. Mr. Deyoung thought being a doctor was better.

Since the Civil War, coloreds flowed North like molasses going downhill, and it went on a hundred years. You will know their names later.

He was twenty-two and had been in Georgia all his life and was going North. A man gave him a horn when he was eight, and he had been playing for a living since. It had been just him and his mother, and at times he brought in more than she did. She died of consumption when he was sixteen.

He played in the hotel band. It was a shame to leave a job that paid so well, but in three months, the girl working the desk would be showing. You never know what they would do when a white woman had a brown baby. She had better leave too or get herself done over. She might even accuse him of rape (she had cornered him, and he gave in, but it didn't matter anymore).

He had been thinking of going North anyway. Some of his friends made it big in Chicago, and he was better than most. He hadn't gone because he was lazy. He packed and acknowledged it for the first time. He would stop up in Michigan and stay with an old flame. It would be a start, then maybe Chicago.

A Mississippian looked down at the gravestone. It was a small tombstone with her name and dates. She was fixed in his memory with the land. He was silent for a long time. He accepted life's pains and joys. Somebody bigger than him made the rules. There would be trouble until he died, but there would be peace too.

His son stood beside him. A man waited outside the gate with a carriage loaded with their suitcases and toolbox. He had had enough of the South. He wanted the youngster to get an education and be somebody. She would have wanted it that way. He picked the boy up and headed for the wagon.

A dark Alabama woman wiped her eyes, and caressed her lithe frame. But her beauty was difficult to appreciate under the circumstances. Letting the child go North with her mother's sister was right. She couldn't raise the child by herself. She was eighteen, and she and her mama were hardly making ends meet. They didn't live like mother and daughter but like sisters and worked at the hotel, where they met a lot of men. The baby wasn't supposed to happen and didn't fit into the life they were living.

Her mother's older sister drank coffee in the kitchen, a good woman with a husband up North and childless. They would provide for him properly; any chance of him turning out right would be slim if he stayed.

The youngster played in the corner. He didn't cry much; there was no sparkle in his eyes. You didn't have to be smart to see that things were going wrong already.

"Well, you better get that child ready 'cause the train's going to be leaving in two hours." His grandmother picked him up, heading for the bedroom.

"His clothes is all ready." She was handsome; it was easy to see where his mother got her looks. She had his mother when she was seventeen and raised her alone. It wasn't what she wanted for her grandson. He needed to be around a man.

"Child, in a moment you and me is gonna be on that choo-choo train going bye-bye." His grandaunt put her cup down and went to the bedroom. It would be colder up North than they could imagine.

A Tennessee woman had had enough of the South.

"Me and that child are going North." She looked at him across the table. "You ain't no help. You come here for a place to sleep when you get drunk, but you ain't no father—ain't no man!"

He slapped her, ramming her against the wall.

"That enough man for ya?"

He walked out, ignoring the boy crying beside her. She picked herself up. She didn't cry. It didn't hurt much anymore. She feared he would come home drunk, hit her, and she would kill him while he slept. The thought frightened her. She had wanted to be grown and on her own. Her mama knew he was no good; it was clear now. She marveled at her stupidity and shook her head, laughing. She was too proud to go back to her mother's house and never regretted having the child. She had her mother's ways; up North she would begin again. Maybe she would find a good man and they would become a family.

A dark figure got off the southbound train; it seemed like the middle of nowhere. It had been years since he had returned South; finally he had come home. A few people remembered him. It was a chance to walk around and sort things.

He visited places where he grew up and played. He didn't talk to many people. He had an old friend, and they did some talking, but not about what was on his mind. His friend knew the sore eating at him, but his friend was a quiet man and wouldn't bring it up.

The last day there, he visited a grave. It wasn't his mama or daddy, but he wept like it was kin. He spent an hour there weeping and thinking. There was an old friend he would visit on the way back North. The old man had introduced him to his wife and had given him counsel through the years. He was unsure if he was still alive.

The train passed a clearing, and he could see the Mississippi River. It was a great sight, but all he could think about was that it had been the burial ground for coloreds. A body would wash up on the shore; nobody could ever identify it. It was usually a colored man, and they guessed the age.

Once, a white man got washed up, and there was so much fuss you would have thought it was the president. Everybody got scared. It was difficult to know what white people would do. Nobody identified the body. They lynched a colored man anyway. It was the way of the South.

It was breezy. The sun was setting, and the stranger moved briskly.

Colonel Jefferson rocked, looking at the sunset and peeling an apple, nodding after cutting the last piece, then dozing. He took these short naps frequently, and it was one of the reasons he walked about late at night. The house was quiet, and his son, John, was in Cape Girardeau and was expected back late. Missy Sarah was down on the plantation.

"Who's there . . . You, Missy?" A noise came from the back porch.

The colonel saw the dark figure and came forward, yelling and clutching his chest, with the knife in the opposite hand. He stumbled as the stranger fled, and blood oozed unto the carpet. He squeezed his chest, looking for the medicine bottle. An hour went by, and Caleb came in carrying a watermelon.

"Missy Sarah?" his voice echoed. "I got that sweet melon you been after me to bring up." He saw the body and blood and dropped the melon and ran for Jesop.

He and Jesop rolled the colonel over. "Lawdy!" The knife was in his belly.

"What happened here?" Missy Sarah was behind them, screaming.

"What is we gonna do? He's dead. It looks like somebody been here. See that chair down over there."

"Mr. John won't be here for a couple of hours. Jesop, you gotta send someone for the sheriff." She paused, looking around, worried. "Don't look like nothin' been taken. Listen, things don't look good." Missy Sarah was thinking and peered at Jesop. "Somebody might think y'all the cause. I seen it happen. We gotta move something around here." She picked up the chair toppled on the floor and inspected the room. The side door was open, and she noticed mud stains on the carpet. "Somebody been here all right, foul play or not." She left the apple peels on the table and cleaned up the watermelon.

Jesop nodded. "Let's do it your way."

Caleb returned huffing. "I done sent Leslie for the sheriff. Won't be back for over an hour."

"I was the first 'un found the body, Caleb. I screamed, dropped the watermelon, then came to the back porch where you were bringing in another one and told ya to fetch Jesop. Then he rolled the body over and saw the knife. He told you to have someone fetch the sheriff. I'm old. If they can tie you in someway, son, no tellin' what could happen. I seen some mighty wrongs."

Caleb nodded, digesting Missy's story.

"No matter what happens, you gonna stay around 'til the funeral, and then head North like you plannin'." Jesop agreed.

"Y'all knows better'n me," Caleb whispered on the way out.

An hour later, Mr. John came. He listened to their story. "Daddy wasn't himself lately. He was peeling an apple over there. He probably heard something outside. He might have had those chest pains again before he slipped. He had a small one after breakfast, and I put his pills out."

Mr. John was holding Missy Sarah. When the sheriff came, Mr. John did the talking, and Missy Sarah nodded. The sheriff had just been reelected. During an election year, they might have been looking for a nigga to lynch.

"Well, I'm sorry 'bout this." He opened the glass door; there were footprints on the porch. "There mighta been someone here," he spoke softly to himself. "Any sign of struggle?" There was silence. "Judging from the wet spot, it was a pretty big melon for a little woman to be carrying. A hurtin' thing." He put his hand on Mr. John's shoulder. "Why I need to use the kitchen so I can talk to these three."

44

"Is it necessary?"

"It's routine. You helped reelect me and you know that I know my job. I need to get their statements down."

Mr. John nodded, and they went in.

After an hour, Mr. John called them to help put the body on the table. He had purchased a coffin the year before. Missy Sarah had found out and came at him yelling like she was about to lay into him like she did when he was a boy.

"Sheriff, do me a favor and stop and tell Jamie. I bought the coffin from him. There's work to do and I got no stomach for it, and Missy Sarah won't be any use for a while."

They didn't know if the sheriff believed them, but the telling went well.

PART TWO

THE NORTH

Chapter 6

Cottages of the wealthy studded the Jersey shoreline, the queen of the eastern seaboard, a playground for the Northern elite since the nineteenth century. People came like flies, and hotels and piers sprouted.

Mr. Boardman got the idea that a plank walk would keep some of the sand out of his trolley and out of the hotels. The boardwalk became a thing unto itself, stretching for miles, and cushioned wheelchairs carried tourists to shops and beaches. There was a taffy war, and prices dropped. Saltwater taffy was sold by the piece and in boxes and was shipped all over the nation; some wouldn't leave without taking a box to a friend to show they had been there.

Hotels and rooming houses were enlarged and new ones built. Coloreds settled in from the beginning, working in construction, building railroads, waiting tables, chauffeuring, and cleaning up. By the 1870s, Atlantic City had a greater percentage of coloreds than New York and nearby Philadelphia.

Caleb and Babe-Ruth and the kids were wide-eyed on the train. There would be jobs, and it was fairer for colored people. Farmlands dwindled, cities merged, and it got colder. Babe-Ruth had packed plenty to eat. The smokestacks told Caleb there was work to be had.

Atlantic City was huge by Jefferson's standards. Grayish row houses and porches lined the treeless street. They passed a small grocery store to their left on the corner. On the right, a flat brick building had a sign showing red paint spilling over a globe and the words "Cover the earth."

"Let me see . . . 1402 Garfield Avenue." Babe-Ruth did the reading. It was an avenue the size of an alley. Caleb carried two bags, and she carried a box and pulled Junior with the other hand, while the girls struggled with small bags. "This here is the house!"

A round-faced woman with reddish-brown skin and a flat nose and a gap between her gold front teeth answered the door.

"Caleb . . . is that you?" She smiled, and they hugged. "Well, ain't you somethin'? Mitchell, come out here quick. Oh my, this must be Ruth."

"Glad to meet you, ma'am."

"Don't you *ma'am* me. Let me look at you . . . You a fine 'un. Call me Mildred." She picked up each child. "Mitchell, man, you better get out here and see this."

Mitchell emerged, putting on his jacket. He was short and dark, with a narrow smooth face and a wide nose. His vest was closed and his collar open.

"What's all this fuss?" He grinned. "Well, well, you Jesop's all right. Welcome. You's a man now. Look just like Jesop."

"Y'all come in. We can't be havin' no street meetin'." Mildred picked up Junior, and they followed her inside.

"Well," Mitchell said, grabbing his shoulder, "how was the trip up?"

"Fine, fine. Thanks for takin' us in. We ain't gonna be no trouble. We left two trunks at the station. Help me go fetch 'em?" Mitchell nodded. "I'll be workin' in no time." They retrieved the trunks, and he followed Mitchell up the steps.

"I ain't worried about you, Caleb. I know your daddy, and I ain't worried 'bout you at all."

The row houses extended the length of the block on both sides, with adjoining walls and porches and you could hear the neighbor next door. The backyards were fenced, and clotheslines ran from the upstairs back windows to windows in the next yard on a pulley (so you could hang and retrieve clothes). Each house had three bedrooms, a bathroom, kitchen, living room, and a basement. Two bedrooms were upstairs with the bathroom.

They moved upstairs with the kids in one room and them in the other; it didn't seem crowded, and Mildred and Babe-Ruth took turns cooking.

The neighborhood was friendly. Sister Jones, the churchwoman next door, had grown kids who lived in other states. There were several families with children. Another store, called Grandma's, was at the opposite end of the street, near the tracks. A block away in the opposite direction, the street ended at Indiana Avenue School, and you could see the front of the school from their porch.

When you were up from the South, you were expected to be ignorant and have little experience of modern living. The Jeffersons were, in fact, astonished, gathering in the bathroom and repeatedly flushing the toilet and examining the pipes. They figured whoever invented a thing as wonderful as an inside toilet could make the bathing tubs with hot water they had heard so much about. Even the colonel didn't have a toilet with running water. The kitchen had a porcelain sink and brass spigot, and there was a gas range. They felt almost rich.

The electric lights seemed magical. Words came from the large bureau with knobs and lights, connecting all over the country. There was nothing in the programming they didn't like, and it brought a new view of the country, which was big on the train, but became bigger as they heard America talking, singing, and dancing.

"Take your elbows off the table and sit up."

There was an idea forming in Babe-Ruth's mind; there would be schooling, and she would be getting them ready for the future. Mildred agreed; she never had children. "If you let them grow like weeds, you got talking animals" was what she said.

Mitchell and Mildred were in the hotel business. She worked as a maid in the Mayflower, and he was the handyman for several boardinghouses. The owner owned some bars, and Mitchell did the cleaning and repairs. Nobody looked over his shoulder, and he did a good job.

Caleb got a job in a week. He had never seen so much lumber. The lot covered ten acres, and business was booming. He followed the foreman to the clock.

"When you come in, you need to punch in here." He was white and about Caleb's age. "If you're late, you get docked one-half hour."

Caleb knew his numbers and could write his name. The boss hired him himself. Caleb did a lot of lifting in the morning; that afternoon, the foreman asked if he could handle a forklift. Caleb said yes; he had driven an old cotton truck and studied the knobs and levers, and after a few moments, he could.

At noon, men gathered on the ground with lunch pails, unwrapping sandwiches and pouring coffee. Caleb could tell he was being studied. It was his first taste of Spam; the thin white bread, called light bread, didn't pack the power of corn bread, which they would have snickered at. He washed it down with coffee, observing their gear. He would buy himself a lunch bucket and thermos. He was getting forty dollars a week, and he would get the right stuff.

"Where ya from, Caleb?"

"Missouri." He slowed the forklift.

"I guess you like this job?"

"More than standin' around talking." He was thinking of Jesop and moved along. At three thirty, the bell rang, and he punched out and wondered what Jesop would think of the punch-out clock.

In the evenings, after a meal and chores, Caleb relaxed on the porch with Mitchell and took account of the day's work and listened to the news echoing from the porches and their living room.

Mitchell's keen eyes and intense black skin made you study him. He was Southern and never mentioned any relatives and was regular in his habits, which made you respect him as older and wiser than his age, which was forty. After dinner, he would join Caleb on the porch. Mitchell's attitude said that at times a man didn't want to talk because he was listening or thinking. Any fool could tell that. A man that worked all day had no time for foolishness.

He'd light his pipe and talk a bit. It went out, and he'd light it again; the radio introduced subjects that they greeted or ignored with silence, a shuffling of feet, or an occasional cackle. Words were kept to a minimum as they mused about the economy, race relations, Chiang Kai-shek, Roosevelt, Stalin, Hitler, and Churchill, wondering how it would all end.

On Friday, Caleb got paid. Babe-Ruth gave him two dollars, and she would save what she could after paying rent and board. The sun was setting; he sniffed the ocean's breeze, looking out at the row houses. He had experienced more change in a few weeks than in all his days before.

Back in Missouri, Jesop leaned in the rocker. The dark-brown blanket covered his lap. Jesop had Jim stand in for him, but Mr. John ran the place now. The sheriff still came around asking about Caleb.

"Read me this letter from Babe-Ruth first. Then we'll go over the newspaper."

Jim Bradford scooted nearer and felt like he'd been adopted.

"The last thing I wanna say is you gonna have another grandchild. We love you and Caleb miss you a lot."

Jim reached for the newspaper.

HITLER INVADES RUSSIA

Today the German troops landed. With lightning swiftness, securing the town, killing thousands, and quickly capturing the remaining resistance . . .

"Son of a bitch!" Jim looked up, shaking his head.

Jesop used to go months without the news. Now Caleb was out there, and if America got in the war, Jim and Leslie might be in it too.

Jesop appeared weaker, and Jim finished reading him the paper. "I better be gettin' home."

Jim was thoughtful on the way home and hadn't been sleeping well because of a recurring dream: *That white boy Randall didn't like him. Jim's eyes said Randall was an ignorant peckerwood.*

When Randall saw the pitchfork, he wanted to ram it down Jim's throat. Everybody laughed when a nigga got scared.

"Here, nigga." He let it fly high.

Jim turned late as the handle dove out of the sun and felt pain and blood spurting from his neck. He would wake up sweating, realizing it was a dream.

It was common for Negroes to have nightmares of being lynched or burned alive. Jim took it as an omen. He would leave the South; it was only a matter of time.

Weeks later in Jersey, Mitchell and Caleb sat on the porch in the ocean air. The neighborhood seemed to be tuned to the same station. The news brought a hush. Caleb was thinking:

Pa is ailin'. I don't know how he gonna fit in when Jim leaves. Jim a goodun. Too smart to stay around white folks, not regular. A white can kill a colored and walk away.

Leslie needs to take Anne and come North. What gonna become of Pa? He continued. *That peckawood foreman seems like a fair 'un. Difficult to know a man though. These Northern boys may a been up here awhile, but they as Southern as me. I got my wife and kids.*

Like most, Caleb had no original thoughts. He listened to Bessie Smith on Mitchell's Victrola, to the radio, and he and Mitchell discussed things from the radio or Mitchell's newspaper. Men wore Bugga Boy caps (puffed on top, with a short bill) cocked to the side. He bought himself one and stopped wearing bibbed overalls and chewed his tobacco at home. He was country, but he would stop advertising it.

It snowed more than they had ever seen, and Babe-Ruth had another boy. George had plump cheeks and thick slobbering lips, sucked Babe-Ruth dry, and ate table food she prechewed.

"Everybody better eat real fast 'cause that bigun over there is a eyeing your plate." Mitchell couldn't get enough of teasing about him.

The three kids were in an upstairs bedroom, and it would be four when George was a little older. They felt secure and insulated, but everything changed the day the music was interrupted by the news:

aTTENTION! THE JAPANESE BOMBED PEARL HARBOR! THE JAPANESE BOMBED PEARL HARBOR!

Nobody heard anything after that, and everyone tried to quiet down everyone else. They sat for what seemed like an hour, then the crowd milled into the streets.

"Let's teach 'em a lesson!"

"Let's join up and kill them slant-eyed sons of bitches."

Men cursed and cried, then dallied and went to bed in anger and disbelief. After a few days, the tension eased. They kept track of the news. Caleb worked overtime and was getting acquainted with the men.

He had noticed Rueben right away. He spoke more properly than others and didn't speak unless it seemed important. He was what was called a race man, hating the way Negroes were treated and pointing it out to whomever would listen. Although annoying, men like him were admired: one of their own had more on his mind than drinking, womanizing, and joking. Besides, he loved sports, which was proof enough that he was human.

Caleb bumped into him on Garfield Avenue. Caleb would see for himself if Reuben thought he was better.

"Rueben, Rueben Robinson. What's yours?" Caleb put his hand out. Rueben took it. He was light, with a flat nose, and tall and muscular and lived several blocks down. He kept track of Hitler, Mussolini, how the war was going, Jim Crow, and baseball. Caleb usually nodded and on occasion added something about Joe Louis, things Mitchell shared from the newspaper, or news he had heard on the radio. He met Jim Longstreet, Samuel Higgins, and Bruce Whitlow, but all three together didn't know as much as Rueben. For Caleb, having lots of information inside your head was a new notion.

They were still playing ball. Joe DiMaggio had gotten Caleb's attention with his fifty-six-game hitting streak, and Ted Williams was leading the league in everything. He wondered what Satchel Paige and Josh Gibson were doing.

That summer was as hot as any they experienced in the South. They drank lots of ice water and got watermelon when they could, eating half and storing the rest in the icebox. The iceman wore a leather apron and a leather shoulder guard and holster with an ice pick and used a grappling to hold and carry the block of ice over his shoulder. He climbed the stairs with children at his heels.

"Stay outta the way! I don't wanna be bustin' no heads."

When he was finished, children peeked through their fingers, protecting their eyes as he chipped away pieces for them to suck on.

At times the heat seemed unbearable, and the firemen opened the hydrants; it drew kids like flies. Parents left their porches and held up skirts and rolled up pant legs, running barefoot through the gushing stream. On such a day splashing in the sun, it was easy to forget there was a war going on.

"Oh, come and get yo crabs!" When the evening shade approached, the crabman pushed fresh crabs resting on a mountain of ice. Some were expecting him. He filled an order and moved along. The guts, called the "dead man," were discarded and the crustaceans boiled, then dipped in a sauce of butter, salt, pepper, and herbs. The men used hot sauce. The Jeffersons became crab lovers.

On weekends, they strolled the boardwalk. There was enough money for taffy and soda pop, and the outing often ended with a dip in the ocean, with the men rolling up their pant legs and splashing with the women and children frolicking like it was a dream.

It was evening, and the children were in bed. Candles flickered and shades were drawn because of the blackout. The women turned in, leaving the men on the porch. Mitchell smoked his pipe, and Caleb spit tobacco into a Maxwell House can, as they listened to the radio.

"I heard they gonna get them Tuskegee Airmen into the war." Mitchell relit, waving the smoke away. Mitchell paused.

"What you mean?"

"Training colored boys to fly in the war."

"You don't say . . . lettin' us be men!"

The war was right against wrong, a chance to stand up and be counted, feeling their strength and getting a day's pay alongside the whites. It was overdue.

George was walking. Butter was scarce, and they received ration cards for coffee and sugar and meat. Babe-Ruth had been faithful to her writing. It was cold in Minnesota, where Jim landed a railroad job and said it might keep him out of the war.

"Leslie is finna bring Mary up North. Said he found kinfolk in Chicago. Pa Jefferson's the same. Mr. John runnin' the place."

With the kids tucked in, she began teaching Caleb to read. Writing his name was all he needed in the South. Most of the Northern coloreds could read, and if they couldn't, they were faking. *Ignorant* was a word Caleb didn't like. He'd rather be called *nigger* than *ignorant*.

It was a different kind of work. He learned the alphabet backward and forward in a week and was able to connect all the letters with their sounds. He spelled words and made sentences; by Christmas, he was reading signs, and by the end of February, he was spelling better than

Babe-Ruth. He read Mitchell's newspaper and delighted in news about the Brown Bomber. Like Babe-Ruth's, his writing was slow and wide like a child's.

Caleb watched the children make castles and throw snowballs. "A man like me was made for the South. I'll always be a Southern boy."

The wind cut through their coats and numbed their toes. They looked like midget hobos, with dripping noses, throwing snowballs and sledding in winter clothes from neighbors whose growing kids had no sibling waiting in the wings. For Babe-Ruth, it was hot soups and corn bread and everyone being tucked in and moonlit icicles and the wind rattling the windowpanes.

Spring brought the smell of the sea, days became longer, and they awakened to budding and chirping. It was good to pack away their overcoats. It wasn't clear to the children what squirrels and insects did in the winter, and their reappearance was met with wonder. In the morning, they opened the windows to the ocean air. There was rationing and less of everything, but life was good. Jessica was in school, the first to attend. For Babe-Ruth, that alone justified moving North.

That Friday, the moon was out, and a cat traversed the pavement under the streetlight, slipping under a porch at the sound of applause. Up and down the avenue, in living rooms and on porches, they gathered around the radio.

"In this corner . . ." It exploded from the radio. Mitchell leaned, motioning for quiet. Caleb moved closer. Mildred and Babe-Ruth whispered as the children giggled. "Weighing 212 pounds, from the great city of Detroit, the heavyweight champion of the world, the Brown Bomber, JOOOOE LOOOIS!"

Mitchell smiled, nodding. It was straight from New York.

"Shhhhhhhh, shhhhhhh!" The bell rang, and Caleb turned up the sound.

"Joe punches a blow to the head, then another. He hits him with the left, then a right to the midsection, and Simon moves away . . ." Cheering echoed through the avenue. "Joe backs away, then comes forward landing a left, then a right . . ."

The cat crossed back with ears perked.

"Simon is hurt! Joe lands another left . . . Simon is down! 1, 2, 3 . . . 10! The WINNAAHH and still heavyweight champion of the world!"

Mitchell relaxed, searching for his pipe, as pandemonium poured into the street. Junior was under the streetlight and ran screaming, pursued by his shadow. Some laughed. Babe-Ruth rushed in, picking him up. The laughter stopped.

"It's just your shadow!" She whirled, taking him inside and glancing back. "Fools!"

Ten minutes went by, and they returned to their porches.

"Gonna be draftin' more a us into Uncle Sam's army soon." Caleb bit down on tobacco, turning to Mitchell in the doorway.

"Y'all show Uncle Sam how colored boys shoot." Caleb nodded back.

In the months that followed, there were more blackouts and rations and men leaving for the war. On Monday, Caleb was at work, and Babe-Ruth was ironing. Junior and George played in the front room. George took the truck, and Junior struck him in the face.

"Stop it!" Babe-Ruth returned the truck and slapped Junior's hand. "You gotta share. Hear me, boy!"

George pushed the truck in front of the screen door. When George was a crawler, Junior didn't mind him. Now George was all over. Junior grabbed some pretzels, put on his cowboy vest, and headed out. Babe-Ruth was upstairs retrieving clothes from the line when Sister Jones hollered up.

"Ruth, I saw Junior walking down the block in his cowboy vest and a bag." Sister Jones looked up the stairs. "I called and he ran. I think he's runnin' away!"

"I'll beat that boy!" Babe-Ruth hurried down and grabbed a switch and rushed out. She didn't see him and dashed to the corner. "Did a little boy pass by here?"

She hurried toward the train depot. Junior headed toward the intersection, his head at knee level with people and cars moving in all directions; across the street, the tracks were double lanes. He paused and looked up at a stranger who saw Babe-Ruth coming. Junior whirled.

"No you don't. We're waiting for this lady!"

At home, Babe-Ruth spanked him until the switch broke and her palm was hot and stinging. He hollered until his cheeks were red, and then his lids lowered.

"Kids will keep you going, honey. You're doing the right thing. Always let them know who's boss." Sister Jones had come in silently, and Babe-Ruth burst into tears. "Now, now, honey, don't fret. You did the right thing, and good will come from it. Wait and see. Listen, I've made a rice puddin'. When you're free, it's cooling in the kitchen."

Babe-Ruth dried her eyes and gazed into the mirror.

"Thanks so much."

Caleb arrived and hung his hat behind the door. "Babe, where you, girl?" She was mending socks in the living room. "I'm making $45 a week!" He took out the bills and popped his fingers.

"Had to spank Junior today. Tried to run away. He don't wanna share." She gave Caleb his $2 and put the rest away.

"Get me a cup of coffee, Babe." She poured, and she could see he was proud; she peered out at the children playing. Things were about to change. She had missed her period, and men were leaving for the war. She feared Caleb would be drafted soon.

Chapter 7

In 1943, the singing of "The Star-Spangled Banner" sent a chill down your spine.

"That flag protects us all!" That was the feeling. It didn't protect the blacks from lynching or Asian Americans from concentration camps, but they all felt like Americans. They were right, and Hitler and the Japs were wrong, and sooner or later everyone would get what they had coming; and if they didn't stop that Nazi, he was going to be over here strangling babies, not checking colors or last names.

When Uncle Sam pointed, you were Government Issue. They drafted Caleb in June with thirty days to report. Babe-Ruth cried, listened to the radio, and read the papers. Then the time came.

"Babe, you'll get a check every month." Caleb's dungaree coat was buttoned at the neck, and the tight-fitting cap's short bill covered his brow. He gazed at the gray canvas bag leaning against the open door.

"Y'all take care. I gotta help Uncle Sam with these Japs and Krauts."

Throughout the land, women cried and hugged their men and hoped for a safe return. Babe-Ruth could feel his heartbeat and held on a long time.

"I gotta go, Babe." He caressed her pregnant belly and turned.

"Honey, he gotta go. He's coming back safe and sound, Ruth, safe and sound," Mitchell nudged.

"Mind yo mama and these 'ere grown-ups." One by one, Caleb lifted them above his head. "If y'all misbehavin', I'll be back and everybody's gonna have a hot seat."

He hugged Mildred and shook Mitchell's hand, then hugged him too.

Babe-Ruth climbed the stairs.

"He gonna be all right. Gonna be fine." Mitchell's eyes followed her up.

The populations were shifting: leaving for war or searching for a better life with better pay than homemaking, farming, or picking cotton; fleeing persecution and prejudice; trying to live better than their parents, hoping their children would live better than them.

The Midwestern state was bordered by great lakes. The north, at the fingers, was forest and farmland; at its palm, a furniture city; fifty miles east, the capital; and farther east, a college town. Still farther east was the metropolis, the automobile center of the world, turning out tanks and jeeps.

In the furniture city, Brother Crawford smiled watching the carpenter finish his porch. He was the first colored carpenter Brother Crawford had known. Crawford's grin widened as he thought about it. Mr. Tom did a lot of jobs for whites; he was charging plenty, but Brother Crawford was getting his money's worth. Why not give the money to his own?

He moved from the window. He had two grandsons in the army and prayed blessings on their heads every morning. Evening came, and he inspected the site. Mr. Tom had cleaned up and would probably finish on Monday. It was a good sign. He was expecting visitors and straightened up the living room.

"I think Brother Stokes will eat some of that pound cake. He got the sweet tooth. The rest may just have coffee."

Sister Crawford nodded and kept working. She enjoyed these Saturday evening gatherings. Some of the men brought their wives, and they enjoyed drinking tea and sewing in the kitchen.

The men were five: two coloreds, a Southern white, an Italian, and a Jew.

The Italian was Catholic, an old ragman by trade. He still worked but didn't need to. He owned his home and some rental property, but working the streets gathering rags, and talking to people, he realized, was the reason he survived. He quoted the scriptures and became known for it. He didn't have any Italian friends who read scripture. They figured loving scripture was for priests and nuns, not for an everyday man. He had carted Brother Crawford's rags away for years. They spent so much time discussing the good book that he began coming just to talk.

The Jew was from somewhere in Europe, old, but sharp, and didn't work anymore. Everyone figured he had money because he was retired and Jewish. He did the ragman's books for free. He joined the meeting, and they were three.

The colored was Southern born and wasn't a churchgoer. He read his Bible, started as a young man, and never stopped. Maybe that was why he didn't like churches. Some of the preachers didn't know their scriptures and seemed to twist it, he thought. He read it, applied it, raised his children by it, and wore it out. He burned his tattered ones; he thought it sacrilege to put them in the garbage.

When he was a workingman, he read at lunchtime. People thought he was strange, and it amazed him that they thought so. He figured it was the most interesting book ever written, and they didn't know anything about it. Why, there was war, famine, pestilence, love, incest, genocide, loyalty—everything you could ask for in a book—and (to his way of thinking) it could make you wise.

The white was born and raised in Dixie. He hadn't known a Jew until he joined the group. His mama gave him a Bible on her deathbed and made him promise to read it. He had done so ever since. It helped him choose a mate, rear his children, and put peace inside. He felt ready for anything.

The three wives went to the kitchen with Sister Crawford. The men turned to the book of Job.

"Now the question is this: when the scripture says, 'There was in the land of Uz a man named Job, was there such a man in the land of Uz or is it a story?"

"Is this a story . . . It's in the book!" The white Southerner tipped his wire rims, grinning.

"Well, let me ask you." Brother Crawford rocked back. "In the Gospel they asked Jesus, 'Who is my brother?' And he said, 'A certain man went down from Jericho and fell among thieves.' Was there a man that went down from Jericho, or is Jesus using a story to illustrate a principle?"

"Why it's a story, an allegory," the white proclaimed.

"Then, it's established that the Bible uses stories, and to say that something is a story doesn't take away its authenticity."

"Quite so." Brother Crawford nodded.

"So the question is, is the book of Job a story?"

Sister Crawford entered and refilled their cups.

"Jesus was one of our boys." The Jew usually said that when they quoted from the New Testament. "Why do we ask?"

"Well, I think it's important. Job is not a Jew, and I think Old Testament scripture is displaying God's love for every man. It's a wisdom book: bad things happen to good people, and we can't always understand why. It's probing the mystery of justice."

"A good point, but we must not be led into thinking that whenever it reads like a story that it didn't happen." The Jew had the floor. "Genesis speaks of people living hundreds of years and God creating the world in six days—is it fantasy because it doesn't fit our notions? . . . Faith, then revelation!"

Later, their wives joined them.

"Wonderful evening."

"Israel will be a nation. It's scripture." The Jew buttoned his coat, gazing at the full moon. "I hope to see it."

"It will be the end of the world then, and I hope to see it too." Brother Crawford gazed up too.

The Jew chuckled. Such eschatology reminded him of Chicken Little's tale and "the sky is falling."

"What they doing down in the woods by the train tracks? It ain't the Depression."

"It's a hobo jungle. They outta work. Used to be more before the war."

Brother Crawford put the lights out, thinking about the twenties and being on the road with white, black, brown, and yellow eating out of the same pot.

Two hundred miles east, Henry Ford was paying, and they kept coming.

Belle Isle stretched for miles and held a hundred thousand easy. They came to cook and relax, to take a boat ride and forget the assembly line. A man untangled his line, tan faced, stout, a worker, glad to be breathing the country air. He loved fishing. It reminded him of Alabama. After a day in the plant, it cleared his mind of the noise and his body of fumes. He fished for bass and threw the rest back. He'd be drafted soon. Women were already taking their places in the factory. He thought about fishing while working and eating, dreamed about it. He loved eating fish but loved catching them more.

He poured coffee and unwrapped his bacon and egg sandwich and dallied, smelling the grass and the scent of flowers, with the sun highlighting the water and pole. He worked the night shift. His Ford was parked beyond the bridge, and he kept it polished. He had an apartment, two suits, and several pairs of shoes, and he wished his folks had come North too. By noon families came with picnic baskets. There was a gleam in a youngster's eyes watching him pull out the big bass. When he was a boy, he didn't watch—he fished.

Another fisherman a hundred yards away noticed some colored men. He was forty-five, slim, and muscular and had been fishing there for years. He remembered the first time he saw coloreds there. He hadn't said a word, and it didn't bother the fish none. Now there were more, and sometimes he felt like the outsider. They were crowding him, changing the music and the rules.

He worked at the plant that made tanks. Some colored fellows worked there too, with some rednecks and women; it seemed like there were more each week. The women were good to look at, but out of place, it seemed to him. The men were the same, glad to be up North, rednecks trying to act the same as him, raised on dough and lard and not accustomed to anything—white niggers acting like they had been up here all the time and had it coming, was how he saw them, and he called them *boy* the same as he did the coloreds, making them bristle. They never would be as good as a Northern white man, to his way of thinking.

He left before noon. Some other whites came early and staked their share of the grounds. There were no signs, but the coloreds got the idea. Nearby, a third white fisherman looked up, stepping into his boat, and pushed off.

Whoever saw a nigger with a boat like this, or a redneck either. Coloreds do a lot of laughing and drinking. They used to be quiet and show they had a right to be here. Now, they're taking over. He paddled down the river until he couldn't see a soul.

In the evening, groups of whites paraded in cars. Belle Isle used to be theirs; now they had to share. The police patrolled, but it shouldn't have changed—it was a crying shame! That was the feeling.

A colored youth took a drag of his cigarette and exhaled through his nostrils and sipped beer, turning away when the police drove by. He and his friends didn't like the cops, and the feeling was mutual. They were there to patrol them, not the whites. The last time there was a rumble, they didn't intervene until the coloreds were winning. Then they ran everybody off, cleared the damn place, but later let the whites back in.

Nearby, another white fisherman packed his gear. He felt relaxed, had caught a few, and had had enough for the day. It was evening, and he worked the night shift and needed some shut-eye. A hundred yards away, a group of whites heard the news.

"Niggas killed a white child. Threw her in the river!"

"They're animals! I hate 'em!"

They in the way and making things worse. When they move to a neighborhood, it gets run down. There goes your life's savings.

The white crowd approached, grabbing whatever and whomever they could. The fisherman ran. It was a rumble, and coloreds retreated until more of their friends came and attacked. The whites escaped in cars, vowing to come back.

Miles away, in Black Bottom, youngsters were forming a crowd.

"Heard the white folks threw a colored baby off the Belle Isle Bridge! Killed him, killed some other people too!"

The old man was angry; so were the young boys. They remembered the black doctor who earned enough for a house in a nice neighborhood. Whites tried to scare him off, but he got his gun and shot back.

"Killed a colored baby!" The crowd grew. Young people were in the streets.

"Junior, you better get in this house!" A mother grabbed her teenager by the ear and pulled him into the house.

The crowd moved on, passing liquor stores, breaking windows, taking whatever they wanted, setting fires, and proceeding to Belle Isle.

"Get that whitey over there!" The black crowd approached groups of whites.

In a white neighborhood three miles north of Belle Isle, a white youth sat on the porch with his hunting rifle. He heard about the killing and looting. He was an A student. His father was at work, and he would protect their home and what his father worked for.

Other whites gathered in cars with bats, knives, guns, and garbage can lids and headed for Belle Isle.

"Kick asses!" They pulled others aboard; they roamed Belle Isle, surrounding groups of coloreds. Shots rang out, and two coloreds lay on the ground. Policemen came and fired into the colored crowd. The coloreds shot back, and a policeman took one in the shoulder.

More policemen came, but the rioting was out of control. They called in the state militia, but it was too big; they needed the National Guard. There was looting, burning, and snipers shooting from roofs. The National Guard shot at will. In the aftermath, there were 332 treated in the emergency room at Receiving Hospital and released. There were 185 whites and 147 Negroes. Gunshots: 12 whites and 9 Negroes. Stabbing: 28 whites and 121 Negroes. Beating: 145 whites and 121 Negroes. Seventeen people died: 3 whites and 14 Negroes. Some whites protected coloreds, and some coloreds protected whites. But it was a race war and in all the papers.

Some said it was brooding for years, instigated by the NAACP and leftist colored newspapers. Colored newspapers called it fascism: thugs and policemen against colored citizens.

The *Detroit News* never confirmed that a child had been killed.

Chapter 8

It was the Pacific; the ship sliced through under the blinding sun. A year had passed, and Caleb finished the letter and began one to Leslie. He wondered if Leslie had learned to read and wondered how he and Mary were doing.

The Japanese occupied some of the islands, and the ship was on alert. Caleb worked in the kitchen, a Jim Crow job. There were a few fights with the whites, but it was always one-on-one and never a race riot. At night, they played cards, talked, and passed a bottle. He never cared for whiskey before, but drinking from the same bottle and acting like it tasted good and didn't burn was a part of the closeness in being adrift. Worrying wouldn't help, so he stopped. They'd transported a colored regiment the week before, all buttoned up, raring to fight.

He thought about his recent return from port and put his pencil down and gazed through the porthole. The local girls liked them. It was a small place, and the colored sailors kept to themselves. Something told him not to go with her, but it had been a long time and after two whiskeys. He remembered the widow on the farm when he was thirteen: it was his first time. He would write Babe-Ruth at another time.

He hadn't heard of the *Pittsburgh Courier* or the *Chicago Defender* when some Northern boys pulled out copies. They dealt with colored issues and concerns in the war and on the home front. It was time to get to the kitchen. He tucked the pad under the bunk with the newspaper, smoothed the blanket, and stepped back. There was order and a place for everything in the navy.

Reuben was in France in the infantry; Atlantic City born and bred, he had lived in Jersey in apartment 5 alone. He imagined his apartment: a few French books lined the shelves next to the radio and the Victrola. The records had been placed neatly between bricks; most were Armstrong and Bessie Smith. There were four French records, and he used to play one daily.

"L'eau est dans la bouteille. Il devrait une facon plus facile pour maitriser le Francais—Assez de choses enfantil . . ." He thought he might go to Montreal—or Haiti—not France.

French was an obsession. It was surprising his school had a class. He took to it instantly, deciding to speak it, knowing he would. Two suits hung in the closet. He had graduated at the top of the class from an all-colored school and finished third in the state in the college entrance exam. Most of his friends took hotel jobs or went to the army. He had worked at the lumberyard saving so he could travel; he wanted to see things and go places, except for the South. The hardest workers at the lumberyard were Southerners; that told him something. Now he was driving for the general because he spoke French.

Eighteen months had passed, and Rueben and friends headed for the Paris bars. The waitress smiled. "Welcome, GIs! We have special menu today."

"Je parlerai de la part de ces mecs."

"Qu'est-ce que vous buvez?"

"Du vin pour tous."

"No, make mine whiskey—two." Jeff held up two fingers.

"Servez vous du whiskey."

The beef was expensive and thin. The room filled with soldiers. They were getting better service, the white soldier at the bar was thinking as he gulped his beer.

"Niggers seem to be running the place!"

More whites entered.

"Got the best-looking women serving them darkies!"

Two military police entered, and the waitress put two glasses of wine on the counter.

"This bar is off-limits to colored soldiers." His partner touched his holster. "I don't make the rules, but I enforce 'em."

"I didn't see no sign. They served me and I'm finishing my drink and ordering a meal." Jeff was six feet and wiry and boxed for the army. "I'm gonna eat it too!"

"Sarg is just doin' his duty." The second MP stepped forward. "It ain't personal, but we can bring as much force as we need . . . It ain't worth the trouble, soldier."

"Drink and divvy up."

A thin man, with yellow teeth and wringing his hands, came from behind the counter. "It's on the house, soldier. My brother got a place a short walk. No problem."

Reuben and the colored soldiers walked the half mile. It was a bar for locals and less fancy. The owner looked like his brother, with more hair. "Tell me your country. Sit, drink."

Jeff finished his second drink. "Felt like turning the place out. We coulda handled that bunch, but why look for trouble. Ain't gotta prove we's men."

The owner smiled and beckoned another round as a waitress glided by. There were rooms off to the side and a big one at the rear with pool and card tables.

Back in Atlantic City, two years passed slowly if you were waiting for your husband to return from the war. Lona had been born in a hospital, and it drained most of their savings. She was walking and talking, and Caleb got all the news in letters. The house was quiet, and Junior and George squatted, drawing on newspapers. The radio was on a ledge, and Babe-Ruth stepped up on the stool, turning it up, and looked down:

"If you don't repent from your sins and turn to Christ, ye shall all likewise perish. Change your attitudes and alter your deeds. Widen your heart and let the light of God in! Love your enemies, pray for those who wrong you, or ye shall likewise perish!"

She released the knob.

"I ask you to bow your heads. Ask God to forgive your sins and change your life. He will come to you and sup with you, and you will be his sons and daughters!"

She stepped down, unaware of the children.

"Pray with me now. Ask God into your life and you will be saved."

Her decision took an instant. Only men and angels could say yes or no.

In the days that followed, she did what she knew: saying a blessing before meals and reading the scripture at bedtime. She reasoned that accepting Christ meant not drinking, smoking, fornicating, attending picture shows, and fighting Caleb. On Saturdays, she went to a church two blocks away. Mildred and Mitchell didn't go to church and knew little about such things, but if it was helping her, they were all for it.

The children began calling her *ma'dear*; it was an expression they had heard.

Mitchell was in the living room smoking his pipe, and the radio was turned low. The candles flickered, and Babe-Ruth was on the couch with the children.

"Ma'dear, why do we have these blackouts?"

"So them Japs don't know we're here and drop them bombs."

"They gonna drop bombs on us, Ma'dear?"

"No. They don't have nothin' against colored boys and girls. They wanna bomb the white folks." Shadows of smoke rings ascended the walls as she led them up the stairs.

Sugar was scarce, and Babe-Ruth baked with whatever she could. She was sweeping the porch when Sister Jones came over.

"I'm gettin' tired of these sirens, blackouts, and rations. Here's your mail, child. A person can't buy enough butter or sugar. Can't make a proper cake. I wish these men would finish their war so we can get on with living."

One letter had writing resembling her own. It was slow reading; she folded and put it into her apron.

"He's doin' fine . . . Told me to tell you hi, and he misses you rice puddin'."

"I think he missing more than that." She chuckled, pursing her lips. "Look, peanut butter! Take it, a whole pound. I got no kids."

Babe-Ruth carried the broom and peanut butter inside.

There were things being written about the war that Babe-Ruth could only feel. The *Chicago Defender* reported the colored view: Uncle Sam was fighting to make the world safe for democracy with a segregated Jim Crow army. French women were told the colored soldiers had tails, a colored serviceman was "executed" in France for having sex with a French prostitute, and one was allegedly killed by an MP for just talking to a French girl.

The Lone Eagles, Tuskegee Airmen, were much in demand; they damaged or destroyed over 409 enemy aircraft, flying 15,553 sorties and 1,578 missions, 200 as heavy bomber escorts deep into the Rhineland, during which not one of the heavies was lost to enemy opposition. The 450 pilots of the 332nd Unit received a Presidential Unit Citation in 1945. General Patton said colored soldiers couldn't handle tanks. The 761st Tank Division distinguished themselves in the field and would receive a belated Presidential Unit Citation more than a quarter of a century later.

The war changed everything: over sixty million died. There was dancing in the streets when it ended. Folks were ready when the first colored units returned to Atlantic City. There was a hundred in the first wave, and they marched down Indiana Avenue, some with only one eye and some with missing limbs.

"That's my boy!" A woman rushed forward.

"Steve, is that you, Steve?"

"Look!" A father stood at attention. They infiltrated the ranks before it reached the center of town. The second wave would be larger. Babe-Ruth cleaned everything to keep her mind occupied and reread Caleb's letters.

A light shone from a window in late November, and a lean figure with a duffel bag moved from Garfield and onto Indiana Avenue with his collar up and hat cocked to the side; a cigarette hung from his mouth as he climbed the stairs. Mitchell was asleep in the living room with his feet on the ottoman and arms dangling. Caleb spotted the corn bread on the stove top and put the duffel bag down. He finished the buttermilk and wiped the crumbs from his mouth. He put the gun (a souvenir won from a soldier in a card game) high on the closet shelf, with the bullets in the duffel, and eased upstairs.

Chapter 9

"Well, well, look what the ocean brought in!" Mitchell's shirt was open, with his suspenders down. "Saw your gear. Man, you a sight!"

That morning, Caleb was on the porch smelling bacon and grits and sipping coffee in the sun.

"Navy didn't hurt me none." Caleb patted his chest. "Fit as a fiddle!" He handed Mitchell a can of tobacco.

"Mildred hugged him, and the children trickled down. George responded slowly at first, and Caleb had something for each one. Then he saw Lona for the first time and just stared. He picked her up and sat with her in his lap for a long time; it would take a while to digest it all.

"Well . . . looka here! This was what I fought the war for!"

Caleb sat around most of the day, and Mitchell came home early and was there if Caleb wanted to talk. They were alone on the front porch.

"Didn't see no Krauts . . . some Japs, water and more water. It was fine with me."

"You a veteran now."

"Yeh." He leaned over the railing and lit a Lucky Strike and exhaled, curling his tongue, making smoke rings, and displayed a bottle of whiskey. Mitchell took a swig.

"Ahhhh!" Mitchell held his breath. "Jack Daniel's. Didn't know you was a drinkin' man . . . You know Babe-Ruth done got religion?"

Mitchell saw the look on Caleb's face and wished he could take it back. Caleb capped the bottle and went inside. He studied Babe-Ruth and leafed through the Bible on the dresser; some passages were in red, and he remembered people carrying Bibles like they were more precious than life itself.

"You sanctified?"

"Yes!" Mildred came in. "I suppose you'd feel better if she woulda been sneakin' around these old tomcats. A man don't know when he's got it good." She stomped out.

He reached into his pocket, taking a long swallow, and hardly talked the rest of the day, but he was thinking.

He got his job back like Uncle Sam said he would. He felt naked when he wasn't working. Babe-Ruth packed thick slices of Spam with a couple of bottles of Coca-Cola and some coffee. He forgot he was mad as the days passed, but it lay beneath the surface: critical, short, dissatisfied. He would keep an account. He had no religious training, but everything he knew came to mind. If his eggs burned, he yelled. If she got sassy, he chuckled.

"Is that the way a Christian woman's s'pose to answer her husband?"

To irritate her, he would take his pistol to the backyard and shoot at the tree stump with the whiskey bottle in his back pocket. The stump was big enough to sit on and would absorb a lot of bullets. The neighbors complained, and Mitchell told him he couldn't shoot anymore. Caleb loved drinking whiskey when Babe-Ruth was watching, smacking his lips after a long swig, sneaking a side-glance to catch her passing judgment. Slamming doors or breaking a dish were probes of her irritability. He had a fair sense of Christian virtues.

He didn't share his thoughts with Babe-Ruth and seemed to be saying that he had changed too. To Mitchell and Mildred, the changes were in Caleb's mind and Babe-Ruth was the same, but more mature and peaceful. Caleb's new friends seemed to be have been chosen with the idea that she would see right through them, and she did.

"I think you a little hard on Babe tonight." Mitchell puffed away and read the newspaper. Caleb nodded and took the sports page.

Months went by, and there were plenty of civil rights activities and talks concerning the NAACP. They felt like everything was about to change. Caleb thought Babe-Ruth might be the same except for attending church on Saturdays and reading the Bible. She was not given to irritability, a virtue to which he contributed.

Caleb can be evil when he wants to be, Babe-Ruth was thinking. *Trying to find my weak spots. I almost hit him the other day. Mildred told him off good. I didn't like her cussin' him though.*

Caleb's goading bothered Mildred more when it was done in front of the children. She was on Babe-Ruth's side.

That Friday, the sky threatened rain. In an alley four blocks away, a black cat sniffed atop a garbage can, and men squatted with wine bottles wrapped in paper bags.

"Don't drink it all, Caleb. Pass the bottle to me." Caleb wiped and stared at the clouds.

"Damn it! Laid me off. Worked my fingers to the bone—gave him one and a half hours' work for an hour's pay. He walks right up to me. 'Boy, I'm gonna have to let you go.'"

The cat toppled the garbage can and licked inside.

"They let me go too, and I gave them twenty minutes' work every hour." Jim had brown skin and red bumps on his face. He chuckled, reaching for the bottle.

"The future's with the union." Caleb held up the paper: UNION WINS DEMANDS IN DETROIT. "They have to stick together."

Jim turned the page. "They say this colored boy is up in Montreal, and next year he gonna be with the Dodgers. Name's Robinson, college boy."

"Let me see that." Ron was almost black, and his mustache was difficult to see. "Ain't that something!" Jim's drinking partner hadn't been at it as long. "That's what we fought the war . . . They say he's a goodun." Caleb read over his shoulders.

"Gimme that back!" Jim gulped and began singing:

"Drink wine spodi yodi, drink wine ba, ba.
Wine, spodi yodi, drink wine."

Jim habitually sang the song when he was drinking.

"Wine, wine, wine: sweet cherry.
Wine, wine, wine: cream sherry.
Pass that bottle to me."

Jim lived with his sister, and he wouldn't have to pay rent for a while. He would still be able to buy food and drink.

Caleb put the newspaper in his back pocket and moved down the avenue by boys playing a game with a disc on the chalked sidewalk. Jack

Robinson's name rolled on his lips, and the gray row houses were a blur. He climbed the stairs, stomping in and slamming the door.

"Laid me off, that's the last." He put the money on the kitchen table.

"We'll manage." Babe-Ruth counted and put a dollar and change in his hand. "Every Friday you bring home $45, not $44.20 like today."

"I did some drinking."

"Well, I always give you $2, not one dollar and twenty cents like now, then I make the budget. I pay $17 a week for groceries, and $10 goes for the rent and electricity. I put $14 dollars under the mattress." She went upstairs and returned with a brown bag. "I missed some during the war, but we got $1,100 dollars here."

Tears welled in his eyes. So what if she got a big head, he was thinking; he didn't care. She had his dinner ready. He washed in the sink and made a sandwich of Polish sausage and went to the living room, where Mitchell shuffled the deck beside a stack of pennies.

"Sit. Let's get it on."

Caleb put down his money. "Got laid off . . . Ruth saved $400—we'll be payin' our share." He grinned, reshuffling the cards.

"Laid off, did ya? Well, Ruth is a fine woman, religion and all." Mitchell peeked over his hand. "You know, Caleb, religion is good for women. They made that way. You won't be laid off long. You a bloodhound when it comes to work."

"If a man don't work, he ain't no man." It was a lesson he had learned from Jesop.

Luther was right. Caleb found a construction job for the summer, and they were back at the lumberyard in the fall.

Reuben came home. The general he had chauffeured wrote a recommendation to Princeton and gave him a copy.

"You got the GI Bill, use it!"

"La guerre ne nous faisons intellegint . . . How do you like my French?"

"Ha-ha. There you go!"

"Plenty brothers died!"

Caleb remembered Reuben had a huge serious side. Caleb was a good worker, but that didn't cover everything. Some of the men in his outfit could be doctors, lawyers, and teachers, and some would. He couldn't imagine Reuben staying in Atlantic City and working for his bosses. What would he have been like if he had been born in the North and gone to school? The thoughts were on his mind.

It was the charter meeting of the city's chapter of the NAACP, and Rueben was secretary and had the papers in order. He didn't go to church until he realized it was a political power base. Twenty were present. The president-elect was the pastor. Rueben had done his homework and would do the busy work; deferring leadership to the older man was good politics.

It was the third meeting, and he coaxed Caleb along. The city only hired colored people for low-level jobs, and they paid taxes like everyone else. It was a long meeting, and as they walked home, Caleb was tired of all the serious talk and told the tale about how the giraffe got a long neck.

Caleb cackled when he finished, but Reuben didn't laugh.

"You know it was funny. Go ahead and laugh."

"That's just the kind of foolishness they expect us to be laughing at. Those are slave tales, and we ain't no slaves."

"I don't care. I been listening to them all my life. My daddy had a thousand of 'em." Caleb didn't flinch.

Reuben offered no further argument. The story was funny, and Caleb was delighted with his rendition. When they parted, Caleb thought some more. As smart as Rueben was, he thought everything white was civilized. There was good in the tales, and they made you laugh. Caleb thought if education didn't have room for a laugh, it needed changing. He would go with Reuben to his NAACP meeting, but he was staying who he was.

When asked to go again, Caleb said, "Only if you listen to my tales on the way home." Rueben agreed. "And speak me some French!"

Caleb was surprised at all the stories he remembered, and Rueben looked forward to hearing them. The NAACP meetings were serious, and Caleb saw men analyzing issues, planning, and drafting a letter to the mayor, which was distributed to all the churches. The city still didn't hire colored firemen, but the number of garbagemen tripled. It was a victory, and they were never going to stop.

Chapter 10

The train rushed through the countryside. Caleb and Rueben were going to bury Jesop. Rueben hated going South and was the only one of Caleb's friends that Babe-Ruth liked.

"Well, let's see what she done packed." Caleb handed him a drumstick. Jesop's age was a mystery. He was never sickly, and he died in his sleep. Caleb guessed he was past eighty. Mildred didn't come, and Caleb figured she knew herself well enough.

"I guess you hafta say yessuh and nossuh to the white folks?" Caleb didn't answer. "Sounds like your pa was a good man."

"Never took no sass. Kept me in line. Taught me to work hard."

"I never knew my daddy. People used to say he was white." Reuben had never talked about his family. "Mama said he wasn't. She was young when she had me . . . pretty, married when I was four. Bastard never liked me. He was dark and didn't like white people, thought I was a half-breed. If I was, it was Indian. Not everything mixed is white . . . I don't believe in God"

Reuben leaned back as Caleb's mouth dropped like he was seeing Rueben for the first time.

Rueben continued. After his mama died, his stepdaddy worked nights and left him in charge. Reuben knew where the pistol was and kept the bathroom door cracked with the light on. Boon, Jim, and Brett were asleep. His stepdaddy constructed the beds. Brett slept on the top bunk across from his, and the younger boys used the bottom ones. His stepdaddy hardly talked to him, but he loved his brothers.

In the morning, his stepdaddy helped them get ready for school and slept until they came home. Reuben supposed he was a good man.

He awoke one night, and a rat was nibbling crumbs from around Bret's mouth. It fled when he leaped up. Brett slept right through it.

Reuben waited with the pistol cocked. He was ten and had never fired a gun. After an hour, it reappeared. Reuben fired, and Brett started screaming with blood all over him. Caleb covered his drumstick.

"Whipped me for killing a rat, almost killed me."

They buried Jesop in the meadow surrounded by the forest, where they had buried Caleb's mother and Louis. Rueben and other men did the digging. Caleb was silent and said things under his breath that nobody could hear. The rain hardly penetrated the foliage around the meadow. The gravestone was small and homemade with cement, and Caleb did the writing. People he hardly knew came. Mr. John looked more like his daddy; Missy Sarah hadn't changed, and the sheriff was there.

Afterward, Missy Sarah handed Caleb a piece of paper. "It's from Jesop. He said to give it to you for insurance." He read it when he returned to Jesop's place:

> *This letter is written by a trusted friend. The colonel came at me and fell on his knife. It was an accident. He might have had a heart attack. We were afraid to tell anybody. Jesop.*

He signed. Only the J was decipherable. It was his mark, and it was on record at the county courthouse.

Rueben was ready when they headed North. Being at Jesop's place, Caleb realized how poor they were and how important his advice was to leave. He wondered if Mr. Bull was alive. He and Jesop and the older men made you feel safe and made being a grown man big and important.

In the months that followed, Jesop, Mr. Bull, and old black men paraded through Caleb's dreams and were on his mind on Monday after work when he hung his coat up.

Babe-Ruth was losing weight and on the couch. She had had these spells since the war after Lona was born. She suffered from anemia and took iron every few months. The radio was turned low, and George was on the floor.

"Boss man said he had to reduce our pay or lay some off."

Mildred came home and took the children upstairs. Mitchell burned trash; the smell of fried pork flowed from the kitchen window.

"How ya, Babe?"

"Better." She straightened her hair.

"Supper's ready. Come and get it!" Sister Jones's voice echoed from the kitchen.

They watched her pray.

"Delicious!"

She smiled at Mitchell and carried a plate to the living room.

"Well, I'll see you tomorrow. Caleb's lunch is in the icebox."

The men cleaned up afterward. And Caleb lit a Lucky Strike.

"That woman can cook. I think you oughta play possum awhile." He chuckled. "Spring might be the time to move to Michigan. Auto plants and heavy industry—real money. I find a job and send for y'all."

"Let's think about it."

He crossed his legs and exhaled a smoke ring. "We'll think all right."

The street was deserted on Sunday morning. Two lights were on. All was quiet except for the newspaper ruffling and the nibbling of a mouse. Babe-Ruth finished dressing upstairs and turned off the light. Downstairs, Mitchell was reading beside his pot of Java, which he took black with a little sugar, blowing and sipping in the quietness.

"Mornin', Mitchell."

He didn't look up. Nobody got up early on Sunday except him. Babe-Ruth went to church Saturdays. All the days in the week, he was civil; someone was always in the bathroom, talking during the evening news, or wrapping the garbage with the sports page. The list of aggravations came quickly to his mind. Sunday morning was his; he glanced up as she moved through and out the door.

He could hear knocking. Next door, Sister Jones opened, dressed in a blue dress and a wide-brimmed hat, with a Bible under her arm.

"What brings you over so early?"

He sipped and frowned at the distant sounds.

"What church do you go to, Sister Jones?" she spoke softly.

"The Tabernacle Apostolic Church of Jesus Christ."

"That's where I'm going. You never talked about your church when I became a Christian. You never preached or made me feel I was less than you."

Mitchel frowned again.

"When I got sick you cleaned my house and prepared our meals, and you haven't said a thing. You the kinda Christian I want to be."

Sister Jones locked up.

He grimaced, turned the page, and continued sipping.

The Tabernacle Apostolic Church of Jesus Christ was a storefront; a neon cross was over the entrance with the words ENTER TO WORSHIP. White curtains covered the window, the choir section surrounded the podium, and drapes covered the baptismal tank, with the River Jordan painted on the back wall.

A boy of thirteen played the keyboard, and the auditorium was filled. Ladies in hats and men in suits and the children were fresh from Saturday night's baths. The worship leader stood with raised hands. If you had seen him the day before (covered with sweat and sawdust), you wouldn't have known it was the same man. Babe-Ruth and Sister Jones took their seats, and ladies helped with their wraps.

They were Pentecostals: sanctified folks, Holy Rollers. Feet quickened, a child bounced on his mother's knees, and his brother giggled. Praise swelled, and the Holy Ghost descended, and they danced in the aisles. Twenty minutes passed. Suddenly it was silent.

"God is here! . . . He's a great big God!" The pastor placed a pile of handkerchiefs beside his Bible, wiping his forehead as they returned to their seats.

I won't be laid off long—Lord, I don't want to be on no welfare.

He sensed their burdens and thoughts:

Lord, this arthritis is gettin' to be more than I can bear.
Lord Jesus, do something with my boy. I done the best I could.
Jesus, I don't know you very well—help me to know you better.
Speak to me today!

"He's here! We take our text this morning from the book of Isaac 55 . . ." He turned to the reader. "Read!"

"Ho, everyone that thirst, come ye to the waters, and he that hath no money, come ye, buy and eat. Come buy wine and milk without money and without price."

"Preach!" echoed from the pews.

He began slowly, the master builder, enunciating, raising his voice, then thundering, slamming his fist, raising a knee to the heavens as sweat and saliva rained and the pile of handkerchiefs dwindled.

"I have tried to the best of my ability [gasp] . . . to tell you about the promises of the Almighty God! I've preached for an hour, ranted and raved. To some it must be a sight. Some laugh. Some dislike me anyway for preaching eternal judgment. I didn't want to preach it, but [gasp] . . . it's in the book!

"I don't care how ridiculous I look. I want to tell it like it was written. People get a little money or education and reason God's Word isn't good anymore. They will find someone to say it's just a story . . . They will have to answer to God!"

"Amen, amen."

"When I go before the Judgment seat [he held up his Bible] and God says, 'Telefero, did you tell them? Did you preach it line for line?'"

"Preach it, brother!"

"'Did you warn them that the wages of sin is death, and the gift of God is eternal life through Christ Jesus . . . ?' I'll say, 'Yes, Lord! . . . Yes, I told them.'"

He leaned, whispering, hands raised, seemingly about to cry.

"As the choir hums, will you give your life to God? Will you come forward to be baptized and have your sins washed away? He'll forget every sin you ever committed—all things will become new!" The humming continued, with his arms outstretched. "Now while the saints in heaven and earth are praying, will you come? Will you give your life to God? His promise is that he will take up his home in you and sup with you. You will be sons and daughters . . . You will never be alone . . . Is there one? Is there one?"

A man and then a young woman came and kneeled at the altar.

"You out there . . . You, yes you! God talked to you this morning when you were washing your face, and you, God heard you when you promised to be a better father . . . Won't you come?"

No more came, and the humming was at its lowest.

"Now, I'm gonna baptize these that have come, but I want to ask you. If you won't come . . . if you just won't come, will you raise your hand and say, 'Preacher, pray for me?' By raising your hand you are acknowledging God, honoring him. You're saying, 'I can't come now, but, Lord, I want to honor you.' The Bible tells us, 'Those that honor me, I will honor, and those that despise me will be lightly esteemed.'"

The pile of handkerchiefs was gone, and they sang the closing song.

Babe-Ruth waited in the greeting line with Sister Jones.

"Praise the Lord, Rev. Telefero. This is Sister Ruth Jefferson. She comes to join the church."

"God bless you, sister." Babe-Ruth was surprised at how small he was. He was clear-eyed and soaked like he'd run a race. "Sister Jones is one of our church mothers. You won't find a better example. Copy her and you'll be off to a good start."

The sign above the exit read LEAVE TO SERVE.

Chapter 11

The streets were cold in late fall. A fog settled on the sidewalk, and boys on their knees shot scummy tops between chalked lines. Four played; one was missing. If you listened, you could hear corduroy britches whistling, genuflecting, taking turns at the shots.

"Hello, Mr. Jefferson."

"How's George?"

Caleb nodded, climbing the porch. Inside, Dr. Concanon—plump, with white hair and a red nose—was thoughtful at the top step, slowly coming down. Babe-Ruth trailed him, and Mildred and Mitchell came out from the kitchen.

"He has polio, and he's got a fever." He paused, putting on his coat. "Keep plenty of soup in him and grease and massage his legs. I'll be back every other day. Give aspirin for the fever and bathe him at room temperature. Don't let him get the chills. If he changes, I expect to hear."

Babe-Ruth nodded, opening the door.

"Some get better, some don't. It's been ten days. We should know something soon. If you don't make him eat, I'll have to put him in the hospital."

Worry mingled with the smell of bean soup, bleached sheets, and kerosene. Windows were opened in the morning and shut when they thought he might be getting a chill.

"Take a little more, George." Babe-Ruth was in his room and blew on the grits and tried nudging it into his mouth (he was her fourth and weighed seven and a half pounds at birth). She had greased his legs with kerosene and wrapped them in flannel like she was told. He looked tired, and she thought he was losing weight. She wiped his mouth with the corner of her apron.

Days went by, and Dr. Concanon reported no change. Babe-Ruth hummed picking beans; the older children played in the backyard while the younger ones napped. She leaned, separating the pebbles from the beans and peering through the window. Caleb came home with glazed eyes, and she avoided his breath.

Mildred arrived, then Mitchell, and he and Caleb sat for a moment.

"How's he doin'?" Caleb looked away and went upstairs.

Babe-Ruth took corn bread from the oven, Mitchell lit his pipe and carried out the trash, and Mildred began setting the table.

"Well, let me give you a hand with this. Rest a spell. You look like you gonna fall over."

Babe-Ruth looked into the children's room; George was sleeping, and Caleb was beside him in the chair. She entered her room and silently closed the door and kneeled at her bedside.

"Lord, you see my boy George, sick with the polio. He can't hardly move his legs. You know I'm doing everythin', but he won't eat and he ain't improving." She choked. "Lord, I ain't nothin'. You done took Louis. Help my boy."

She had only recently learned to pray. Sister Jones said not to put on airs and say pretty words but to tell God like you see it, and if your heart is clear and your hands clean, he'll answer. She finished and slumped to the floor.

A half hour went by. George was still. Then sweat beaded on his forehead and chest, darkening the sheet. Caleb felt his brow.

"Babe . . ."

She rushed in as rumbling came from the stairs.

The sweat poured. Then his eyelids flickered, and he looked around. After a while, his legs moved, and he tried to rise.

"I hungry."

"Good God Almighty!" Babe-Ruth put him on her lap, and Mildred mopped his forehead. "The fever done broke!" The woman removed his wet underclothes.

Caleb slipped downstairs, returning with a Spam sandwich and some milk, which George gobbled up. Mitchell eased out, reaching for his pipe, and Caleb joined him in the kitchen and put the coffee cups into the sink and took down two glasses and the bottle of Jack Daniel's.

They changed the sheets. Babe-Ruth tucked him in and put the lights out and reentered her room.

"Thank you for savin' my boy. I'm gonna dedicate these kids to you and serve you the rest of my life."

The fever didn't return, and George improved daily. After several months, he was himself. Babe-Ruth thought God had taken Louis the same as he had healed George. That George was fully recovered was enough for Caleb. George was never in the hospital, and nobody else had anything but a cold. Caleb thought perhaps he never had polio at all.

It was spring, and Rueben handed Caleb an envelope as they walked down Indiana Avenue coming from work. Caleb read it slowly.

"'Accepted to Princeton.' You on the GI Bill." Rueben was grinning. "Have a job lined up?" Caleb finished and looked up.

"Where there's a will! Uncle Sam's gonna help."

Rueben never acted like he was better than Caleb, and they felt like brothers. Caleb gave the letter back.

"I bet you gonna be a lawyer. You'd be a goodun."

"I thought about it. I got it in my mind to study languages . . . Might give the law a try."

They turned at Indiana Avenue, and Rueben stopped at the corner store. Caleb continued home. A half hour later, Caleb came out to the front porch with a cup of coffee and saw him leaving. It was strange that he would be in there for ten minutes. Caleb noticed it several times after that, and a few weeks later, he followed him in. Caleb had seen the owner before, but he sensed something. The owner's daughter's eyes lit up when she saw Rueben. She had the old man's forehead, with a pretty face.

"Hey, frenchy!"

Rueben winked back. Caleb bought his tobacco and left. It would be lynching business in the South; he remembered when white women were around and he and Jesop would look down or the other way. Jesop forbade him to talk or even look at white female children and said it was just giving some cracker a license to kill.

Weeks went by. It wasn't Caleb's business, but he figured that if he was any kind of a friend, he'd say something. He did a week later.

"You betta stop talkin' French to that white girl. It's nothin' but trouble."

Rueben chuckled. "It don't mean nothing. She never met a nigga she thought could think, let alone speak French."

Why fool with the man's women when we got them in all shapes and sizes and all colors (was the way Caleb thought about it). Perhaps it was harmless in the North, but it still seemed dangerous and stupid for a smart man like Rueben.

The days were stormy. Caleb had five growing kids and an upstairs that was crowded. Babe-Ruth got on his nerves at time, and he remembered how Mitchell behaved when he was upset with Mildred and tried to do the same. Mitchell said he had never struck her in all their years but had felt like it at times. Sometimes Caleb got so mad at Babe-Ruth that he wouldn't answer to irritate her, and she felt like striking him too.

That Saturday, Junior and George played cowboys in the living room. Caleb took his gun down from the closet and cleaned it. He always kept the bullets in the dresser drawer. The man he won the gun from was going to college and had his sights set on being a dentist. Caleb had never seen a colored dentist and the only one he had ever seen was in the navy

He had met a lot of men like him in the service, colored with dreams of going places and seeing things and doing things that colored men hadn't seen or done. Perhaps that was why Joe Louis was so important: there could only be one Heavy Weight Champion of the world. Who could imagine such a thing! Seeing the Pacific was like heaven (deep, vast, unfathomable). He looked at Junior and George playing. Childhood was special, he was thinking and wondered if they would be dreamers; he thought things would be better when they were grown.

Reuben visited Princeton, and it was all arranged. He had a job and the GI bill, and he would get a small loan. He thought if he did well in the first year, he might win a scholarship and get additional money. He would work at the lumberyard as much as he could until the last day of August.

Caleb left Rueben and headed home. Dinner wasn't ready, so he had a cup of coffee on the porch. He finished and was about to go back in when a shot rang out, and he dropped his cup and ran to the corner. Rueben stumbled out bleeding from his scalp. Mitchell and the neighbors came running.

Blood splattered as Caleb tried to help Rueben up as he sank to the pavement.

"Ahhhhhhhhhhh!" Caleb charged the store, but Mitchell had him by the throat.

"The man got a gun—you got chillun!" Mitchell had help tackling him. "I got one too!"

Blood pooled around Rueben's matted scalp, and he sighed his last breath. Babe-Ruth turned away.

The ambulance and police came and put the store owner in one car and his daughter in another. Mitchell held Caleb by his belt, with Babe-Ruth on his other side.

They called it self-defense. The store never opened again. In the days that followed, Babe-Ruth fixed Caleb special meals like he was a sick child and brought him writing materials and stamps so he could write Reuben's brothers. Mitchell drank whiskey with him to keep him company. Caleb took time off from work and gathered Rueben's things; he packaged most of them for his brothers and gave Babe-Ruth the French records and slept in and lay around all day.

People from the lumberyard and about fifty from the NAACP came to the funeral service at the church where they held the NAACP meetings. His brothers had that pensive look like Rueben. Caleb could see that they were no ordinary men.

That night, Caleb watched Babe-Ruth sleeping. The whole world could turn to manure as long as it wasn't her family. When he and Rueben buried Jesop, he hadn't shared his feeling. Jesop used to be big, strong, and frightening, not used up like he was in the coffin. He could have told her about the men in the navy like Rueben, with that same look, colored men that flew planes, drove tanks, and spoke foreign languages. *He was going to Princeton, damn it! Why couldn't he be somebody?*

Caleb dressed and was out of the house. Lunchtime came, and he grabbed his pail. He drank two cups of coffee and toyed with his Spam sandwiches.

"I hear they gone be laying some off pretty soon." The man beside him devoured a mackerel sandwich. Caleb wasn't listening and noticed the headline: LOUIS BEATS AUGUSTUS IN THE SECOND ROUND.

"Let me read it when you're done." Caleb saved every Joe Louis clipping he could. He had even heard him speak after an exhibition bout in the navy. He reopened his lunch and sniffed. The day went swiftly, and he was thoughtful going home.

Babe-Ruth sewed by the window, thinking about the children: *Jessica is ten, with bulging eyes and tall, making you wonder when the rest of her body would catch up. Anne acts like Jessica, except usually giving in. George is four, two years younger than Junior, cut from a different mold.* She scanned her ancestors for similar streaks of mannishness. *He accepts life's ups and downs and has a great tolerance for pain and has it in his mind to master Junior. They fight every few days, and he doesn't mind being whipped. Lona is a quiet, peaceful child and happy being the youngest.*

She thought about Mildred and Mitchell. They never had children, and the reason was a mystery and unimportant. They had made them feel at home and loved being aunt and uncle. It was an inconvenience, but not a burden. If it had been, they would have known.

Mitchell had a way of acting that made you respect a certain decorum and at the same time left you feeling welcome. Mildred's secret was contentment. When they married, she knew he would fulfill something she needed. She used to talk more. Mitchell knew when to talk and when to listen and was no fool.

"George, you betta' stop whooping that woman!" Mitchell chuckled as George pulled his britches up over his hot behind after Babe-Ruth gave him a spanking. George cried louder. Mitchell was the only one laughing. "Leave that woman alone!" Mitchell roared. Finally, they all laughed in spite of themselves.

Caleb was going to Michigan alone to find work. Babe-Ruth had savings to tide them over until he could send for them. There wouldn't be an argument. His decision shocked everybody. Mitchell supported it, but he was shocked too. Caleb would miss them; it would be like being back at sea.

PART THREE

THE MIDWEST

Chapter 12

Mr. Deyoung's brick Tudor was palatial on the edge of Little Italy. More Latvians were arriving, and he hired some. Eastward, his Dutch neighbors were well off and prospering. His son, Dr. Dan Deyoung, was off to Pakistan to do surgery and teach. He had brought him up right.

Little Italy had a business area lined with restaurants and grocery stores; olive oils and pickled foods and hanging pepperoni lined the windows. The houses were well kept, and many had gardens and grapevines in the back and winemakers from the old country inside.

Farther west were Negroes and poor whites and streets leading to the train tracks and dirt roads. Maurice sat dreamy eyed beside the window. He was in his thirties, but he looked older. He savored his reefer and whiskey and looked adoringly at his manicure and then at the clarinet in the open case. He'd played in the same band and at the same hotel since he migrated from the South. It didn't bother him that coloreds had to enter the hotel from the rear. Years had passed, and touring bands asked him to join up, but the invitations were fewer. He was never going to make it big. The thought had settled in.

A few blocks away, Tom Fenton finished washing dishes. Young Tom had left for school, and he needed to hurry to the job site. He had two men working for him that needed supervision. It was unusual for a colored carpenter to go on his own, but he had to choose between going solo and trusting the whims of a boss. It took a while, and he underbid on jobs at first. Now they knew what he could do, and word spread. He had more jobs than he could handle and was getting offers from other contractors, but he liked the independence.

He would teach young Tom the trade when he got older if he showed an interest. There was more opportunity for colored people in the North, and he realized young Tom might want to do something else. Last night, they had a boxing lesson. Maybe the boy would be another Joe Louis. He smiled as he locked up and hurried to the truck.

In the same neighborhood, young Henry looked up at his aunt Lucille and grinned. His uncle watched him put on his wraps and head out.

"That boy is thrivin'—and you the cause."

She savored the compliment. When they learned she couldn't have children, she cried for a week. Now she was blessed to raise her sister's grandchild, and it was good for everybody.

Henry scampered to the park to play basketball. He would be chosen if he waited for the losing team to leave. The big boys never showed up early on Saturdays. They teased poorer kids unless they were tough. He liked the North; his clothes were as good as anyone's, and he was accepted. His mother's memory had dimmed; he read her letters and wrote back, but Lucille was his real mama now.

A few blocks away, Carter threw a rock and darted into the alley; he was unsure if he heard glass break and hadn't looked back until he got home. He leaned against the locked door, catching his breath. These streaks of devilment brought exhilaration. The apartment was quiet. His mama was at work, and he had everything the other kids had. He wondered if he had hit his target and thought about the BB gun in the hardware store. He took his dinner plate from the oven and imagined himself in the big leagues like Jackie Robinson.

Caleb found work in Michigan in two days. The factory was on the edge of the city and had three hundred workers and made steel auto parts and supplied cement to builders. He worked from 7:00 a.m. to 3:30 p.m., with a half hour for lunch. He and another fellow went halves on a loaf of bread and some rings of bologna and split what remained for dinner.

In the evening, he took the gravel and dirt roads to the forest by the tracks. There were about twenty of them, and they laid planks over trees and built a trench with a tarp to keep rainwater out. The stew heated up, and Caleb threw in bits of ring bologna into the pot.

"I got five children in Alabama." A white dipped in, filling his bowl. "When I get enough money and can get a place, I'm bringin' 'em up."

Caleb leaned against the tree and wiped his tin bowl clean with bread, then filled it with coffee and lit a cigarette.

It was a clear night; they kept the flames high. He rolled up in his blanket and rested on his grip.

It was a week later and 8:00 a.m. when the mailman came in Jersey.

"I hope it's good news." Sister Jones eyed Babe-Ruth sifting through the letters; Babe-Ruth found what she was looking for and leaned against the railing.

"From Caleb." She looked up. "Got a job." She finished and put it in her apron. George played in the corner. She was thinking of Reuben as she gathered up the blocks.

On Friday morning in Michigan, Caleb rolled up his blanket, dusted himself, and hurried to the river and washed, then trotted across the tracks and up the gravel road past old brick houses to the corner store and put sixty cents on the counter.

"Two pounds of ring bologna and a loaf of bread, please."

He stuffed the package into his duffel bag. The factory was ten minutes away, and he arrived early with time to punch in and drink a five-cent cup of coffee, black with two cubes of sugar. The building was lit up and more mechanized and noisier than a lumberyard. It wasn't friendly, but he figured it was because they were about bigger things; at lunchtime he ate alone.

Men gathered around the punch-out clock; they had seen these country boys before and were wondering who was this man from Jersey with a Southern accent, short hair, and pants high up on his waist.

"So you're from Jersey, eh?" The buzzer sounded. He was skinny and mouthing a toothpick and stepped to the clock, putting his card in. "Been to New Yawk?"

Caleb shook his head and punched out.

"Pick any cotton up in Jersey, boy?" The man behind him chuckled.

Down by the tracks, the houses on the gravel road were made of yellow brick, with three stories and long back porches. A few had lawns, and some had concrete patios in front and small gardens on the side or in back. There was a house with a "for rent" sign. The street—level apartment had a flat roof and smokestack. Halfway back, it shot up two stories, which made it shaped like a shoe. Caleb could see a light on and knocked. The door opened, and the aroma of bread and yeast filled his nostrils.

"What can I do for you, young man?"

"I saw the 'for rent' sign. I'm looking for a place to rent."

"Let the young man in." An old man grinned, widening the door. He was about seventy, with brown skin and silvery-gray eyes, about the best-looking old man Caleb had ever seen.

"My name's Brother Crawford and this is Sister Crawford." She was short and light skinned, with freckles, and had all her teeth. "What's your name, son?"

"Caleb . . . I was tellin' yo missus I'm lookin' for a place to rent so I can send for my family in Jersey." He dusted himself and transferred his gloves to his duffel bag, setting it inside the door.

"Sit down, boy, sit right down."

"Ma'am, that's some good-smelling bread."

"You just come right on in." She led him into the kitchen and added a butter dish and a jar of honey and reached for the coffeepot.

Brother Crawford had a look that could be unsettling if you were up to no good. It was Caleb's best meal in a while, and he forgot they were watching. Brother Crawford laughed, and Sister Crawford covered her mouth. The apartment was on the third floor and was unfurnished except for a potbelly stove, a gas range, and a refrigerator. They said he could pay whatever he could until he sent for his family.

It was a joy not to be sleeping outside and have running water. He felt like his ship had landed. Weeks went by, it was payday, and he loaded cement.

"Country boy, come do some drinking with us tonight." Peabody was short, with a triangular head and a scar above his right eye. "We'll take you home afterwards, if yo wife don't mind." He slapped Caleb's back.

Caleb refused the offer. At three thirty, he punched out, cashed his check, and sent money to Jersey. He bought a brown sofa for eight dollars, five down and promised to pay the rest in a week, then shopped for groceries.

It was Tuesday in Jersey; it would be Babe-Ruth's last prayer service, and she wore her Sunday clothes.

"I want to talk with you, Sister." Rev. Teleofero shook her hand, then turned to Sister Jones. "I want you to come too."

The service ended, and they waited outside his office. Babe-Ruth remembered their first meeting. After ten minutes, his door opened.

"So, you are heading for Michigan." He paused. "It concerns me." He spoke slowly, putting his elbows on the desk, folding his hands, glancing at Sister Jones, who Babe-Ruth could sense was nodding. "You are young in the Lord."

His skin was clear and velvety, and his eyes were soft. A faint scar blended into his right eyebrow, and she imagined his perfectly straight teeth were false.

"I know Rev. Clemmons in Michigan. He's white, but as good a man as you'll find. This letter will make you a welcomed member. I don't want you to take a year to meet the saints." He handed her the letter. "God bless you, my child."

Locking doors echoed in the sanctuary. The reverend offered them a ride, but they preferred to walk and dallied on the steps and walked home under the streetlights.

"I'm never gonna leave you, child. Even when I'm gone, I'll be with you."

Chapter 13

In 1948, the Brown Bomber fought a bum a month, Truman retained his presidency, Mao Tse-tung replaced Chiang Kai-shek, Chuck Yeager broke the sound barrier, and Jackie Robinson completed his rookie season with the Brooklyn Dodgers.

Babe-Ruth's and the children's belongings were packed. Mildred had prepared sandwiches. It was all she could do to keep her emotions in check. Mitchell was steady, hugging Mildred and loading the luggage onto the cart he fetched from the station.

"It's time to go. They gonna do fine."

She cried as their train pulled out of sight.

Back in Michigan, Caleb had furnished the apartment and stocked the refrigerator and the cupboards and stood at the sink, wincing as the water struck his knuckles, then dried them and lit a cigarette. He was thinking of two days ago: he had chugged down his coffee, punched in, and loaded cement like he did every day.

"Hey, I bet you miss the smell of cotton up here, don't you?" Chet pulled up with a wheelbarrow. Caleb acted like he hadn't heard and was tired of the country-boy jokes. At day's end, he washed and punched out and noticed Chet and others gathered a block away. Chet shouted out, but Caleb kept walking.

"Bet you'll talk to me now!" His fist grazed Caleb's jaw. Caleb countered, and Chet was down, and Caleb's right cross stopped Peabody as he rushed in. And it was over.

Blood dripped from Caleb's mouth. *They didn't want a fight, or they'd have won.* The crowd dispersed, and his back dried on the way home.

The next day, word spread, and men found reasons to visit the dock and look him over.

"Young man, over here." The supervisor beckoned. "What's your name?"

"Caleb, Caleb, sir."

"Well, Caleb, who taught you to work like that?"

"My pa."

The man grinned. "Dan Yocum. Call me Yocum. Let me see those hands. Go in before you lift another bag and have the nurse wrap 'em proper."

Caleb bent over the sink, remembering, and clenched his fist again. He didn't relish street fighting, but it wasn't broken.

On the train, the children were on their best behavior in their Sunday clothes. Babe-Ruth was pleased as passengers dropped cellophane-wrapped candies into their hands.

"Look, Ma'dear, cows!" George's face pressed the window.

God, you done kept us around a lotta good folks. Babe-Ruth gazed at the countryside.

Be with Jesop in death and take him to your kingdom. I know he was hard at times, but life is that way too, and if he didn't have it in him, how was he gonna survive? How was any o' us gonna survive? Mr. Bull must be gettin' close to meetin ya, Lord, and so must Missy Sarah.

The ride took all day, and after lunch she dozed. She awoke with the kids still napping and wondered how long they had slept. The train stopped, and she spotted Caleb in the crowd; they were the last to get off.

"We fine." She patted his chest. "You look good."

"Hey, doin' fine, better now since y'all come. Don't need much." He hugged the kids and grabbed a suitcase, pulling George toward the pickup. "Belongs to Brother Crawford, our landlord. You'll like him and his missus."

"What happened to your hands?"

"Been working hard."

The neighborhood was mixed; Babe-Ruth noticed it right away. In Jersey, there were whites downtown and plenty at the train station. She thought about the colonel and Dr. Concanon and remembered Southern whites squatting in huts along a river, poor and unwashed, living on flour and fatback. Her pa gave them vegetables, especially tomatoes to cure scurvy. Folks called them rednecks. Her pa never did; he said they were poor and hurting like themselves. The prevailing sentiment was that they were trash, fodder for lynching parties, and if a white couldn't make it in America, he was a shiftless peckerwood, about the lowest creature God created.

Caleb led them along the side of the house to the back steps. Babe-Ruth noticed the racially mixed gathering in the landlord's flat as they climbed to the porch on the third floor and viewed the grassless backyard. Caleb watched her inspect the rooms and the stocked refrigerator and cupboards.

"Well?"

"Fine, Caleb, real good."

There was a knock at the door, and Sister Crawford introduced herself and Brother Crawford, and she brought fried chicken, potato salad, rolls, and Kool-Aid.

"What a fine-looking family." Sister Crawford hugged Babe-Ruth.

They set the table, and Brother Crawford eased back downstairs to his guests. Night came quickly; there would be time to explore in the morning.

The street was half colored, with a lot of large families. In the house on their right, the family had a yellow-skinned daughter; she was well dressed. They owned the house, spoke, but didn't mingle. To their left were the Simmons, white, with ten children; everything seemed out of control. When Mr. Simmons wasn't at work, he was working on his car or drinking. His wife looked worn out.

Strange fragrances came from the Italian's house across the street. Babe-Ruth wondered how the food tasted. Their yard was meticulously pruned, with grapevines running along the side of the house into a backyard and garden. Marco was ten and mannerable and played his trumpet for an hour every evening after dinner. Babe-Ruth enjoyed listening. He dressed nicely; his family spoke but kept to themselves.

Four blocks away, the viaduct went over the train tracks to Franklin School. Some of the Italians attended a Catholic school, but the horn player went to Franklin. Once a family was established, they could open an account at the corner grocery store. On the paved road two blocks down was a colored barbershop. Haircuts were twenty-five cents, too much for some families with children. Chonsey Park was a block away, and she could view the playground from their third-story window: a ball field, a half basketball court, and sets of swings and monkey bars.

On weekdays, she rose at six; fixed Caleb grits, bacon, and coffee; and woke the children before he left for work. When they were ushered off to school, she did her cleaning and washing. At lunchtime, she'd begin picking beans (sorting dried, packaged beans and removing small pebbles and the ones that floated). She usually listened to *Our Gal Sunday* and *Just Plain Bill* on the radio as she ironed or sewed while the younger ones napped.

It was a spring day, and she was in the kitchen. Steam spewed out through the window. She wondered when the Detroit Tigers were going to get a colored player, and she sipped tea and thought about Mildred and Mitchell. The children were healthy, and Caleb seemed like his old self. It was all she ever wanted and the reason she had stood up to Jesop.

About half the children at Franklin School were colored. A third had a drawl. You could tell those who were from large families by their clothes.

Junior decided that his teacher was smart by the look in her eyes. When they were well behaved, she read *The Adventures of Tom Sawyer*. That and recess highlighted his days.

He sat in the back with two friends. Carter was tall for his age and good looking when his mouth was shut, which was rare. He had a round face, and his narrow eyes sparkled over two huge beaver-like teeth. His clothes were new and well fitting. Beside him was Henry, his first convert.

Henry was smaller, with dark eyes and his bushy hair combed back. At home there were lots of rules, and his adjustment had been slow, but he had found friends. They giggled as the teacher recited.

"Stop it!" The girl in front pulled her pigtail from Carter's hand. He froze as the teacher approached.

"You three separate!" She would give them notes for their parents and hoped that would be the end of it.

That Friday, men lined up at the clock. Chet placed his arm on Caleb's shoulder. It was the first time they had spoken since the fight. Chet looked boyish extending his hand, and Caleb took it.

"Cal, let's have a drink?" The bar was two blocks away.

"I'll have a short one with ya." Caleb massaged the change in his pocket.

"Hey, take your hands outta your pocket, and let old Chet take care of things."

Patrons huddled in small groups, and the jukebox blasted the boogie-woogie.

"What can I do for you, fellas?" The bartender's tropical shirt exposed curly hairs, and he put napkins down.

"Two beers! . . . Busy eh?" Caleb lifted the glass, and foam ran down the sides. "Good, very good. Come here much?"

"I like one after work." Chet chuckled. "Washes the tiredness out. Easier to put up with Mary's mouth. You got a mean jab." They bumped shoulders laughing. Liquor bottles lined the mirror; the laughter was contagious. "Hey, you with me?"

"Sorry, man, I was thinking."

"You get paid for thinking?" They roared. "Another beer?"

"No, gotta be goin'." Caleb took his hat out of his back pocket; a husky-voiced woman laughed in the back booth. "Make it a whiskey and I'll stay and watch the scenery."

The drink was strong and good. The woman had a long gorgeous neck, and it made them feel like they were having a good time.

"Big day tomorrow."

"Right." Chet squinted as they moved onto the pavement.

Chapter 14

Rueben's and Jesop's deaths were still soaking in. Caleb burped, patted his shirt, and found a cigarette. Dinner (pinto beans and corn bread, a sweet onion, and Polish sausage) was over, and it was time for the bathroom, a second cup of coffee, and the radio.

"Hello, America and all the ships at sea!"

Walter Winchell reviewed the day's events. Clattering came from the kitchen, and Caleb moved closer, turning up the volume, as the children drifted in.

"Today, I bring you the craze of the nation. The Brooklyn Dodgers are playing inspired baseball, and at the end of the broadcast I will interview the rookie of the year and the first Negro to play in the major leagues."

"Shhhhhh, y'all come in and listen. You gonna be hearing Jackie Robinson." His look was serious. Finally it started.

Winchell: How's it going, Jackie?

Robinson: Just fine, Mr. Winchell. We're fighting for the pennant, and I'm having a good year.

W: You had a great one, the rookie of the year. Congratulations!

R: Thank you, Mr. Winchell.

W: There still has to be enormous pressure. How are you holding up?

R: I'm doing well. I'm playing hard. Mr. Rickey said to be tactful and I'm doing it to the best of my ability.

W: Tactful! . . . Still, it must be a heavy load having the eyes of your whole race upon you, indeed the nation?

R: I don't know. I think I'll be able to look back and tell you better. Right now I'm concentrating on winning the pennant.

W: Thank you, Jackie. Well, there you have it. This Robinson is not only a great athlete, he's an articulate and thoughtful man.

Caleb turned the radio off. "That was Jackie Robinson, the first Negro to play major league ball."

"That's a white man," Jessica spoke for them all.

Caleb thought about Reuben and the men he met in the service and how they made him feel. "That's an educated man! Education! He's been to college. It's not color that makes you sound proper. It's the learnin'!"

"How does learnin' do it, Daddy?" Junior was on his knees.

"Learnin' is being taught how to behave in the world. How to speak like people that have something, to do the hardest jobs that pay the most, jobs you have to be smart to figure out, like a doctor or teacher. That's why we sending y'all to school. 'Stumps and trees grow on land. Education makes the man.'"

It was a bewildering notion penetrating minds where imagination and foolishness competed for space.

Babe-Ruth beheld them through the cracked door and finished scraping the dishes. "Big sister, you better come in here and help out."

Babe-Ruth would attend church tonight. A month had passed, and she had put it off too long. She was a little afraid of Rev. Clemmon's white church. She thought it would probably be Bible class night like in Jersey.

It would be a good outing, she thought. She'd take Junior, and it would be dark when they returned. Perhaps someday Caleb would come. She could read his thoughts before the war; now she feared him when alcohol was on his breath. He took to Brother Crawford though, and she hoped something good would come from it.

Ten blocks was a short walk, and there was too much on the radio and in the newspapers for a young Southern woman to understand. Prayers went up for Caleb, the kids, her sisters and their husbands, Sister Jones, Mildred and Mitchell, friends back in Jersey, and old dead Jesop.

The Apostolic Sanctified Church was the first Pentecostal church in the state of Michigan. Since 1907, three generations worshiped together:

whites, coloreds, Mexicans, and Indians through the race riots of 1919 and 1943; poor folks from Georgia, Alabama, Kentucky, Texas, and Oklahoma; and descendents of the great Azusa Street Revival of 1904.

Six formed the deacon board, brothers serving, praying for families, judging, and burying one another. They said when Jesus came, the tempter's power was broken. America was segregated, but theirs was a higher plane—holiness, they called it. The neighborhood was poor, but the building was big, with freshly painted white brick and a neon cross.

The auditorium was full and brightly lit, with the choir seated behind the podium. It was Bible-class night like Babe-Ruth suspected, and she felt peaceful leading Junior down the aisle. It would be different to worship with white people, but the thought was a dim one as they slid into their seats. The music was gospel and country. A colored man led the singing and after a few songs gave way to the pastor.

The service was similar to the services in Jersey. Babe-Ruth felt at peace, and they waited in the greeting line to meet the pastor.

"Praise the Lord, Rev Clemmons. I'm Sister Jefferson from New Jersey." She handed him the letter. "It's good to be here."

He read it quickly. His jaw was square, and his blue eyes twinkled.

"Good to have you, sister." He smiled; she felt like she knew him. "How is Rev. Telefero? I haven't seen him since last year in Upstate New York." His manner said, "You're one of us."

"Sister Clemmons, come meet Sister Jefferson."

"They call me Ruth."

She met five ladies and liked them all, especially Sister Clemmons. *White people*, Babe-Ruth thought, gliding under the streetlight, holding Junior's hand, *they're the same as us.*

In 1949, Israel became a nation. Some thought it was the beginning of the end of the world and that it said so in the Bible. Harry Truman was sworn in as president. Mao Tse-tung and the People's Republic of China took over Peking. The auto industry fueled the economy, the CIO ousted two communist unions, and the steelworkers' strike won a pension.

Things would get better. You could hear it on the radio and see it on the faces of workers who dreamed of higher wages, an automobile, and a house, immigrants (Irish, Italians, Latvians, and Dutch) striving to live in all-white neighborhoods and be a part of the middle class with a fresh change of clothes every morning.

Coloreds were dreaming too. They knew they were as good as anybody. But the color line said white was better, straight hair and light skin were better, and some purchased skin whiteners and hair straighteners. Caleb was up before the sun, and Babe-Ruth fed them and ushered the older ones off to school. She was pregnant again; it would be her sixth. Caleb dreamed of having his own home and a car. A home was on Babe-Ruth's mind too. In the evening, there was dinner and a little time listening to the radio. Caleb smoked a few cigarettes after dinner and had his final cup of coffee. On church nights, Babe-Ruth returned home refreshed.

It was Thursday, and the sun spilled through the window onto corn bread cooling on the stovetop. The children would be arriving, and she draped a gingham cloth over the pan.

"Y'all stay right where you are. I'll be right back." She motioned to George and hurried down the back steps to observe her children's behavior in the streets. She didn't know what prompted her, but she sensed that it was important.

A group of children turned unto the gravel road; her three were walking along with Henry and Carter and others she didn't know. They passed a drunk who was holding a rolled newspaper and weaving down the sidewalk. He suddenly vomited, lifting his head and trying to focus, as the children jeered.

"Come in, now!" she screamed, and they came running, following her up the back stairs and into the kitchen. "My children mocking a grown man?"

"It wasn't us, Ma'dear. It was those other kids." Big sister covered her mouth.

"We're just with 'em." Junior searched for a better answer.

"Shut up! Kids that don't show respect is trash. We ain't trashy folk and don't hang with them that is. I never want to see it again." She turned away. "Wait 'til your father gets home!"

Hours passed, and Caleb moved up the driveway. The children greeted him, but he sensed there was something wrong. Childhood was a special time, and he had a good time too. Babe-Ruth avoided his breath.

"Caleb, you gotta do somethin'. They was in the street disrespecting a grown man."

"Call 'em in." He bent over the spigot, splashing his face, and took the leather glove from his pocket. "Send 'em one at a time." One by one they lay across his lap. "I better not hear of it again." It was over, and he put away the glove.

Babe-Ruth's pregnancy was barely showing. It was after dinner, and she and Caleb were alone.

"George said he's gonna be a baseball player like Jack Robinson." She rocked, patching pants.

"If he gets an education, he can be whatever he wants." He glanced over the newspaper. "Babe-Ruth, they's colored men younger than me with plenty learning. Things hafta change." He turned to the back page.

She noticed Henry and Carter among the boys playing in the yard. Something about them was hard to put a finger on.

"You know, Caleb, it won't be long 'til we can buy a house."

"Lotta nice places where colored can buy." He stopped reading. "Mr. Yocum got an old Packard he'd sell me for $250. Says I can pay a little at a time. Might consider it in a month or so."

The boys left for the park. She paused at the window and took a black dress from its plastic and felt its cascading pattern. It was a perfect fit. It would be nice to wear to church at special events. It was secondhand and was sold for a dollar at the rummage sale. A rich girl wore it once, and her parents donated it to the Salvation Army. Babe-Ruth covered the dress and patted the money in her apron. They would get that house if things kept going good.

She had a good view of the playground. There were two groups, and she spotted Junior's blue sweater. Play ceased, and they circled. Two were in the middle. It didn't seem like a fight. She winced as the circle tightened. She had seen it before.

"Did you know Bo's mama's on the ADC. The state's taking care of his family. My daddy and yo daddy is feeding them suckas!"

Jeff wiped his forehead and accepted the applause of the kids surrounding them.

"ooooooooh!" chanted an instigator.

"He's talkin' 'bout . . . yo mama!" another agitator chimed in.

Bo appeared unmoved. Past generations had made the rules. He could have warned he didn't play the dozens and fought. To fight now was to lose face. "Jeff, they tell me yo mama is a maid for them white folks. She MADE for her white boss. He be juggin' her regula'. Why you think all you

Smiths is light skinned? Yo daddy ain't light skinned, boy. He be shootin' blanks. I'm gonna pay her to come and clean."

"OOOOOOH, OOOOOOH!"

"Y'all ain't got the money, Bo. Yo sister done told me. I been juggin' her. I give her bologna. Says all she get at home is government surplus rice and flour—no meat, just U.S.A. government peanut butter. I been giving her MEAT!"

Jeff turned, sweating, feigning a grin. "Boy, with all the maid work you mama doin', don't she have time to wash your drawers?" He held his nose, pointing to the graying undershorts showing over Bo's pants. "If I was you, I wouldn't take my shirt off and show you wearing the same filth every day—gimme air!"

"OOOOOH, OOOOOOH."

Bo looked away. And a tear slid down his cheek.

"OOOOOOH, OOOOOOOH, OOOOOOOH!" an agitator catapulted into a summersault. "The winnnah!"

Babe-Ruth grimaced and adjusted the curtain. Five minutes later, Junior and George eased through the gate and climbed the back stairs.

Chapter 15

"I put special treats in."

Lucille wrapped the scarf around Henry's neck and handed him his lunch bucket.

James emptied his coffee cup, and she ushered them out. She had forty minutes before going to work and poured herself a cup. They had worked and saved, had a good home, and now they could share it with Henry. She would write her sister and Henry's mama tonight.

Blocks away, Vera turned to Carter.

"I expect you to behave at school. If you get a good report card, we'll look at that BB gun you been talking about."

She watched him run down the street. Carter would go to the Y after school, and their neighbor would come over and warm his dinner and watch him tonight. Tim would have her home by nine. He was a widower with no children and was a hard worker. Something could come of it.

Caleb put his leather gloves in his back pocket, remembering the night before. It was over, and Babe-Ruth poured his second cup of coffee.

"I want y'all to study hard at that schoolhouse, hear me? 'Spect y'all to do better'n me. In a year we're gettin' our own home. There'll be two bathrooms, a backyard full of grass with a swing and some bars and big enough for a ball game. You'll have to yell to hear from one end to the other. The living room rug gonna be like a cushion so you can walk around naked without gettin' cold."

The children gaped. It was better than eating.

Babe-Ruth was trying not to laugh. "Caleb, you gonna be late if you don't hurry. You kids ain't got all day. If you gonna be somebody, you better eat them grits and get ready for school."

The sun was shining, and Caleb was thinking of Rueben and about breakfast and the spankings. He chuckled on the way out. Babe-Ruth began cleaning and reread the note that Junior brought from the teacher, which had been on top of the refrigerator and put it in the trash.

Groups of children merged nearing school. The bell rang, they took their seats, and the teacher did a roll call. Two were missing, and she looked at Junior, then turned to the blackboard.

Two blocks away, Henry and Carter inhaled the fresh air and disappeared behind bushes, retrieving poles and cans of worms stashed the day before.

"Cal will miss a good time." Carter chewed a blade of grass. "He doesn't deserve to go after what he done. Imagine taking a note home from the teacher and getting a whipping for what the teacher wrote? I don't ever remember a thing like that. It may be the first time in the world." Henry nodded. "The next day he says to me, 'What did yo mama do?' Do you believe it?"

Fresh air filled their nostrils as they ran through the graveyard and over the tracks and into the fields with poles bouncing.

"My aunt's gonna find out, and I'm gettin' the whippin' of my life."

"Hank, she'll never know. I've done it many times. Mama ain't figured it out yet. Wait 'til you see the river!"

Their shoulders bumped as the river came into view. Carter mounted a rock, kicked off his shoes, and cast. The sun warmed their backs, and the stream tickled their toes.

"I got one!" Carter yelled.

It was big. He gave in and let it run. The bobber dove. Then the fish glimmered as he reeled it in. He took out the hook. Then it jerked, splashing back and swimming away, as he spit out the blade of grass. "Shoot! Biggest one I ever caught."

Henry's line tightened; it was the first bite of his life. "It's as big as yours!" He reeled it in, strung it through the gills, and tied it down.

The sun beamed, more fish lined their strings, and they munched Hershey bars. "Carter, I'm going in." He had gone to pee and returned naked.

"See the foam whirling over there! I don't think you better."

Carter is bigger, smarter, and usually makes the decisions, but I caught the first fish my first time trying. Why do I always do what Carter says? He's jealous. The thoughts rushed through his mind as he raced along the shore. "Last one in's a rotten egg!" He jumped in and came up thrashing.

"Help!"

The sun was dazzling. *What if Henry drowned? His mother would hate me, and so would everyone at school. I'm older, and skipping was my idea . . . It's almost like murder.* The thoughts came as Carter rushed along the shore and dove in. They gasped and wrestled . . . and drowned.

The sun beamed into the afternoon. School bells rang, girls played tag, and boys chased boleys (large marbles) heading home. The moon and stars appeared, highlighting foaming currents. Scattered wraps faded in the shadows.

Tragedy was not new to the neighborhood. Fourteen-year-old Alonzo Rice choked on his vomit in a drunken sleep. Evelyn Pierce, a white girl, froze on the railroad tracks as her twin brother jumped to safety. Charles Drew broke his neck diving into a shallow creek and was lucky to be able to walk, but he was unable to turn his head. A ten-year-old girl four blocks away was dragged from her bed and raped and killed. They arrested the brother at first. The real killer was a white man who had seen her in Sunday school. Junior used to speak to his daughters, but stopped.

Days later, the afternoon was like evening. It sprinkled, then poured, as children scurried into the funeral parlor. It was the first time most had seen a corpse. Henry and Carter didn't look like themselves dressed in suits and displayed in purple-velvet-lined boxes with brass railings. It was a picture to be stowed away, held under like a beach ball, until the time was right.

Babe-Ruth rocked, remembering Junior running from his shadow in Jersey. He wouldn't eat certain foods, so she prepared him special meals. He began to stutter, and at school he brooded and daydreamed, feeling nastiness in his throat and covertly spitting phlegm onto his chest.

"The capital of Argentina is . . . Bogotá."

Mrs. Levy knew the deaths of Henry and Carter was affecting him. He had been one of her best students, and now he wasn't trying. He shared a bit of history with the class.

"The Jews killed Jesus."

"Who told you that?" He could see that Mrs. Levy was angry.

"A big boy," he countered.

"You tell that big boy he's wrong!"

She was pretty and smart, but he didn't like her anymore.

The next day, a classmate put a quarter in a Noxzema jar inside his desk; when the class went to recess, Junior took it and came home with potato chip crumbs around his mouth. Babe-Ruth noticed the crumbs right away.

"Where did you get the money for those chips, boy?" She wiped his mouth with her hand.

"A man gave it to me for catching his dog, Ma'dear."

It was a sufficient answer, but the lie lingered. He thought about stealing and lying when he slid into the hot tub on Saturday night and again the next day in church. He came suddenly upon a growling dog and thought it was Lucifer himself, not knowing the dog was chained or that a car barely missed him as he fled across the street.

She was worried about Jessica too. She had burned her right cheek on the potbelly stove a year earlier, and it left a scar. She seemed frightened of Caleb, whom she adored, and he didn't notice. Rather he ignored her and was repulsed by the facial scar and her guarding Babe-Ruth whenever there was an argument.

"Scarface!"

And he said other hurtful things, which Babe-Ruth tried to soothe. "Ma'dear, why does Daddy hate me?"

"He don't hate you, girl. It's the alcohol and some meanest that got inside of him—he ain't hisself."

Babe-Ruth worried about Caleb, who was staying away weekends. It was endurance that mattered in a drinking bout, and on occasion he drank two-fifths of whiskey in a night. He laughed when the man fell from his chair, and Chet put twenty dollars in his pocket.

"OK, put your money down. I say this nigga can outdrink anybody here and walk away. Here's twenty dollars to prove it."

Sometimes he couldn't remember things. He looked over at Chet snoring. He didn't know the people, but they were Chet's friends. Ten dollars was missing from his wallet. He had stashed most of his money in the Packard. He won it back playing cards and was there all day drinking and eating pig's feet.

Four days later, he had the drip and was afraid to sleep with Babe-Ruth. Chet went with him to the doctor and left with a sore butt too. Caleb secretly washed his drawers and put them in the laundry and didn't touch Babe-Ruth for a month.

On another weekend, he was in a fight and had a swollen jaw and bruised hands. One weekend lasted four days, and he didn't go to work on Monday; he told Mr. Yocum his mama had died. Babe-Ruth didn't understand, until the flowers came. Then she was ashamed.

She told Rev. Clemmons, and they began praying regularly for him.

"Open the damn door!" It was a week later and Saturday afternoon. Caleb stumbled in and vomited and fell asleep beside it on the floor. She ushered the kids away. Seeing their father that way wasn't right. She cleaned him up and checked his wallet; half his check was gone. If she hadn't been a Christian, she'd have beaten him sober.

Caleb's carousing continued in the following weeks. She continued praying and stayed out of his way.

"Junior, stop that damn stuttering. Ruth, can't you teach him to talk right?"

He missed work again, and his job put him on notice. Almost losing his job told him something. He thought about Junior and tried talking to him. *Why is she always so steady, damn Christian, blaming everything on me, turning the children against me?*

For two weeks he stopped drinking and was in control. He was sure of it.

"I'm the boss of my home. I come home when I gets ready and I go when I please."

Chet nodded, teasing with a sneer, hinting that Babe-Ruth was keeping him out of the bars. His abstinence lasted another fortnight, enough time to assure himself he had licked it and to secure his job and pay the back rent. He smoked more cigarettes and had a shot with Chet to show he was all right.

Caleb was thirty-four, drawing a regular check, a grown man. He smoked his Lucky Strikes, drank an occasional shot or two, and listened to the radio. There were men like Brother Crawford, spiritual men, who had the idea that this world was a stopover, men with eyes bent on doing the right thing as they saw it, trying to save their souls, but there was more to it. Some were dreamers like Reuben, who didn't believe in God or heaven but had some idea that was better than anything they ever saw or felt, an idea that made living bearable and gave them a reason to get up in the morning.

Men like Caleb talked with their fists, worked with their hands, relished their food, and enjoyed burping and sitting in the bathroom, relieving themselves and having a cigarette, doing the thing at hand; sensing their strength, feeling good when they get their check, and cursing when they were shorted. There was stupidity in such men—grunts of war, builders of cities, survivors that kept getting up and coming.

Caleb remembered lying in his vomit and the children watching and promised himself not to drink heavy anymore. There was more to life than feeding kids, so he purchased a gray suit and black alligator shoes, silk socks, and a polka-dot tie. He went back to the bar and found that yellow woman with the long neck. He and Lillie became a pair. And if he brought home most of his check, it was his business.

Chapter 16

Junior knew he would be spanked for failing the second grade. He walked through the graveyard, along the tracks, and through the field. He had put in a good last day of school, and he would have learned and recited properly if Mrs. Levy had been nicer. He would rather be spanked by Caleb; he knew it would hurt more, but then it would be over.

Babe-Ruth read the report card and stared out the window. It had been a difficult year: a different school, Henry's and Carter's deaths, and Caleb drinking and now gone three days, probably carousing with Chet.

"Mama, I'm sorry. Me and that teacher don't get along. She don't like me."

"Watch your mouth. You got no business passing judgment on no grown person. You and me goin' to that school and talk to that teacher."

"When's Daddy coming home?" He lowered his voice.

"Soon. You know, sometimes things bother him like they bother you, only bigger 'cause he's a man. He's not himself . . . having trouble with his drinking. He'll be all right." She squeezed him and could feel his heartbeat and sensed he was not all child.

A stranger knocked, and she inspected the room.

"Mrs. Jefferson?" He stood, hat in hand, in a dungaree shirt and jacket. "I'm Yocum, Caleb's supervisor."

He was big, with a round face and blue eyes, with flushed cheeks and nose, and she directed him to a chair, where his huge red hands rested on his knees.

"Where's that husband of yours? We ain't seen him since he got his check on Thursday . . . Sick?" Junior was standing guard. "He's out there drinking? Running with those fellas? No good can come of it."

The vanilla curtains screened the sunlight.

"How many kids you got here?" Junior held up five fingers. "I want to tell this boy something. Your daddy's the best workingman I have ever seen. And I've seen them all. If he's back Monday morning, he still got his job . . . Tell him

Yocum said so."

"Mr. Yocum . . . thanks." And he was gone.

"Get your hat. We're going to that school." She leaned into the kitchen, taking her apron off. "Jessica, watch 'til we get back."

Junior tried to keep up, then sat outside the classroom, watching them talk. He couldn't hear. It wasn't mean talk, but it wasn't friendly either. They finished, and he prepared for the worst.

"Thank you for coming, Mrs. Jefferson." The door opened. He had been whipped for less.

"Somethin's not right between you and that teacher, boy." They passed a malt shop, and she hesitated, then went in. "Two Whirla Whips, please." They walked home eating ice cream.

Imagine that! Junior thought his ma'dear was like Solomon and David in the Bible. She didn't lie, cheat, or steal, and you couldn't always figure her out.

Evening came, and Junior was waiting for Caleb and hoping for another reprieve.

"Daddy's home!" Junior rushed him. The others came running, and Junior was in Caleb's arms before he could climb the stairs. "Daddy, where you been?"

"Go back and play." Junior and Jessica leaned against the railing, looking up with ears perked.

"Junior didn't pass the second grade . . . I think it will be all right though . . . He ain't no dumb child. He'll be all right . . . Mr. Yocum was here." Babe-Ruth paused, then realized he had heard. "Says if you there Monday, you still got your job."

"I'll be there." He entered the bathroom wrapped in a towel.

She rinsed pots and noticed Junior and big sister leaning on the railing below. Caleb reentered the bedroom and came out in his sport coat.

"Where you goin'?"

"Don't be questioning me, heffa!" His fist shot out, and her scream brought rumbling from the stairs. Jessica and Junior rushed in. Babe-Ruth's nose was bleeding, and she tried rising but couldn't. "Stay out of my business!" He turned to Jessica. "Scarfaced heffa!" and slammed the door on the way out.

Babe-Ruth wouldn't attend the Friday service with a swollen face; she found dirt and dust everywhere, crumbs under the stove, in back of the refrigerator, and the silver dollar she had lost months before. She scrubbed and waxed, washed and ironed every wearable item she could find, and turned bad garments into rags. She made corn bread and chili, which they washed down with Kool-Aid. Babe-Ruth and the children had a prayer meeting in the evening, and Sister Crawford came up and saw her face and cried.

On Sunday, Caleb returned; he was away the entire weekend and hardly talked. The children lingered in the kitchen. When he was snoring, she huddled on the edge of the bed.

He was back at work on Monday and at home leaned over the sink, cupping and drinking as if nothing had happened. She was cutting bread, and Junior watched.

"Don't you wanna go and play?" Junior walked out slowly. "He all right?" She didn't answer and set the table.

After a week, her facial swelling was gone. Caleb seemed more like himself for a while. But he came home drunk and mean on Friday. She didn't know what to say and didn't say a word. Her silence irritated him more. *There she goes again, old sanctified Babe-Ruth in control.* He slapped her, and she didn't scream. *Oh, you ain't got nothing to say . . . You better'n me, too good for me!*

He got his gun, pushed Junior unto the back porch, and fired. Gun smoke flowed into the room as Junior rushed back in crying. She screamed, and Caleb looked like he didn't know himself anymore.

"What was wrong with a man to shoot over his child's head just to scare me?" Babe-Ruth told Rev. Clemmons, and he spoke to Caleb, who was embarrassed with the colossal stupidity of it still sinking in.

Weeks passed. Was he crazy? She was thinking, what if he could see what he's become? She was thinking and washed a wine bottle, filled it with tea, and filled her glass. The children watched for his Packard to arrive, and they were ready. He entered, and she staggered forward with her blouse loosened, garbling her words and waving the wine bottle.

"Have a drink, honey." He was speechless as she flopped into his arms. The children laughed. He did too. She felt she had made her point.

Almost losing his job and shooting over Junior's head were taking their toll. Over the next few months, he seemed to be trying. He was home more weekends and drinking less. He would relapse, then steady himself. On paydays they saved a little, with some left over for sweets and pop, even a yo-yo or baseball cards.

That weekend, five boys dallied outside the grocery store.

"Thumbs down!" Marco emerged with a sixteen-ounce bottle of soda; he didn't have to share his jumbo carbonated delight.

"Thumbs up!" Junior gave each two of his Good & Plentys. They strolled.

"Hear about the Smiths?" Marco waited for their attention. "They got a television set."

"A what?"

"A movie box that shows pictures like the show."

"You kidding?"

"Mrs. Jones has one." Freddie worked her yard. "She let me watch a puppet show. It was great."

"Think she'd let us watch?" Marco's soda pop was almost gone. He wiped the bottle, and Freddie took a swig.

"*The Lone Ranger* and *Cisco Kid* are on Monday, Wednesday, and Friday. I'll ask her. I bet she'll say yes."

Babe-Ruth had been watching the boys dallying down the sidewalk and moved away from the window toward footsteps coming up the back stairs.

"Where you? . . . I want my half of the savings."

"What for?" She backed away.

"My half! This ain't no discussion. My half or I'll go get it myself!" He had his pay in his pocket and gave it to her but kept two dollars. She was speechless. Their savings were stashed away, and she retrieved his half.

It was two hundred dollars, and it felt good in his pocket. Later he handed Lillie a hundred and had bought a fancy shirt, some slacks, a pair of patent leather shoes, liquor, and a haircut. That weekend, Lillie cooked eggs and chops for breakfast, chitterlings for dinner, and there was plenty to drink. He returned home Sunday evening.

On Monday, Lillie looked in the mirror, applying lipstick; waitressing was hard, and the pay was low. She thought she was the best she had ever seen from the neck up and everything else was above average. She used to think she would meet someone special; at thirty-five, the notion was fading.

She exhaled and put the cigarette in the ashtray, turning to the mirror. She received tips, mostly from men who came in for coffee or a meal and to look her over. She liked the attention, but mainly the tips. She was for their imagination, a fantasy they could almost touch. Having children was for others; she always looked good and thought she always would. There were no close friends since her mother died; she never knew her daddy and knew how to take care of herself.

"I'll have a refill, you beautiful thing."

Joe sat with a group that regularly lined the counter at 6:30 a.m. He had three mouths to feed and couldn't stand his wife in the morning. If he had been observant, he would have known it wasn't how she looked, but her grouchiness, which she had learned from him. Beside him was Peabody, a Northern-born, red-eyed bachelor, perpetually unshaven, and couldn't grow a beard, the price of heavy drinking, talking dirty because it made him feel like a man. He coughed and sipped, pushing the donut between his jaws, a vagabond with a job.

"Gimme a refill."

Lillie stared and poured. It was men like him she loathed. She knew men, had them catalogued, and he was a weasel. He snarled, lifting the cup, undressing her with a stare. Caleb looked at the clock, put two dimes down, and drained his cup.

At work, Caleb loaded fifty-pound bags and kept working when the lunch bell rang.

"Caleb!" Mr. Yocum tugged at his shirttail, amused. "After lunch, go help Josh with the furnace. There's thirty cents more an hour."

Josh was fifteen years older and wasn't a talker. Now he had to be. His jaw bulged with tobacco.

"You gotta wear this shield and apron. When you shovel the coal in, move away quickly. I'll be unloading right behind you. Drink a little water every couple hours, whether you feel thirsty or not, or you'll be dry before you know it." He paused, spat, and continued. "I have seen fellas plumb out faint."

They worked without words, a good pair. In and out, fueling the furnace, pouring hot metal into molds. They stopped, watered up, and back again. Caleb's sleeves were rolled up to his elbows, and sweat covered his arms.

The next day, he wore a thick shirt and kept the sleeves down and wrapped a bandana around his neck. He brought a towel and some Vaseline for the tiny burns. At lunchtime, they ate in the vestibule. Josh's wife made him a good lunch, and Caleb winked his approval.

Babe-Ruth brushed her hair as Lona watched. Jessica was twelve and was bothered when Caleb did and said hurting things. The scar on her cheek was very visible, and Babe-Ruth wondered if it would fade or worsen with time. She was short, with big feet, a sign she would grow. Ann was Caleb's favorite. She could unstick a zipper, make Halloween costumes, and do other magical feats usually reserved for moms. A worried expression appeared when Babe-Ruth thought about Junior. George ate whatever she put in front of him, slept like he was dead through thunder and lightning, and still couldn't whip Junior. Little sister was still content just to be a part of the family.

The other children were in school, and Babe-Ruth and little sister strolled to the bus stop. They would take it to the east side, where she did day work for Mrs. Richards on Monday, Wednesday, and Friday; she would be home in time to see the kids arrive from school. Sister Crawford would fix the kids' lunches. It was their secret.

If she earned $1,000, she would have the $1,200 they need to pay down on a house. Mrs. Richards was paying $24 a week, and in a month she would have over ninety dollars; in ten months, she would have it all. *Owning a home wouldn't make life trouble-free, but giving up is the same as being dead.*

Mrs. Richards's husband was a doctor, and her children were grown. It was a large white house with a spacious lawn, with four sleeping rooms. She loved to have guest and entertain; having a part-time housekeeper was a luxury she never afforded herself until now.

"Why don't you sit and have some coffee, Ruth?" She had been watching Babe-Ruth folding laundry through the basement door.

"I'll be up in a minute."

They drank coffee. Lona had a glass of milk and a cookie.

"I see you have special plans for the money."

"Why do you say so, ma'am?"

"It's obvious. Your husband is working and you said you could only help me for a few months. Sounds like you have plans."

Babe-Ruth smiled. She wouldn't talk about her business. People were just like her papa said. He seemed to talk to her more after he got sick, and he said that sometimes they didn't like seeing you get ahead even if it wasn't affecting them.

"Well, I better finish up. We gotta get that bus on time and be home."

Mrs. Richards grinned. It was good to have company, and she hoped Babe-Ruth would continue to want the work.

At home, Babe-Ruth cooked rice instead of beans because it took less time, hot dogs for the kids, and two pork chops for Caleb. She made gravy and a batch of biscuits. After dinner, she would clean, and tomorrow would be washday.

The thought of the $1,100 she saved in New Jersey spurred her on. She loved the poetry and comfort of the scriptures, and at bedtime she read and prayed. She would miss some church services, but she thought God would understand.

Chapter 17

A man dying in the gas chamber in Arizona gasped, "Joe Louis, Joe Louis, save me!" The war in Korea, McCarthyism, and the fear of communism hovered over the nation. Dr. Bunche won the Nobel Prize; Jackie Robinson had a sterling year; and the names of Langston Hughes, Lena Horne, and Sammy Davis were on everyone's lips.

Caleb sat with Chet sipping beer. Caleb looked twenty-five—clean shaven, bushy haired, with his sleeves rolled back and muscles gliding under his skin as he blew away the foam.

"The colored man is moving up." It was four o'clock; he had worked an hour overtime and drained the last swallow.

"Listen!" Chet put his drink down. "Man, we working like dogs. The white man still controls everything."

"Not anymore. I done bought a house on Windell Street. We been savin'. I sign the contract at lunch break. The man brought it to me."

Chet's mouth dropped. "Better have another before you go."

"You drinking by yourself." Caleb left him sitting at the bar.

Babe-Ruth was always a wizard at saving, he was thinking as he walked into the sunlight. *And I'm good at making it. We done it in spite of our troubles . . . It came together fast. It's a done deal.*

Babe-Ruth stuffed boxes, tying and lining them against the wall, while big sister served supper. Three weeks ago, the tax check came, and she took Caleb to see the house. She saw how pleased he was, and she knew it was theirs. And if they wanted to holler and stomp until the roof rattled, it was nobody's business.

"Mama, George won't stop playing with his food! I told him three times and he keeps doing it." Big sister knew he was doing it to aggravate her.

"Well, he better not!"

Nobody made it through life on their own, and Babe-Ruth reminded herself to thank Brother and Sister Crawford. Caleb sat down, and big sister put two pieces of sausage next to his black-eyed peas, and Babe-Ruth poured coffee.

"I signed." He handed her the papers, and they watched him eat. Then he was alone, listening to them packing, and stuffed the last bite into his mouth and joined them.

The next morning, he loaded the truck with Brother Crawford in the driver's seat, looking at him through the mirror; Brother Crawford was remembering when he bought his first place. They drove slowly through Little Italy.

The Dazzolas were ready to sell when coloreds, Latvians, and Southern whites began moving in. Some of the lawns were groomed, with deep backyards and fences concealing gardens, grapevines, and fruit trees. Tenement houses were on the corner.

"I remember when no coloreds could buy here." The new siding was part of the deal. They pulled up; the house was gray, with two stories and a nice lawn. A Cyclone fence enclosed the backyard, and it smelled of tar and painted wood. They unloaded. Then the last item was in.

"That's it . . . Thanks." Caleb followed him out.

"Take care of that fine family, hear."

Caleb thought about Mr. Bull and Jesop and put his gloves in his back pocket, watching Brother Crawford's truck pull away.

The front window perched above the lawn and street, and Babe-Ruth ran her fingers over the red and blue tinted glass squares bordering it. They worked all day and finally finished unpacking; she prepared chili for dinner, and the day was done. Big sister and Ann snuggled on their mattress on the floor, whispering about girls down the street. Junior and George rested their heads on their hands, peering out at the moon. Lona was asleep in the little room next to the girls', and Caleb turned the final light out.

Nine people lived in the house on their right. A room was rented to Mr. Solum; there were four kids, and both parents worked. Mrs. Clay lived downstairs with another "grandchild" and did some day work, but she was retired. Her husband was dead and had left a small pension.

Mrs. Clay was a churchwoman, a church mother, and nursed a fledgling church until it was past the storefront stage. Then she would find another struggling congregation needing her considerable skills, which were ice-cream making, barbecuing, baking, giving rummage sales for the building fund or raising funds for a Sunday school bus, and advising women. Like most church mothers, she was cheerful and on the plump side.

It made you wonder. What did she get out of it? What was she like as a youngster? Perhaps she had been like everyone else and grew into her matriarchy, but one sensed her earlier years were awkward, biding her time, preparing to be old.

Her daughter had two girls and two boys. The third boy she kept was a "grandchild," and what that meant wasn't clear. He had some of her blood and needed someone. Sister Clay made you look her in the eyes and listen up.

Mr. Solum survived the First World War and the Depression and had full use of the house. He liked children, and if a child behaved properly, he was easy to get along with. Pipe smoking and tobacco chewing were his only vices; he chewed outside and smoked in the kitchen and on the porch. It wasn't that it bothered anybody. He was a gentleman, and there was an order and place for things. He had a suit and a pair of polished black shoes in his closet; he wasn't a churchgoer except for Easter and Christmastime, but he was devout and regular in his ways.

The Jeffersons' basement was cool. The Dazzolas left an old washing machine, a fruit bin with canned peaches and cucumbers, two brown sacks of rat poison, and two full wine barrels. The wine was sweet, and Caleb went for a cup. He drank after supper, and a week later he invited Chet. The next week, Chet brought a friend, and the following week, there were four.

"Junior, come down here!" Caleb looked up, grinning. "Meet my oldest boy." Junior shook their hands and eased back upstairs. "He's a goodun. Never no sass."

The men left, and Caleb felt the concrete floor and patted the furnace and leaned back in his chair. No more potbelly stoves, he was thinking, putting his legs up; it was all his.

Babe-Ruth searched on her hands and knees, then winced.

"Why did they leave those barrels of wine? Where's my black dress? Big sister, you seen my black dress?"

"No, ma'am."

"I know we brought it here." She had searched the closets, boxes, and dresser drawers.

"I'll look in the storage room."

It was her favorite dress, and it would be an incentive to lose weight after childbirth (it would be their sixth). She knew she had packed it. Big sister entered with a wooden sword on top of a pile of black cloth. She held up the pieces of the dress cut into a mask, a square bandana, a sash, and a cape.

Babe-Ruth covered her mouth in horror. "Call 'em in! Who did this?"

The silence was short.

"I did, Ma'dear."

"You . . . ?"

Junior nodded. "Yes. It's a secret. I'll slip out at night and protect people, swoop down and rescue them from bad people on the streets, like Zorro." Even George laughed.

"Shhhhh!" She motioned the other children out. "Gwan." She observed him; he was strange, but not dumb or crazy. She rubbed his fuzzy head as his siblings listened outside the door, confused, expecting a whipping.

In the summer of 1952, the war in Korea was a newspaper war to men like Caleb, who had done their time. Tuskegee Institute reported it as the first year without a lynching since they began keeping records seventy-one years ago. Jackie Robinson batted .308 and had 19 homers and led his team toward the fall classic with the hated Yankees. Willie Mays was in his second year and struggling after a brilliant first season. Caleb and Babe-Ruth followed baseball on the radio whenever they could.

The adults in the neighborhood kept to themselves. Jimmie Jones and Ignacio Lamodo were the high school star receiver and quarterback, with their exploits in the papers every week. Their younger siblings (Lamodos, Italian; and Joneses, colored) were always ready to fight.

"Cross that line, Leo, and I'll knock the stuffin' outta ya!" Billie Jones had been hankerin' to get a piece of Leo Lamoda since they were in the fifth grade.

"I crossed it, whatta you gonna do?"

They rolled, kicking up dust. Leo got on top, and Harry Jones decided Leo was too small and landed a straight right to the head of Joey Lamodo. It was Joneses versus Lamodos again, with everybody swinging.

"OK, knuckleheads, stop it." Their older brothers Ignacio and Jimmy intervened.

"He started it." Leo's face was red.

"I'll finish it too."

"We don't care who started it. Break it up!" Ignacio grabbed his brother by the collar, and Jimmie held Billie. "Jimmie, Let's make 'em kiss."

Leo and Billie broke free like they were being branded. Everybody laughed, and it was over. The truce affected everyone. Billie and Leo became friends. When one had a party, the other was invited. The parents didn't socialize, but they were fair-minded, and everyone showed respect.

Fat Mike lived in a brick house around the corner, and his father was a barber. In spite of Mike's size, he was an exceptional athlete, quick, with a rare combination of toughness and fairness, and he could take a joke.

Terry, next door on the other side, was skinny, with buckteeth and a stutter like Junior. He had eight siblings; half were girls. His father had factory work during the day and was a part-time janitor at a bakery in the evening. His mother did hotel work. The bakery job provided an unbelievable assortment of pastries: raspberry and blueberry Danish, pecan pies, cakes with multiple convoluted shapes and frostings, holiday cakes decorated with every variety of color (a step above their usual extraordinary fare), including assorted fruit breads. Neighbor kids dreamed of being adopted. Terry and his siblings had cavities and missing teeth.

Their twelve-year-old cousin was deaf and dumb, but he was treated like a brother. He was skinny, with an asymmetrical face. He didn't know sign language and grunted and babbled, further twisting his features; it was hilarious. He had a short fuse, but his cousins remained patient until they got his message. The respect was contagious, and he was accepted as one of the gang.

That Friday, there was a half day of school. Junior, George, Terry, and Mike were shooting marbles when barking erupted.

"Caesar's the baddest dog around." Mike peered around the corner.

Caesar (a bull mongrel) and a German shepherd were at each other. Caesar was overpowering; it was brief, and the German shepherd whimpered off.

Caesar turned; his crossed eyes shot a shiver down their spines. His face was brown on one side and white on the other, with spiked teeth and an almost-absent nose. Muscles enclosed his neck and shoulders, which were brown, becoming reddish, and turning white on lean forelegs. He whirled as if wearing a cape and pranced out of sight.

"Belongs to the Wilsons."

"Ever sic him on anyone?"

"Naw, everybody leaves him alone. Don't throw things or try petting him. If another dog comes, look out!"

Hours passed, and they were on the steps by the store, munching Snickers bars. Caleb's Packard honked.

"That's a television set!" Terry stood up.

"How you know?"

"Nothing else comes in a box like that." Mike tried to keep up.

"Come in." Caleb carried in the box, and the children followed. Babe-Ruth directed him to the living room. "Put it there."

He unpacked, attached the antenna, and turned it on. Jessica went back to the kitchen. She had watched television before and didn't relish a roomful of smelly boys. The neighborhood had plenty of girls her age, and she had found two she especially liked. Ann Marie lived on the corner, and Gloria, only a few blocks down. She had been looking in her closet, lamenting her scarcity of clothes. Unlike boys, what she wore was vastly more important than the amount of sugary delights she could consume. She had thought about being a boy but realized being a girl was better.

Junior was fascinated by women young and old. He thought them superior in ways and found their conversations foreign and fascinating.

He would think in later years that they inhabited a different world—a kinder one. He would marvel at their sensitivities and unbelievable pettiness. One clear objection that would later emerge against the Christian hell would be that there would be women there. To burn for eternity he thought hideous, that it should happen to a woman—the worst of them—unthinkable.

That Friday, the barbershop was humming; three barbers were working. Pictures of hairstyles lined the walls with the picture of Harry Truman on the calendar in the center. Puffs of hair were scattered under the chairs. Mr. Manny had the floor, and the presidential election was the subject.

"I don't think our boy can do it." He looked into the mirror at the elderly man in his chair. "Light on the sides?"

The man getting a haircut nodded. "You're right. Stevenson a smart man . . ."

Mr. Writ was waiting, the seat beside him was vacant, and Caleb and two men stood. Mr. Writ was the undertaker and wore a soft tweed suit and a smile.

"How are you today, sir?" Caleb admired his dress.

"Oh, it's your world. I'm just living in it." It was Mr. Writ's favorite line.

His funeral establishment was the subject of taboos. Children took special note. If you stepped on his lawn, you had to bite your finger until it hurt to remove the curse. Stealing from him was a curse, and vandalism was worse. The saying was "Raise my grit, and I'll send you to Writ." And he gave the best trick or treats by far.

Mr. Manny turned his client, who met Mr. Writ's smile.

"Don't be smiling at me! Quit staring! I got no business for ya."

After his haircut, Caleb tightened his belt and stretched, smelling of talcum and aftershave; the avenue was busy.

Babe-Ruth was at the window; it was six o'clock, and Caleb wasn't home. She massaged her abdomen and looked at her swollen feet. He would only have half his check. She caressed her face in the mirror and brushed her hair to the side. She thought about his missing suit and put the lights out.

"Junior, put on your shoes and walk to church with me." He eased away from the television to find his shoes.

Big sister observed from the doorway.

"It's gonna be fine, big sister."

"Ready." Junior swung through the door.

It was a clear night. Everyone seemed to be on the opposite side of the street; Babe-Ruth didn't notice Junior shiver as Caesar emerged from a porch.

The prayer service was short, and the church mothers migrated toward Babe-Ruth. Sister Clemmons hugged those in her way. Sister Jones dallied in little conversations, waiting by the door.

"Praise the Lord, Sister Ruth." The gathering of women surrounded her and drifted to the vestibule, kissing, embracing, and hugging (not asking about what was not their business). Junior watched and dozed as groups lingered and the choir practiced: SING 'TIL THE POWER OF THE LORD COMES DOWN. SING 'TIL THE POWER OF THE LORD COMES DOWN.

"Girl, I thought I could go no further." Sister Smith swallowed tears. "I knew what he was doin'. Then I put it in God's hands. That man of mine wrestled until the Lord pulled him in."

Sister Williams leaned forward, and their cheeks touched.

"He was nineteen and a man . . ." She paused. "But he was still my boy. I couldn't stop worrying. He was out all night. Then he moved out and went from bad to worse. I just prayed. Years passed. Girl, I had given it over to the Almighty! Then he got a job, married, and began to change. Sometimes they come to church with me. She a wonderful daughter-in-law. I'm still praying."

The choir continued as Junior slept.

"She had a child outta wedlock—broke my heart." Sister Jones spoke louder because of the singing. "It was the next thing to being dead. The father was no good . . . just using her. Everybody could see it but her. She the one that sang that song so wonderful tonight. She went back and finished night school and is working at the bank. My husband always wanted a boy and him and the child are together all the time . . . God will make things turn out."

Sister Richardson wiped her face before sharing.

"When my Jeffery went to prison, I thought it would kill me. At times I wished I was dead . . . HALLELUJAH! I though life could get no darker, but it did. Then, HALLELUJAH! He got out early on good behavior and is working regularly and studying at night school. HALLELUJAH!"

Junior awakened at the shout, and the room was shining. And if you were a boy feeling your mama's burdens, you almost saw them—muscular, with golden wings. Babe-Ruth was uplifted; he could feel it in her hand walking home.

Chapter 18

On Windell Street, a breeze passed between the houses, as a rat slipped through the coal bin and onto shelves, sniffing the brown bags and buttered bread on the trap. Junior sat up at the sound, then went back to sleep.

In the morning, Babe-Ruth served pancakes before Saturday chores. "Hurry up, I got plenty of work for everybody." She wiped her hands.

Big sister rushed to open the rattling door.

"Can't nobody hear?" Caleb pushed past to the sink and guzzled water, then dowsed his face. Junior stopped eating.

"Want some pancakes?" Jessica began picking up plates. Caleb didn't answer.

Junior put his plate in the sink, standing between his parents.

"Don't be staring me down, woman!" She screamed as he swung, and Junior dropped the plate, rushing to the basement.

"Daddy, don't!" Jessica was beside her on the floor; the others screamed.

"Heffa!" Jessica got up when Caleb entered their bedroom. He didn't come out, and Jessica eased to the basement, then ran yelling upstairs.

"Junior ate the rat poison!"

"What you say, gal?"

"He ate the poison!"

Babe-Ruth rushed down, and Caleb scraped his head coming behind her.

"Call the ambulance!"

She tried gagging him. He stiffened and jerked, and his eyes rolled back. Then he vomited. Caleb tried protecting his head.

"Jesus! Jesus! Jesus!" His breathing was shallow, and she put a rag under his head.

Ten minutes went by, and rumbling came from the stairs. "What's going on?" The ambulance attendants leaned over and flinched when Junior jerked.

"He ate rat poison." Ann squeezed his hand as they loaded him onto the stretcher and rushed upstairs.

"Eh! . . . Go to St. Mary's Hospital."

St. Mary's Hospital was six blocks away. Caleb and Babe-Ruth sped past the EMERGENCY sign and parked.

"I'm Caleb Jefferson. They brought my boy in."

"The doctor will be with you as soon as he can. He's with him now." The nurse was stocky, with a round face and firm voice. "You need to fill out these forms. Doc's good, but you've got some waiting to do."

Babe-Ruth began writing. The clerk typed, and the nurse returned to the back. Caleb lit a cigarette and paced. Babe-Ruth finished and handed back the papers and sat.

She's praying, Caleb guessed; there was nothing to do, nothing to say. The ambulance attendants came from the back and left quickly. Caleb was thinking about the awful dream back on the farm when Mr. Bull rescued him from his nap. It wasn't a dreamworld like at the bars when he had a buzz on. Rat poison was in Junior's blood, and if the doctor couldn't treat it, he would die like some crazy white who killed himself. It wasn't right.

How in the world? I worked myself to the bone—sick or well. Spanked him when he needed to be and taught him respect. I'll kill the little bastard, wring his neck—it's a shame, a pissin' shame! Babe-Ruth's praying, blaming me, I bet. I don't care anymore. Nobody ever stood with me. Let them stare. Piss on them! God, I hope he's all right.

"I want the doctor." An hour had passed, and a lady carried her child to the desk. "He got a fever . . . Has fits when he gets a fever."

The clerk looked up from her typewriter. "The nurse will be right with you. You'll have to fill out these forms."

"We need the doctor now!"

"He's with a dangerously ill child." The clerk looked at Caleb and Babe-Ruth. "Fill out the papers. He will see you as soon as he can."

Another half hour went by, and Caleb lit another cigarette and went to the window. The nurse returned and led the new arrivals to the back.

"Doc's still busy. Let's work on this fever. Have you given aspirin?"

Caleb paced and smoked, and another hour passed.

"Mr. Jefferson? He's resting now." Babe-Ruth squeezed Caleb's hand and followed him in.

"Come in. We've pumped his stomach and stopped the seizures." The room was white and smelled of medicines. Junior was unconscious and surrounded by machines, with tubes coming from his mouth and nose. The doctor reminded him of the pilots in the navy—boys seemingly wearing their fathers' leather jackets, goggled caps, silk scarfs, and pistols too big for their britches, good pilots, prepared to die for their country. "It'll breathe for him until the poison's gone. We must report poisoning. What happened?"

They waited for the police, who questioned them and left, and the nurse took Junior to his room. Caleb drove Babe-Ruth home and returned.

They're blaming me. Caleb could tell by the look in their eyes. *It's my fault. Go ahead, put it on the man. He's all right. That's what's important.*

Night came, and he sat by the window in the hospital room, watching the machines. *Childhood's a special time. Why he gonna do something like this for? He's trying to understand our problems, things too big for a child's mind.* He thought about the shooting over Junior's head to scare Babe-Ruth. Junior was frightened, and it was a crazy, stupid thing to do. Did it drive Junior crazy? He hoped Junior wasn't crazy, then dozed.

Babe-Ruth rose early and took a cab back to the hospital. Caleb and Junior were asleep; she closed the door and walked back home. She would relieve him after church.

The doctor removed the tubes from Junior's body. By noon, he was awake and ate and didn't talk, and Caleb didn't force it. Babe-Ruth returned. Caleb left and returned after three hours and sensed he had spoken.

Back at home, the next morning Caleb returned from the hospital and dressed for work. Babe-Ruth poured him a second cup of coffee, begging him to eat something.

"Junior doing good. They'll probably let me bring him home tonight."

At work, the sweat poured from his neck and arms, and his stomach growled. Lunchtime came, and Josh motioned to take a break. He was headed out, when blackness and thunderous smoke overcame them. Caleb dragged Josh out, who was unconscious and covered with soot, but talking and making sense when the ambulance arrived.

They shut the unit down, and Caleb cleaned up and sat around the rest of the day observed by the nurse.

He quivered driving to the hospital. He looked in on Josh, but he had already been discharged. Then he signed the papers, and he and Junior headed home. He parked and looked over at Junior.

"Trying to kill yourself?"

"Daddy, does Jackie Robinson drink like you?"

"Watch your mouth, boy!" There was a way a boy ought to address his father. The silence was long. "No, I don't suspect he does."

"Why you do it then?"

"That's enough."

A boy had to show respect to get an answer even if he was asking the right questions. It was wrong for Junior to confront him like he was a child.

Caleb changed his clothes, and they ate in silence.

"Going to your prayer meeting tonight?" Caleb had left the table with his plate unfinished. Babe-Ruth nodded. "I'll drive you." It was an unusual offer. "The furnace blew up today . . . We lucky to be alive." He steered out of the driveway and down the alley. She watched big sister put out the kitchen lights and didn't hear him. "It could've been worse."

She was thinking of the look on Junior's face. The car stopped, and she closed the door. "Thanks. I'll be able to get home. Get some sleep."

"I'm gonna park and come in."

She waited on the curb. They had never been in church together. She sat in the pew, smelling his workman's body, fishing back in her mind for the words he had spoken in the car.

Rev. Clemmons took his text, nodding to the reader. "Read."

"You are gods, I said all of you are sons of the Most High. But you will die like men; your life will end like that of any prince" (Psalm 82:6-7).

"Last night I labored on the sermon that I was to preach today. It would last about an hour. I had been studying and praying over it all week. I had become proud of it too. It had a great measure of inspiration. It was God's Word.

"When I opened my Bible just now, this passage jumped out at me. The sermon I had prepared was God's Word, but it was not God's Word for today!

"This is the sermon that the Lord would have me bring. Now, you must pray with me as I preach it because God hasn't told me everything that's in it. What is man? What kind of creature is he? Who are we anyway?"

His words rained, Caleb was alone, and the earth was new. The sermon ended, and Babe-Ruth waited while he talked to Rev. Clemmons. They were in his office a long time. The church was almost empty when Rev. Clemmons came out of his office.

"Sister Betsy, could y'all take Sister Jefferson home?" He turned, holding Babe-Ruth's hand. "I need to be with him awhile. Don't wait up."

Caleb was in the reverend's office with tears running through his fingers. He accepted a handkerchief, and confessions flowed like an imprisoned soul finding an open door. He talked about the navy, drinking and carousing, the deaths of Jesop and Reuben, and about him and Babe-Ruth fighting and its effect on Junior and Jessica.

"Today when that furnace blew up, I think the Lord was talking, trying to make me stop and think. Preacher, I wanna be baptized. I need to change. It ain't no good the way I am."

"You never been baptized, son?"

"Been to church only for NAACP meetings and a funeral."

To most, Caleb was a buck who worked hard and took the pay he had coming, a country boy, returned from war a whiskey drinker with a bit more savvy, but nobody, not even Jesop, knew him deep inside. He had never talked so openly to anyone; he finished and stared into the preacher's blue eyes.

"Now, my son, upon the confession of your faith . . ." They had gone upstairs to the baptismal tank draped behind the pulpit. The auditorium was empty; on the wall was the painting of the River Jordan. Rev. Clemmons was beside the baptismal pool, with a hand on Caleb's back and the other on Caleb's crossed arms; Caleb was in cold water up to his elbows and wearing a white gown. "on your belief in the death, burial, and resurrection of our Lord Jesus Christ . . ." Caleb had always believed there was a God, but he had never met him. "I now, indeed, baptize you in the name of the Father, the Son, and the Holy Ghost."

The chilling shroud engulfed him; he emerged gasping, reawakened.

Weeks went by, and it was letter-writing time. Writing was a skill Babe-Ruth intended to keep.

Dear Mitchell and Mildred:

I hope all is going good. I been keeping both of you in my prayers. We all miss and love you both a lot. The kids is doing well and so is me and Caleb.

Michigan is a bigger state than New Jersey and Caleb was right. There is a lot of work and chance to make a better living. We bought us a home. It is a good house and something to be thankful for. It has four bedrooms, a bathroom and a kitchen and a storage room too. Caleb has been working a lot and we even got a TV set. The kids is getting big.

I can never thank you all enough for helping us get started. You know how this man works and his job is going good. He done bought himself a Packard car for two hundred and fifty dollars from Mr. Yocum. It's a good car and he drives me to church at times and takes the kids and me to John Ball Park sometimes for a picnic. Sometimes we get to watch a baseball game. We even saw the Kansas City Monarchs play the Birmingham Black Barons. It was something.

Caleb tried to show me how to drive a couple of times but he got fed up with me after a while and stopped. There is an old gentleman next door named Mr. Solum and he said he would give me a try. We having the first lesson as soon as I get done with this letter. It's time to go. I'll write again. You all is in my prayers.

Love, Ruth

She pasted on the stamp and tucked it inside her Bible.

"Big sister, watch the kids while I have my driving lesson."

She knocked, and Mr. Solum came out.

"I guess you ready to do some drivin'." She nodded and followed him to his car. He wore his gray hair like a crown. "Let's see what the man done taught you." He sat beside her and lit his pipe, then thought for a moment and put it back into his pocket. "Afta you back it out, and you can do it, we'll just drive up and down the alleys awhile. When I think you're ready, we'll go to the streets."

She was surprised at how easy it was and hadn't realized how much Caleb had taught her. She had the choke and the gear down and eased into a rhythm. Caleb's yelling made her nervous, but Mr. Solum's manner brought confidence, and she settled in.

Soon they were in the street, and she rounded the block seven times and honked.

"After a few more times, we goin' downtown, and then when you're ready, we'll hit the highway. Did you read the little book I got you?"

"Yes, I did."

They came back from downtown, and she parked and noticed Jessica and George in the window. She would show Caleb when she was ready. He had an attitude about women drivers, and she was itching to prove him wrong.

She was no modern woman, but she could read and write, and she was learning to drive. When the kids gathered around, she remembered how meek Jim Bradford was (he had taught her to read) and was determined to be the same way. Night was falling. Caleb had been coming home late and was spending a lot of time with the reverend. She didn't know how it would turn out, but she was praying.

The church calendar for the regular week was divided into five services. Sunday had the high services, and the parishioners stayed three hours in the morning and three in the evening. The last hour of the morning service followed Sunday school and was inspirational. Babe-Ruth felt its effect the rest of the week and said it was like manna from heaven, and it was difficult to sustain a depression afterward.

"If more people could have the encouraging word of God preached to their hearts, they wouldn't need so many of those head doctors." She said it often, and she was ready for the week.

The music was a mixture of the new and the old, country and gospel: "Precious Lord Take My Hand," "Gonna Be a Great Wake Up That Morning," "Amazing Grace," "Confidence," "I Hear Angels." It was uplifting, and folks cried, laughed, and made a joyful noise.

After the Sunday night service, they ate in the basement cafeteria. On Monday, there was a short prayer meeting at noon, and in the evening, another short prayer service, followed by choir practice. Most stayed around afterward to visit or seek counsel from Rev. Clemmons. He would be the last to leave.

Sometimes he'd counsel folks until the wee hours of the morning. One of his sons or a deacon stayed around, and if he were counseling a woman, he kept the door ajar. There was a row of chairs outside his basement office near the cafeteria, where people waited. Some just sat to visit.

Tuesday was young people's night. Wednesday, Bible class in the afternoon for an hour and in the evening for those who worked. Friday was "saints meeting." When two or three were gathered together, the scripture said the Lord was there. They referred to any Christian as a saint and felt you needed the Holy Ghost to live saintly.

The old white brick's ambience permeated the neighborhood. To the neighbors, it was a lot of churchgoing, and the Holy Rollers seemed like unusual folks.

It was Wednesday before the afternoon Bible class, and Rev. Clemmons sat at his desk with his wrinkled hands covering his face. The silence was broken by sniffles. As a boy, he cried over his dead dog, and he cried easily. He had been praying for Caleb, and he rose and looked at the Bible on the shelf. He took it down and turned the pages. It was unused and given to him many years ago. He remembered it like it was yesterday.

The year was 1919. He had planted a church and had left the South for the army and settled in Chicago. It was a storefront; he and a bunch of ladies canvassed the neighborhood, going door-to-door. He preached in the parks, and they purchased a small piano for outdoor meetings. The church grew, and before long they were in a building that seated 250, not counting the choir loft.

He was young and unmarried when the woman gave him the Bible. He was giving a revival to inspire the church and bring in new members. He prepared a sermon for each night, and everyone brought friends and relatives. It was a great effort. A society gal pulled up in a Cadillac. She parked in front and sat in the front row, right under the pulpit, and looked like she belonged in the movies or on the cover of a magazine.

It was a difficult sermon to preach, and it took all the Holy Ghost he had. Afterward, she got in line to shake his hand and stared into his eyes.

"Praise the Lord. Come back again." He moved to the next person.

"I'll be back."

She came every night and sat in the same seat with her legs crossed. He took a special fast on Wednesday. He could feel all the things God made a man who was twenty-eight and unmarried to feel. He was doing something for the Lord, and Satan had sent someone to trip him up. The crowds grew. Each night she came, dallied, and he shook her hand.

It was the last service of the revival and Friday, and she went to the back of the line, caressing the Bible. He greeted the people, praying, and she stepped forward as the last in line.

"How you doing, sugar?" Parishioners were by the door, and the two of them were alone.

"I'm doing fine, sister. How about you?"

"I been watching you. I think we can do fine together. You been noticing me too. And you like what you see. Why don't you lock this church up so I can give you the sweetest jelly roll you ever had?"

Their eyes met, and he took her hand.

"Sister, you out there doing whatever you do. Sometimes you win and sometimes you lose. Now, tell me. When you lose and it's going to happen and you're hurting because the devil has you by the neck and there's no way out and you can't breathe . . . don't you want one righteous man left to reach out to the Lord for you?"

Her face went blank. Then she frowned, and tears rolled down, little-girl tears from far away, deep inside, from places she had forgotten and from another time. She pulled her hand away, and the silence was deep and long. Then she raised her head.

"You take it." She handed him the Bible. It was new and had never been opened. "You'll get more use from it than I will." She walked away.

"I'm saving it for you, sister. When you're ready, it will be here."

He leafed through the pages; he still expected to return it someday. It was time for the afternoon prayer service. Caleb would come tonight. They had been meeting for weeks and talking for hours.

Babe-Ruth was hopeful, but she felt like she didn't know Caleb anymore.

"Reverend, what's going on with Caleb?" She had waited after the Wednesday afternoon Bible class and shook his hand by the door.

"I'm expecting him tonight. He's in the valley of decision." They moved to the side near the alcove. "Grace is surrounding him. So far, so good. Keep on praying." He paused and held her hand with both hands. "One thing, he's hit you for the last time."

She pondered his words and massaged her stomach going home. She had a poor singing voice, but she felt in tune. Perhaps the reverend would talk to Junior someday.

There was a nudge, and she looked down into Caesar's crossed eyes and patted his head and hurried up the steps. There was a letter from Sister Jones, a good sign. She would read it later. She would serve turnip greens and pork chops. Mrs. Clay brought George and Lona from next door. They chatted. Then she thanked her and got busy. The children settled down with coloring books, and she went to the kitchen and made herself tea and brought them cookies and milk. And she sat by the window and read the letter, meditating on the words.

She sang setting the table. It was peaceful, expansive, like a child marveling and bursting with hope. She thought about life before she found the Lord and wondered how she had survived.

The greens sputtered, and she lifted the top and lowered the flame.

"Where's Daddy, Ma'dear?" She looked at Ann but didn't answer.

They finished dinner, and she covered Caleb's pork chops and wrapped the corn bread in the cloth and put them in the oven. Ann helped clear the table. It was getting late, and she imagined he went directly to church. She shared about her encounter with the crossed-eyed dog.

"That's Caesar. Don't mess with him, Ma'dear." Junior shook his head.

It was strange, she thought; she could sense when a dog was mean. He was peculiar though.

At ten thirty, she rolled over and looked at the clock. Morning came, and she cleared her throat, realizing Caleb's side hadn't been slept in. Perhaps he was in an accident, she thought. The child inside kicked, and she hurried to the window fogging the glass.

"Lord, help us!"

PART FOUR

BACK SOUTHWARD

Chapter 19

Caleb filled his Packard with gasoline. Three days before, he had headed home and driven past the bar. He hadn't seen Lillie for weeks and had been tempted to go in for a drink, but he kept driving. He had been almost home when he turned his Packard around and headed back. Lillie wasn't there, but he stayed for a drink; it was his first in a month.

"Why don't you buy me a drink and I'll have it with ya, suga'." She had a long body. They drank beer and then whiskey. It was Friday, and what business did he have going to anybody's church? What had gotten in him?

He squinted and tightened the cap on the gas tank. He had watched her put on her blue-and-white hotel uniform, observing him in the mirror and combing her hair.

"Keep on sleeping, suga'. There's some bacon and grits there. I'll be back at four."

She left, and he tried lifting his head. He must have done good, and he dozed until he heard sirens, then got up to find a Lucky Strike. After some bacon and grits, he lit up again. The apartment was small, with a few pictures and plaster of Paris lamps. He turned on the radio and grabbed a beer and checked his wallet.

She came back home man hungry. He hadn't seen a picture show in years; they returned and drank some more. She didn't care if she knew his name. He felt like a bar whore she picked up because she needed a buck. The shadows crept back. Had he been dreaming, standing in a pool of cold water and telling someone everything in his heart? Wasn't religion for women? His mind was out of joint, he reasoned, mixed up because of Junior and the poison and the explosion. Guilt had him by the throat, and religion pounced. How did the reverend know what was good for him anyway?

"Where's the whiskey, gal?"

He could drink a man under the table and find a woman when he needed one. Damn them all! He didn't need a plan to take care of number one. He wondered if he had ever loved a soul and reasoned he loved Jesop all right. The rest were life suckers, leeches. Rueben understood, and that was why he was single.

It was getting dark, and he directed the Packard southward and would do odd jobs on the way. Nobody knew the future. He drove until he was tired and pulled over to the side of the road and bedded down.

It was Friday morning and a week later, and Maurice drank his coffee slowly. A twisted brown bag bulged in his pocket as he looked at Lillie working behind the counter and winked.

"What's a fine-looking woman like you doing working in a place like this?"

"I gotta eat." She hesitated, refilling the cups of the men at the counter, then looking in the mirror and starting another pot.

She hadn't seen Caleb for weeks, and she had noticed Maurice before.

"Is coffee and donuts all you eat? It's bad for your teeth."

"Know where I can get something better?"

"Yes." She dipped her pinky in the cup.

"I drink my coffee black. Never knew adding a little sugar could make it taste this good."

She dallied, then moved behind the counter.

"I get off at eight. Pick me up and I'll fix you a real dinner."

"I'm busy tonight, but we'll make it soon."

It was another day, and in the alley just off Windell Street, brown bags twisted around whiskey bottles lined the window ledge in late afternoon. Chet swallowed and hurled the dice.

"He's gone." He paused.

"Who's gone?"

"Caleb." They squatted with bloodshot eyes. "I'd a left a long time ago if I had all them kids." Peabody stooped and hurled the dice. "Hot damn, you niggas better have something in your pockets."

A block away, men carried a bureau, putting it in their truck, next to the television set. "That's it."

A passerby looked up as Babe-Ruth closed the curtains, and the truck pulled away. She had called them and wouldn't try to keep what she couldn't afford. The neighbors had seen it before.

Two houses down, a man went inside, thinking, *What's she gonna do? They'll have to go on welfare.*

Another was thinking, *Never did think much of them. She mighty proud though.*

Some didn't like them in the first place. Still, there were other thoughts: *A good-looking woman. I'll just wait and see.*

It had been thirteen days, and Mr. Yocum said Chet hadn't seen him.

"Everybody, come in the living room." Babe-Ruth wore Caleb's long-sleeved denim shirt. "Your daddy's gone . . . There gonna be some hard times ahead, but we gonna come through this shining on the other side." She had their full attention, and big sister folded her hands, while Lona played with her fingers. "God will be with us, you'll see."

She finished, and they could feel a blanket of peace spreading over them, a light in winter.

In a week, the money was gone. Babe-Ruth picked greens from the garden for a meatless supper.

"It's good, Ma'dear." They dug in after the prayer. They hadn't taken the garden seriously before. Corn bread with margarine sopped in turnip greens and seasoned right hit the spot.

"I'm gonna be havin' this baby soon. We gonna need help." They were silent as she chewed. She was thinking about the poor in the twenties eating government food and living in shacks. Lona didn't like greens and looked up from her mush. George had cleaned his plate. Junior listened intently. She got up and put her dish in the sink.

"I'm going to social services tomorrow."

On the west side of town, Maurice looked out the window. The street below was quiet. Lillie fried the chicken and was still in her work clothes, with her hair down. He had peeled potatoes and reached into his jacket hanging up and put the fifth of gin on the table.

"Naw, we gonna have wine with this meal." She put glasses and a bottle of Bronte on the table. "Gin for later!"

It was his best meal in months. They cleared the table, and she put on a Sam Cooke record. Maurice put away the dishes, and she reappeared, with the dimmed light showing her figure.

It was daylight, and most came on foot. The flat brick building's parking lot was filling up. Chairs and writing tables lined the walls. White clerks—men freshly shaved and women with perfumed breasts, who had showered and put on deodorant and wore ties and high-heeled shoes—leaned across at the white trash and niggers.

"Did you fill the form on both sides?" he said it often because he knew half the time they didn't. The nigger reminded him of the one his daddy used to work with, and the man behind him of his uncle Fred—check that. He looked away. He didn't know these people, didn't know anything about them.

They lined the walls, white and colored, poor, trying to get help, feeling their sameness.

The colored man nodded. *They think they are better than we are.* He could see it in their eyes. They wouldn't move this slow if they weren't poor.

The white behind him felt the same, impatient, with nowhere to go. *Lord, I'm ignorant, what am I gonna do? I need some help. Somebody gotta help me and my babies until I get back on my feet. Having a job don't make them better than me,* he was thinking.

The clerks listened and filed the papers; their superiors checked them and put them in stacks. They can hardly read, he thought. Can't fill out a simple form.

At lunchtime, the lines were still long.

"I'm sorry, we gonna only have two clerks working for the next hour." They were just going to have to wait. They didn't have anyplace to go anyway. What kind of a job would it be if they had to work through the lunch hour.

A clerk put on her flats and hurried out. She had a sandwich in her handbag, which she would eat quickly and walk two blocks away to look at a couch. When her next-door neighbor sees it, she wouldn't rest until she had a new one too.

Need to smoke me a couple of cigarettes and walk around the block. The male clerk was thinking and was disgusted and didn't care who saw it. *I gotta get away from these sons a bitches awhile.* He was glad he was not like them, glad he finished high school and passed the civil service exam.

After lunch, the clerks and administrators returned. The afternoon went slowly; the line dwindled, then picked up wall to wall again.

Gosh, they look like the same ones that were here this morning. The clerk straightened his tie. "Ma'am, I can't do anything until this form is completely filled out."

"Excuse me please. You're sitting on my hat." A colored man dusted his hat off, thinking that the peckerwood whose butt was on his hat was there at the welfare office just like him, but when he gets a job, he'll act like he had never stepped foot in a place like this.

Babe-Ruth had been there six hours. It was good to breathe the outside air. Her swollen feet ached. She noticed the nice cars parked on the street. Her head began to clear, and her throat was dry. Things would get better; she didn't know how or when, but it had to.

Two days went by. It was 10:00 a.m., and she was expecting the social worker. She heard stories about them coming around to see what you had, if you drank, or if your husband was back. Lona and George were down for naps. There was a knock, and she looked at the kitchen clock; she could see a young white woman at the door.

"Hello, I'm Mrs. Tezon, from the Social Services Department." She was thin and in her early twenties.

"Come right in." They moved through to the kitchen. Her face was narrow, and she had blues eyes and wore a beige jacket with matching skirt. "My husband's gone. I've got five children, one on the way. We're outta food." They stared. "I won't need help forever. When I wean this baby, I'm gettin' a job."

"Have you ever worked?"

"Not full-time, but I can."

"You intend to take care of them yourself?" She walked through the rooms. "Do you mind?"

"No, go ahead."

"You're my first client." A breeze flowed from the window. "You're a good housekeeper."

"Thanks . . . I'm a religious woman, Mrs. Tezon . . ."

"We can help." She took a pen and paper. "First . . ."

It would have been a good photograph. They had just met and were friends. There was frankness, questions, and answers, and Mrs. Tezon spelled out what must be done before the baby arrived.

"Can I call you Ruth?" She put her handbag on her shoulder.

"Babe-Ruth." She followed her out.

"My card."

Babe-Ruth watched her get into her car and reentered the kitchen. She opened the cupboard and inspected the bag of corn meal.

Chapter 20

Food was scarce in the months that followed. Babe-Ruth didn't always know how bad it was. Her growing boys spent their days selling pop bottles, running errands, begging other children, and politely drooling over Mrs. Clay's cooking. Mrs. Clay would never tell. The girls were hungry too and lamented their comparative lack of clothes.

The wind patted the face of a nightwalker shuffling through leaves blanketing the sidewalk. "You gotta wake up, gal . . . I'm fixin' to have this baby. Call me a taxi." Big sister staggered, rubbing her forehead. Wide-eyed, she pulled her bangs and opened the phone book. "You hafta stay home from school tomorrow." Babe-Ruth dressed as she talked. "There's macaroni and cheese mix in there. Make sure everybody's in before dark and things is locked up." Jessica nodded as she dialed. "I don't want no visitors. I'll call soon as I can . . . I'm gonna do fine."

The taxi ride was bumpy. She groaned as they checked her in and rushed her to the delivery room. After an injection, it was a dreamworld. It was a boy, and the pain and throbbing faded into the days.

Then she was back home watching them huddled around, kissing his cheeks and rump.

"ooo."

He was smooth and soft chocolate, shining to beat the moon.

Smack. The smooching resounded as the children took turns. He was a gift that spoke for itself.

She had entered the labor room days before with no husband at her side and no ring, sensing their thoughts. The Kitchens never believed in common law, never thought it was right.

"If a man loves you and respects you, he needs to put it in writing and say it in front of people."

She had her Bible and could have opened it and showed them the writing:

"Ruth Kitchen, this 20th day of October, 1934, is here married to Caleb Jefferson before the Lord and the Reverend J. Pugh and the people listed below." It wasn't what she did or thought about. Decency couldn't be taken away.

The room was cavernous and white and smelled of iodine. She screamed getting onto the table as the nurse took the Bible and wiped her forehead. She couldn't breathe. Then life ripped out, wet and warm, and the pains waned. And she was somewhere else.

"Whaa!"

She heard.

"You have a boy." But it was only sounds until she came back and tried lifting her head. It was a boy, and he was all right, she thought he said. The doctor put him on her abdomen, and she caressed his scalp and inspected him. She was remembering it now as she watched them kissing his cheeks and rump.

She named him Jesop. He was strong and sucked until he had enough, and they slept.

Big sister was the boss.

"Shhhhh!" She was caring for Mama. "Y'all go upstairs, and I don't wanta hear ya." She was sixteen, missing school, and knew what was needed.

Ann brought in Babe-Ruth's supper. The corn bread was sliced and crisp and layered with margarine buttressed in a moat of steaming butter beans and pot liquor.

"Someteet, Ma'dear."

"Gal, look what you done! . . . Have they eaten?"

"Gonna call 'em down now."

The days went that way. The church had given them enough to pay the mortgage for a while, and in her mind it was a loan. She rented the upstairs out, and they would share the bathroom. There was still the hospital bill to pay, and she vowed she would pay it even if it was with a dollar a week. They had received some government surplus, and having enough food brought a kind of ease. A few weeks later, Mrs. Tezon stopped by. There was a conference between her and Babe-Ruth. Mrs. Tezon glanced intermittently at Jessica, who could hear her name being mentioned. It wasn't worrisome when they were talking about you and were on your side. It was about school, her being a young lady, her responsibilities, and how she was holding up. Mrs. Tezon looked directly into Jessica's eyes like she was grown and at the same time like she was a child needing direction.

After she left, Babe-Ruth called Jessica in. "Big sister, I want you in school tomorrow. You been missing too much."

There was more color in Babe-Ruth's face. They gathered around her bed with comic books (Blackhawk, Superman, Batman and Robin, the Lone Ranger, Zorro, Wonder Woman, and the Red Rider), passing the new ones to their ma'dear, and they trickled down from the eldest to the youngest. Closed in with her children and an occasional visitor was a peace they wished would last forever.

They weren't the first in the neighborhood to get government surplus. At the end of the block, eight families in the large tenement were on ADC. The building had a stench. There was a colored family and a Mexican family, and the rest were whites. It wouldn't occur to you at first, but after a while, you noticed things. One of the men had all of his fingers looking like thumbs and talked like his tongue was too big. Another's face appeared small for his body. The women were emaciated and unkept; the children were shoeless, unwashed, and underfoot. The homeowners regarded them as trash but seldom said it directly.

"I don't want y'all playin' down at that corner."

"Whose child are you?" The child coming up the steps with her Freddie with an empty pop bottle in his pocket stopped, feeling abhorrence in her tone.

Babe-Ruth would shop on Monday, not Friday, when the neighborhood came to buy and show off. How you ate measured how you were doing to Southern migrants who could still taste the lard and dough of the Depression.

"No, don't give me that one. Show me the bigger one." The robust colored lady with her cart filled gestured, flanked by her husband. The butcher moved quickly, eager, holding up the larger roast, his neck bent. She knew what she wanted, a big spender—demanded her money's worth.

"Gimme a fifty-pound bag of them spuds." A stout lady with two freckle-faced boys pushed her loaded cart forward. The produce man nodded and rushed to the back.

The cash register chimed. There would be no fooling with children who wanted to study what penny candy to buy. Some customers bought on credit and some with cash, and others cashed checks and paid their bills. Loaded grocery carts formed a line; a boy bagged and when necessary carried bags to the cars and trucks.

On Monday, the clerk looked at the array of groceries, cigarettes, and beer being purchased by the occupants of the tenement.

"You have three dollars left." The clerk looked restlessly at customers in line with small purchases.

Babe-Ruth pushed the groceries toward the cash register. Junior stood beside her as she put the items down and checked her list. At home she had powdered milk, cheese, peanut butter, and cornmeal from the government surplus.

The clerk checked the register, then took the cash from Babe-Ruth's hand and gave her thirty-one cents back.

"Junior, get a box of Tide soap, and hurry." She took two cents from her purse, and Junior quickly returned.

Junior loaded the red wagon. He didn't see much sense in buying soap. There was nothing in the groceries but essentials. He noticed the five-pound bag of sugar, and he was thinking maybe she would make a cake on Sunday. He pulled the wagon home, thinking that receiving government surplus was a disgrace.

The next day, Baby-Ruth was cutting carrots and realized Jesop was choking when he turned blue and couldn't scream. She turned him upside down and ran toward St. Mary's Hospital six blocks away.

"Call the hospital and tell them I'm coming!" He dangled as she kept running and beating on his chest like a drum.

"Whahh!" It shot out. She inspected him and the carrot and went back home.

A wine bottled sizzled in the Missouri heat, and the remaining drops evaporated. Caleb turned over and snored as the sun blackened his skin. Ants foraged his body, but he slept on.

In Michigan, ten-year-old Junior pressed his ear to the ground like he had seen the Indians do in the movies. They could hear things far away, and so could he; he shook the ant from his ear and concentrated. Next door, Jeffrey was in the kitchen with a chocolate pastry in his hand, watching Junior listening to the ground and chuckling as Junior lifted his head. Jeffrey took a bite and frowned and heaved the remnant into the trash and wiped the frosting from his lips. He licked his fingers and looked into the square white box. A Bismarck caught his eyes, and he removed the nutty, powdered sugar and chocolate Danish surrounding it. Beside the box, lemon-filled Long Johns covered with white frosting lay on a paper tray. He grabbed the Bismarck and skipped into the backyard.

Junior stared through the Cyclone fence at the casually held Bismarck.

"Hey, Jeff, what ya' doin'?" Jeff took a bite and hurled the rest into the garbage can. "Got any more sweet rolls, man?"

Jeff leaned against the fence. Since his father took the evening job cleaning the bakery, pastries had become commonplace although they cost a whopping nickel apiece at the store.

"What you listenin' at the ground for?"

"How would you like to ride me up and down the alley for a bag of sweet rolls?"

It was an interesting proposition. It appealed to Jeff. He had no sporting interest. He derived some pleasure from watching dogs fight and from pulling the limbs off grasshoppers.

"You do it first." Jeff grinned, thinking it strange to be listening to the ground.

Junior could almost taste the sweet rolls as Jeff hopped on his back.

"Giddy up!"

What if the guys could see me riding this fool and kicking him to a gallop? The thought made Jeff laugh. "Giddy up!"

Junior's mouth watered. He would get a dozen if he gave him a good ride. *I'm glad no one is out here,* he was thinking as he raced back.

"Giddy up!"

He sprinted the last thirty yards and stumbled to the ground. Jeff rushed inside and returned with a white bag: chocolate, nutty, Bismarcks, cream filled, and twisted glazed. Junior panted and squatted behind the garage. Ants gathered as wet crumbs dropped between his knees.

The sun went down in Missouri. Caleb's skin cooled, and sleep roared on. The moon beamed down dreams, and he moaned. He snored. Then groans returned. Branches sagged, and he awakened in a foggy field and thought about a woman two weeks ago; they had drunk two bottles of wine. He held the bottle up and let it drop; it would be Sunday, and he wished it were Monday so he could find work.

Paved roads revealed cracks the winter had left. Little Jesop was fourteen months old and weaned in the spring of 1953. The one-story brick building had no shades, and the parking lot was filled. Inside, men sat in rows, filling out forms. Clerks examined papers and directed them to offices in the back. Babe-Ruth put the paper down. Her writing was legible in the first two letters, then trailed off into wriggled lines. The clerk looked at the writing, then at her.

"Go over behind that wall. You'll be meeting with Mr. Fox."

There were few women in the room, and most were clerks. She held the paper tightly and eased behind the partition.

"Have a seat." He took the form and read it quickly. "Mrs. Jefferson." He nodded. "My name is Fox. What can I do for you?"

He was over 250 pounds, with caramel skin, and neatly dressed, one of two coloreds working.

"I need me a man's job." She paused. "I've got six kids to feed."

"Your husband gone." He nodded and glanced at the paper. "Having trouble with the welfare people?"

"No, Mrs. Tezon's a fine woman. I ain't raisin' my kids on welfare. I need a man's job."

"Oh, you do, do you . . . Let me see what I have here for a man."

He took out a folder and returned to his desk, studied it, and made two phone calls. Then he made a third.

"Well, here's your man's job. It's piecework, and it'll be rough. If you can't cut it, they'll have you outta there in a week. Pays $65 per week. It's a man's job, all right."

She said, "Thank you, Mr. Fox," and shook his hand, but the words wouldn't come out.

Dinner was special that night, with bits of beef in the pinto beans, margarine melting over corn bread, and Kool-Aid.

"I got something important to say." She cleaned the last morsel and put the spoon and empty glass on her plate. "We got us a job today. I'll be startin' tomorrow so we need to have a house meeting. We can clean up afterwards." They surrounded her on the bed. "I'll be working at the Kensington Brass Company on the three thirty to midnight shift. I don't want the state to raise my family. You can hold your heads up because we support ourselves. We's as good as anybody, white or colored. Never forget that." They nodded as she continued.

"Now we have to have some rules. Big sister, when I'm not here, you in charge." She looked at the others. "I'll leave for work at three sharp, and leave Jesop in big sister's care." She turned to Jessica. "I expect everyone to obey you, or they'll answer to me. I want everyone in before dark, and no visitors unless I approve beforehand."

She turned to Ann. "You a good cook. I want dinner ready at five, and be fair with the servings." Then she turned to Junior. "You the oldest boy. Act like it. You're eleven. Boys became men at twelve in the Bible. You gotta make the fire in the furnace and keep the basement and outside clean and the grass cut. George'll help. Help your sisters. Look out for 'em.

"You have to take turns watching little Jesop. After supper, I want everything washed and cleaned so this house ain't full of rats and roaches. Now, we gonna do well. I don't want no writing on the walls or tearing up. If we don't tear things up, we won't have to buy it again. Then we can make some gains." She had their full attention. "You know, kids, we's special. If anyone says you don't have a father, you tell 'em you're sons and daughters of God! He's the best father there is. He gonna be my husband too. He put us here for a purpose. We a light on a hill put here to show that with his help a single woman can raise six kids and raise 'em right. And we'll have something left over to give."

Summer felt better when their mother had a job and they knew they were as good as anybody. Jessica and her sisters could sleep in, and there would be baby-sitting and small jobs for cash and shopping and visiting and playing jacks and double Dutch and caring for the younger ones when Babe-Ruth was away. For Junior and George, after chores and their paper route, there would be baseball to play and listening to it on the radio and Kool-Aid and popsicles and swimming. At times, there would be windfalls of pastries, earned or otherwise, and the joys of being boys frolicking in the earth and sun.

Babe-Ruth had no idea how to raise boys, and she knew it. She thought she would keep them busy hustling for money or playing ball or Boy Scouting. She figured that they were mulish and you had to beat them at times and make sure it hurt so they would remember the infraction.

Summer didn't last long enough. Then it was fall, with less daylight and school and football in the peewee leagues. Junior and George's team was the only one without uniforms, but they wore old shoulder pads and Jim Thorpe—type leather helmets to keep them in the game. George was as big as Junior and was able to play even though he was younger. There were always plenty of activities at the church, with plenty to eat, mixing culinary delight with indoctrination.

It got colder. And Junior shoveled the coal into the sleeping furnace. It crackled and burst into flames. He added more and rattled the grate, then dumped the ashes into a cardboard box and hosed it down until the cardboard was soaked. Puffs of smoke and ash speckled his hair as he handed the hose to George.

"Don't just stand there. Pitch in!"

George turned the water off. The rest of the family was asleep. The *Herald* guaranteed delivery by 7:00 a.m. They had five minutes to dress.

They moved through dark streets with gray newspaper bags over their shoulders. George shivered and buttoned his coat as they passed drunks in doorways. Caesar appeared, startling at first, then sniffing and intermittently disappearing in and out of shadows and doorways.

Each house or apartment had a story fabricated from fact and fiction:

At the green apartment building, each of the four units received a paper. The occupants were colored and well off. The man in the back apartment was rarely at home, and papers collected for days. The one beside it had six telephones and belonged to the numbers man. Sometimes his table was loaded with pads, sometimes money. Policemen visited at times and were presumed friendly. The two front apartments belonged to an uninteresting teacher and a mailman.

The white lady in the dirty blue house was a witch. Old tubs and plumbing fixtures cluttered the front yard in what she called a garden, and they were careful not to trip. The paper was put inside the screen door without slamming it, or she would report them for chipping the paint. She paid at the central office, and they saw only her silhouette and imagined she never slept.

The white family in the small gray house was on public assistance. The father was in prison for raping and strangling a twelve-year-old colored girl a few blocks down. They paid on time. Junior and George didn't speak to the children anymore and wished their mother would mail in their payment too.

The gorgeous colored woman in the corner house was a generous tipper. She didn't have a husband, and the house was neat and well kept. White men slipped out on those dark mornings. They had never seen the same one twice. They thought she was like Jezebel in the Bible, whom they heard about in Sunday school.

Caesar reappeared beside a porch, and they let him in. Delivering to seventy-five customers took ninety minutes, and they stopped at Russo's. The old Italian sold papers too. They were competitors but friends. His thick mustache was curled like handlebars. He sorted the fruit beforehand and left them the ones that were bruised and going bad. Their bags bounced on their shoulders as they spat out the rotten parts and chomped down, heading home.

The city was stirring. It was time to wash and get ready for school. Junior dozed the first hour. Then the free milk awakened him, and his mind picked up the reading and arithmetic. He shook his head in disgust thinking about the Dodgers losing the series again. He hoped he could make an early collection and buy donuts for him and George.

Northern High was bordered by four neighborhoods and was half a century old. Two hundred freshmen and sophomores gathered in the cafeteria for homeroom. Some would quit at sixteen and earn more than their teachers. The teacher scanned the list: Jessica Jefferson, Steven Jones . . . Rufus Robinson, Gunner Stein . . . Peter Strasin, Mya Vaults,

Leo Victorio, Valtis Vsekus? He paused; his hair curled over his spectacles as he searched for Valtis, who held up a note and passed it forward.

Jessica wore a pink blouse and blue skirt, with white socks cuffed over oxblood loafers. She sat in back of Tom with his freshly trimmed flattop. The bell sounded, and she looked down when he turned around.

First hour would begin in six minutes. After math came English, science, a forty-minute lunch break, then home economics and civics. The final bell rang, and she hurried to her locker and down the stairs.

"Hey, girl, wait up! What you in such a hurry for? You know all we gotta do tonight is study." Gloria's breasts made Jessica appear childlike.

"I gotta get home so Ma'dear can leave for work." Their pace quickened. "Glo, did you see that Tom?"

"Yes?"

"Well . . . ?"

"Well . . . you know what I mean, girl."

"Right. He's all right if you like 'em tall." They laughed, holding hands.

Gloria helped Jessica and Ann prepare supper. Afterward Ann went upstairs, and they studied at the kitchen table.

"Don't you think Mr. Jones is handsome?" Jessica looked up from her civics book.

"I don't know, handsome or not, he's gonna be givin' a test tomorrow."

"Aren't you liking no boys?" Jessica rested on her elbows.

"I'm gonna be a nurse."

After a few hours, they relaxed and laughed a little. Then Gloria napped.

Gloria's mother arrived. Her blue hotel uniform showed beneath her coat. You could see where Gloria got her looks. Jessica watched them get in the car and put the porch light on.

Mary glanced over at Gloria as she drove. "How you, girl? You like Jessica's family, don't you?"

"Is Maurice gonna be staying with us long?"

"Awhile."

She had Gloria when she was sixteen, and they were often mistaken for sisters. Maurice was in the living room in a black silk undershirt, sipping whiskey.

"What took you so long?" He had smooth caramel skin and a thin mustache and a pinky ring on the hand holding his drink.

"Had to pick up my girl."

He helped her with her coat.

"Night, Mama." Gloria looked from the top step. And a shiver surged through her

The Kensington Brass Company was changing shifts. Walls shot up two stories, smokestacks exhaled, and racks of keys dropped into churning barrels of soapy water and rocks. Goggled workers shaped metal into latches, dropping them into baskets for drilling, hooking them to chains for the furnace and shower, and dumping them into trays and on to plating for a copper coating. *ooooooz, ooooooz, ooooooooz.*

It blasted in their sleep: three for a shift change, two for break time starting or ending. Long and continuous signaled an emergency.

Thin-gloved women assembled copper-colored locks. A man wrote on a pad and handed it to an assistant, who picked up the phone and called the engineer. *ooooooooz, ooooooz.*

Churning barrels halted; cutting ceased; bending, drilling, firing, and plating stopped. They removed goggles and shed gloves. Fifteen minutes was time enough to have a cup of coffee and a roll, to relax and light a cigarette. They opened lunch buckets, poured coffee, and inhaled cigarettes.

A tall thin man, his shirt open, exposing the blond hair on his chest, finished half a sandwich and returned the rest to his lunch bucket. He was getting $1.85 an hour, big money, but that didn't mean they owned him.

The old-timer was Italian, short and squat, with gray hair and a knowing look. He got $2.50 an hour; he knew his job, knew it inside and out. The foreman left him alone.

Gonna go out this weekend and do me some hunting. Boy, I hate it here, but they is paying me for it. He was up from the South, a puffy-jawed bull of a man, and put away his lunch box.

I'm gettin' me that brand-new Chevy if I can get a little overtime. He was tanned, almost brown, a toothpick of a man, up from the South too and always planning. *ooooooooz, ooooooz.* It was a good pause, then time to get back.

It was a few more hours before supper, and John looked at the clock. He didn't mind work if he had a good meal packed. The sandwich his wife packed looked good.

Job's bad on the hands, bad on the nails too. Lu, they called her for short. She was forty but looked younger and gave her age as thirty-two. *Gotta take some personal time and take care of my nails and hair. A woman needs to do these thing.* She put the mirror away and got up.

Babe-Ruth arrived home smelling of sulfur and cigarettes. She was thinking about Junior always begging for the pastries next door. She had bought a dozen glazed donuts and made a pitcher of lemonade and made him eat and drink until he was stuffed. She thought it would cure his incessant begging, but she was wrong. She inspected the rooms. Last night the house was dirty, and she woke them all up. She had been tired, but she did it anyway and could see the lesson took. She undressed and slid into the tub and dozed, then awakened and went to bed, and blasting horns and the smell of tobacco and sulfur saturated her dreams.

That Saturday morning, she was tempted to sleep in, but she had too much to do. Ann got them ready to work with buckwheat cakes. A twenty-pound bag could go a long way with a little margarine and Karo Syrup. There was plenty to do in a house with seven people. It never got completed, but they would stop around three in the afternoon. They were always expecting chili Saturday evening. The rest of the day would be preparation for Sunday school, then dinner and bathing.

She trekked down the alley in old clothes. It went for miles, and you could walk downtown without going on the main streets. It was a day for rummaging.

Today they refer to it as recycling, but then it was surviving. The junkman collected junk, and the ragman, rags. The junkman liked objects of heavy metal, and most of the kids imagined they were melted down. Occasionally an object was fixed and resold or resold to somebody that knew how to fix it. It was never really clear what the ragman did with the rags. They weren't good enough or clean enough for the rummage sales; rumor was they would be used to make paper. It didn't make sense to kids. Sometimes ragmen made a good living, but they were careful not to show it, or people would want a better price.

Rummage sales were standing or weekend affairs. The standing ones were the enterprises of industrious women who didn't have to sell everything at once, so things could be held and sold according to demand.

The most famous was Bertha's. Anne was a healthy competitor. The stores stood on the fringes of the commercial district. Bertha's storefront adjoined her home, and she could open and close whenever she wanted. She had regular hours; at times she rented the space for weekend sales. The Salvation Army specialized in furniture. Their clothes were neatly ironed and on hangers and too expensive for some.

Anne and Bertha arrived early at other weekend sales so they could carry off the best buys for resale.

"I saw your mama in Bertha's!" It was always said in a signifying fashion, a put-down. It was better if Babe-Ruth did her rummaging privately. She got there early. The great pickings went fast; she had to compete with Anne and Bertha. Babe-Ruth kept her eyes peeled for Sunday clothes and good shoes. There were three big sales, and she returned with loaded shopping bags. She trekked down the alley relaxed. Rummaging put her mind at ease. It was one of the reasons she rarely missed.

Once she returned, the boys were playing ball in the alley, so she turned on the main street and entered the house from the front so as not to embarrass them. She put her bags away and looked out the kitchen window. There was a little extra, and she went to the backyard and beckoned George and put a coin in his hand and another into Junior's, which fell to the ground. It was a dime, and some boys snickered.

"Thanks, Ma'dear." Junior ignored them, putting it in his pocket. He had it right as he thought about it later. If you weren't proud of your own and their efforts, something was wrong with you.

When he was fifteen, her rummaging brought him a tweed suit. He never liked getting dressed up before, but that suit made him feel dashing. He'd hang it up and step back. He didn't know anyone with as good a suit, secondhand or not. Years later, he would describe the suit to his children, and they would marvel at the wonder in his eyes.

Chapter 21

It was another country. Korea was a memory, Louis and Dimaggio had come and gone, and Jackie Robinson's Dodgers lost yet another series. Johna's tree stood like a tower on what had seemed like a village and was taller and more grandeur. Caleb leaned on its huge trunk and looked up at its green towering overhead and remembered names and faces. He had found work on the Jefferson plantation and at the new factory, where the jobs were sucked up by farm workers pushed off the land by machinery. He pocketed his pay and moved up the small hill toward home.

He found himself standing over Jesop's grave looking at Jesop's name and the date he had written on the tombstone. Caleb guessed he was in his late eighties. It was strange to go there each payday, and he didn't understand why he waited until he got the job. He hadn't drank since he started working regularly. He made no promises and took it a step at a time. At home, he ate pork chops and a can of beans, washed quickly, and changed into his new overalls. There was a young gal a few miles down that he would call on.

"Tell Geraldine to come out here." He handed her mama two bags of groceries.

"Geraldine, you got yoself a visitor, girl."

She was seventeen and a woman all over. He took the cellophane-wrapped pastries from his bib. Her mama went in, and they talked, then walked awhile. Then he laid his jacket under the tree.

They headed for the house in the moonlight. Saturday, he would do farmwork, and he would be up at the strike of dawn.

Seasons passed slowly in the country. On Friday, he brought his money home and put it under a plank. He had fixed things up. Geraldine came early, smelling like flowers. In the morning, they carried home the groceries. She talked a lot, and he didn't mind.

Months went by, and he was in Cape Girardeau and saw his old Packard. Selling it had kept him in booze when he first arrived, but it was time to buy it back. They wanted three hundred dollars, and it needed some work. He had more than enough and sealed the deal the following week.

"A new car, Caleb!" Geraldine was waiting when he drove up, and she jumped all over him like it was a Cadillac.

The next morning, he took her home. Her mother moved slowly.

"Thank you, Caleb. I'm sorry, but my legs is swelling again."

She looked older than her forty-five years (six pregnancies and five miscarriages) and was minus some teeth. They hadn't seen the father for years and had subsisted on government surplus and their garden until Caleb started coming around.

"Caleb, come in, let's talk." She sat, and Geraldine put away the groceries. "Geraldine missed her monthly flow. She gonna have your child."

Geraldine grabbed his arm.

"What's done is done. I'll keep bringing groceries and add some cash."

"I knew you'd do the right thing."

Caleb was true to his word and worked some overtime. When she started showing, he found a midwife and made the arrangements. The time came; it was the weekend, and he didn't miss a day at the plant. It was a boy, and Caleb named him Rueben. Geraldine was back on her feet in a day.

In the winter, he grew some wheat. On Saturday, he noticed a large trailer at the car lot in Cape Jarrod. It was in back and the size of a small house, with white aluminum siding and wide windows, a bedroom, sitting room, and a closet of a bathroom with shower off the dining room. He thought about it for a month and bought it for fifteen hundred dollars and parked it next to the water pump beside his shanty.

Back in Michigan, Babe-Ruth's boys were growing and hustling to get what they wanted and what they thought they needed. She turned at the door. "Be home before I get off work." She was fond of the trick or treats herself.

The boys were free to roam. Cal and George ate dinner hastily. Cal was a hobo and George a clown; Ann and Jessica were gypsies. The older sisters would escort the fairies, Jesop and Lona, around the neighborhood.

The boys quickly pillaged the neighborhood (Mr. Writ still gave the best treats), with their bag starting to bulge as they chomped apples. At eight thirty, they stopped at Campau Park for the bonfire, where the policemen provided free cider and donuts.

"One donut at a time, one at a time! There's enough for everybody."

With the fire warming their backs, the great ape, King Kong, exploded on the silver screen—Halloween was everything it was supposed to be! Afterward, they trekked home with bags bulging. George reached for a Hershey bar as a stranger approached.

"I got more'n you." He turned to Junior.

"Let me see what you got there." The stranger grabbed George's bag and fled. "I'll take it all"

"He took my brother's candy!" Junior yelled to someone approaching that they didn't know but had seen before.

"My candy!" The new boy rushed after the thief, and George screamed louder, joining the chase. The pursuer was fast. The surprised thief looked back and tripped, and the newcomer put him in a half nelson.

"Give it back! Now, tell him you're a dirty coward, and you'll never do it again!"

"I'm a coward, and I won't do it again."

"You left out something!" He bent his neck toward the ground.

"I'm a dirty coward, I'll never do it again."

"Kiss the ground!"

"No!" Drool dripped from his mouth.

"Do it!" He pushed his face into the ground. "Next time I'll break your arm."

"Thanks." George recovered his bag.

He said his name was Tom and accepted two Hershey bars.

"Live near here?" Junior opened his bag.

"Three blocks down." Tom accepted two more candy bars, and he was gone.

What a Halloween! they thought and put their bags at their bedside and slept with candy in their mouths.

The next day, young Tom set two bowls of rice down and poured his father a cup of coffee and slid pork chops unto their plates. He talked about Halloween, but old Tom's mind was somewhere else.

"Aah!" Old Tom sipped coffee. "You did good, son. How was school?" The boy nodded. "How's the boxing?"

"I'm fighting for the state title tomorrow at the civic center. Can you come?"

The old man nodded. He'd be tired, but he couldn't stay away.

Then he had that dreamy look, and young Tom could tell his father was musing. He was forty-five when he married, and everyone thought it would never happen. He was a natural hermit, they thought, unmarried and not running with the gals. There was no cure for a man like that. Lisa was twenty. It was a happy time. He was already a contented man, and life got better, he thought, as he watched young Tom eating. He was strong too and had her natural goodness. Looking at the boy brought it all back.

She was even lovelier when she started showing.

"I'm gonna have this child and turn around and have another."

She had found the man she wanted. The boys her age were too trifling for her taste. She wanted someone with his anchor sunk so they could dig in and live. He was a carpenter and didn't have to go begging to any man. When the day drew near, she was ready. There was no need to go to town and see a doctor; she hadn't vomited once. She had a midwife, named Bartha, like her mother had and like those before her.

"Oh, it's a boy all right. He must be some kinda boxer 'cause he's making a fuss." She'd hold her stomach.

Night came, and he waited in the yard. There were no screams or hollering, and he bit off a plug of tobacco and waited, chewed, waited some more, and paced. Then he heard a baby crying, strong and healthy, and waited a few minutes, giving them time to clean up. Ladies wouldn't just have things any old way, he was thinking; a table had to have a tablecloth, and a window, curtains. They made life better.

Finally he went in. They were three, and he was proud. Bartha looked startled. The baby was swaddled in Lisa's arms, with blood soaking the sheets; she was sweating and pale.

"Tom, she's bleeding, and I can't stop it!" Bertha was pressing with a hand inside and the other on the belly, but it wouldn't stop. Lisa was cold, and he took the baby. Then she closed her eyes for good.

Old Tom had reverie in his eyes as they stared.

"You got a gal friend, Tom?"

"No, sir, but I'm working on it."

"You get a goodun, hear . . . Your mama was a goodun. Get a goodun."

"Yes, sir . . . What was Mama like?" There were no pictures, and he had heard it all before.

"She was a pretty woman with skin the color of a penny, and strong. I didn't need to beat off no suitors. Boys her own age were plumb scared. She had pearly teeth, straight, and she was big. You know what I'm ferrin' to—big!" They smiled and reared back cackling. "She was my one and only. That was it for me. I didn't have one before and never will again."

There was water in old Tom's eyes, and the youngster put his hand on his shoulder.

It was Saturday afternoon. The boys had finished the chores and were in the next alley playing football. Babe-Ruth had returned from rummaging when smoke seeped under the basement door and through the vents.

"Get the baby!" she yelled upstairs to Jessica and dialed. "This is 611 Windel. Our house is on fire!"

Big sister rushed down with the li'l Jesop.

"Is everybody out?"

"They in the yard." Smoke filled the rooms as she grabbed the green tackle box and rushed out.

In the alley on the next block, Junior threw a spiral; George caught it and paused.

"A fire! On the next block!" They rushed toward the sounds of fire engines, remembering the ambulance sirens and blood in the street when a truck hit an old man.

"It's big!" George was front running and suddenly relinquished the lead. Within the abstract adventure, a horrible possibility emerged, and he bolted to the front again.

A crowd surrounded his home, and fire and smoke streamed from the windows. Babe-Ruth was holding Jesop. George slithered through.

"Ma'dear, is everybody out?" She nodded, and he buried his face in her apron, as she winced, looking over the crowd.

I wonder if she got insurance? I hope she had sense enough to have insurance. A short black man shook his head.

What she gonna do? That house was all she had. Five kids surrounded the skinny white lady from the tenement.

"Stand back. Everybody stay back!" The fireman waved, still aiming the hose. The crowd grew, and another fire engine pulled in. Glass cracked as smoke burst through windows.

She always thought she was something, a colored woman from the next block was thinking. *Let's see how she deals with this.*

Poor woman. She was doing the best she could. It's a shame! A robust white woman held her son by his hand and dried her eyes.

A middle-aged colored man smirked. *She's a proudun. This'll bring her down a notch.*

Babe-Ruth squeezed the green tackle box. A thin yellow woman, with some missing teeth, cried and hugged Junior, who moved behind Babe-Ruth. The firemen broke windows, chopped down doors, and directed hoses.

"Not much left." The fireman tipped his helmet and wiped. "Just a frame!" They drew in the hoses and put a rope around the area. "Lady, don't try to get in for nothing. It's dangerous. Seen some get killed trying."

The crowd thinned. Mrs. Clay hugged Babe-Ruth and slipped an envelope into her apron.

"Junior, George, y'all be stayin' with Mrs. Clay. The rest of us is goin' with

Sister Grant. It's all arranged. Behave and be useful, you know what I mean." Junior and George disappeared inside Mrs. Clay's door as Babe-Ruth surveyed the ruins.

Chapter 22

Maurice never knew his daddy. He must have been a good-looking man; he chuckled at the thought while inspecting his teeth. Childhood was good; he was hungry and hurting at times, but those memories faded, and the good ones remained. Mary was one of his women. They met at the hotel. It was a way to spend time; he puffed his reefer in his undershirt and exhaled shaking his scotch and water, looking into the sun.

"Mama, I'm home!" Gloria took her coat off skipping upstairs. "Ain't Mama home?"

"She gonna be." He put his drink down following her up to her room.

"What you doing in here?" She backed against the wall as he closed the door.

"Cool it, sweetheart. Some things need learning. I'm the teacher"

She bolted past, slamming the door on his hand.

"Little bitch!" He carried her back in and put her on the bed. "No one can hear!" He was too strong, and she held her breath . . . Then it was over. "You been wanting it and you got it. Tell your mama, and she'll hate you for it!"

It rained hard for two days. She stayed in her room most of the time, saying she wasn't feeling well. The world seemed different. She kept looking in the mirror and going to the bathroom; at school she felt like people were looking at her.

"What's wrong, girl? You have a hard period?" Jessica shook her head and wouldn't talk anymore.

Her mother sensed the possibilities. And she cried.

"Girl, what's wrong? I can tell there is something."

"Nothing, Mama. I'm all right. Nothing to worry about."

Maurice denied it, but she sensed Gloria wasn't a child anymore and kicked him out. *I feel like a fish outta water. I don't know what to do or what to think. I'll stay close and see if she gets her flow. God, I'm sorry.*

Cal and George were living at Mrs. Clay's and almost done delivering their morning papers; the aroma of breakfast filled the air. The Holly House was the kind of restaurant they planned to eat at someday. Colored people in starched white hats and uniforms cooked and served. It was well lit, with white trimmings on brick. The paper vendor was beside the door; only the coin box was locked.

They had sold two papers earlier and were two short. Junior pretended to insert two dimes and took what they needed. Then a blue Ford pulled up, and two men got out.

"Well, boys, how's business?" Dark hair showed under his hat; he had a round head and crooked teeth. Junior's throat felt dry; George's head dropped.

"Get in the car."

They got in the backseat with the taller detective with a red nose and large ears.

"Didn't pay for those papers, did ya?"

"No, sir." Junior looked down.

"Ever hear of Walter Jones?" Jones was the no-nonsense colored detective assigned to the colored neighborhood. Rumor was he'd pistol-whip you if you got out of line. "We'll turn you over to him. He'll know what to do."

"John, I don't think these boys want to go to reform school. They've learned their lesson." The one with them in back looked at his partner.

"I don't know. They've been doing this awhile and will get into bigger things. I say we hand them over to Jones, and when he's finished, he'll put them where they belong."

Would it be better to be whipped by Captain Jones or Babe-Ruth? The thought was on their minds.

"I think they learned their lesson . . . Give 'em another chance."

Junior handed over the dimes and two nickels.

"Here's what we got sellin' the papers—the tip too. Take it! We'll never do it again."

The one in the front seat weighed the coins in his palm. "All right. Go! If we catch you again, we'll run you in."

They never looked back.

It was no adjustment for them to live at Mrs. Clay's. She had watched them drool over her food, and she cooked extra. A cook could tell when a refusal wasn't real, and she wouldn't tell. Mr. Solum, Ol' Smokey, who rented a room, was the man of the house. Junior ran errands for him and afterward stayed and listened to his stories.

"Junior, why don't you go and fetch me some Days Work [tobacco]. You ain't done nothin' all day."

Mr. Solum loved to fish, and if you got him telling stories, you realized what an art it was. Silver haired, puffing a dark-brown pipe the color of his skin, crossing his legs with precision and relighting, he had a way about him that made Junior want to become an old man.

Living was easy; sports and the paper route provided excuses to be on the streets.

"Hey, young bloods, what you hangin' around here for?" Damon leaned; a cigarette hung from his mouth as he showed them a condom. "You can get these inside, but you have to be eighteen." He was the sex expert. The condom was proof enough. "I use seven a week. Sometimes a couple a night. Y'all will be need 'em in about ten or twenty years."

Junior was loitering and chewing gum when Ray Pritchard staggered by. Ray had been a catcher in the Negro leagues, with home run power. Junior thought he should have made it to the big leagues. Mr. Solum agreed.

"How you, Mr. Ray?"

"How you, young man?" Mr. Ray walked straighter as he disappeared down the street.

"Man, can't you hear me calling you?" Jim put his arm on Junior's shoulder. "Sometimes you in a world by yourself." Jim was the older of Mrs. Clay's "grandchildren," thirteen and tall for his age. "Tell Grandma the coach is takin' me and the boys to a ball game, and I won't be home 'til dark."

"What game?"

"Deliver the message!"

Living in another woman's house was trying for Babe-Ruth. She and the girls helped clean and cook and picked up after themselves. Mrs. Grant wasn't accustomed to being served. When Caleb left, there wasn't enough food, and Babe-Ruth almost didn't pay the insurance. She eyed the green tackle box on the dresser, which contained the insurance papers. People from the factory and church sent food and money. It would take the insurance company several months to rebuild. Babe-Ruth said when God humbled you, things get clearer.

She was off work for most of the week, and she and Gloria's mother got better acquainted. Mary was sending Gloria South to live with her aunt. Mary had to be at work, so Gloria would stay overnight at Sister Grant's, and Babe-Ruth would see that she boarded the bus.

"I know you don't like it, but I'm sending you to my people. I can't handle things the way they are, and I can't protect you." She put the money and the tickets in her purse.

"Mama, I don't wanna go."

"Mama loves you, child, and knows best. I'll be down as soon as I get some vacation. Then we'll make some plans."

That Friday, Gloria was packed and ready. Babe-Ruth imagined raising her herself.

"Gloria, that bus is taking you to Georgia where you auntie's waiting." Babe-Ruth had prepared a basket of chicken, peanut butter and jelly sandwiches, with Pepsi cola and potato chips. "Don't get off for nothing except the bathroom. When you do, tell the driver that you'll be right back. Your mama's doin' the best she can. She loves you."

They put Gloria's belonging in Sister Grant's car.

"I'm gonna miss y'all." Jessica watched them pull away. She thought they were being moved around like checkers, with no concern for their feelings. She didn't know what was wrong, and she couldn't do anything about it anyway. They promised to write weekly and to be together again when they were grown.

After a few weeks, Babe-Ruth rented their apartment back. Brother and Sister Crawford were like relatives, and Babe-Ruth and the kids settled in. Months passed, and it was taking more time to repair the house than she thought.

"Junior, take this sweet potato pie down to Sister Crawford . . . Don't worry. I baked two." Babe-Ruth knew she couldn't repay kindness, but it was important to try. The insurance would replace the major furnishings. She thanked God she had kept the policy current.

She stopped in every couple of weeks to see how the construction was coming along and thought her hundred-year-old house was almost new. Finally they went home.

Everything smelled of plaster and painted wood. Beige plaster walls were bordered by new woodwork.

"We scrubbed these floors 'til the Lord decided to give us new ones." She was delighted by the freshness and bright rooms.

"Good, Ma'dear." Jessica skipped upstairs.

Babe-Ruth ran her finger along the front window's latticework. The tinted glass squares were unchanged.

"Come!" she yelled upstairs. "Let's thank the Lord for our new home."

They kneeled around her bed, intermittently peeking up at her praying. It was their mother's religion, and it worked. God was good, and he made their ma'dear strong and had provided them a new home. Church people were nice and on their side and could be trusted, and it was all right to have to bathe on Saturday night and be inspected and listen to long sermons on Sunday and pray before meals.

Babe-Ruth finished the prayer, and the children escaped to their new rooms.

Jessica wrote Gloria weekly and always got a letter back. She missed a lot of school and had overdue homework. It was Monday and 8:00 p.m., and she studied at the dining room table. There was a knock at the door. Only certain visitors were allowed when Babe-Ruth was at work, and Jessica hurried to the door. Mrs. Tezon wore a blue suit and hat (Jessica liked her style).

"How are you, Mrs. Tezon? You know Ma'dear isn't home?" Jessica was admiring her outfit.

"Why, I've come to see you, Jessica." She walked in, taking off her hat. "I haven't had a chance to see you since your mom started her job. I've been thinking about you, though."

"Like a cup of coffee?"

She nodded. A rumbling came from the stairs. George and Junior said hello and retreated upstairs. Ma'dear had a cup before work. "I'll warm it up."

"How's school?"

"I've missed a lot and I'm behind. I'm not gonna pass at this rate."

"If you don't, you'll have to go to summer school."

"I'm sixteen, and I'm thinking about getting a job. Ma'dear never spent a day in school."

"The times are different." The coffee perked, and Jessica took down a cup and saucer.

"Do you take sugar and cream?"

"A little of both. There are people twice your age looking back, wishing they had stayed in school."

"But, I don't have the clothes, and I've missed too much. Want to know something? I'm not smart. When Gloria was here, we worked together. I was riding her coattails."

Mrs. Tezon held out her handkerchief. "Jessica, do me two favors: First, keep working as hard as you can until the term finishes, and we'll sit down and talk about summer school. Second, I want you to read this book, Ain't I a Woman, by Harriet Tubman. We'll talk about it when you're finished. Read ten pages at bedtime."

Jessica ran her fingers over the cover. "I'll read it."

"Remember, I'll be back."

She locked up.

"Everything all right, big sister." Junior leaned in from the stairway.

She nodded and reentered the kitchen. "I'm fine." She needed to finish her studies, and she had ten pages to read.

Chapter 23

Back in Jersey, Mitchell had all the space he needed, and if he didn't read the newspaper, it wasn't read. At times he imagined a house full of noise; Babe-Ruth hadn't written for a while, and it worried him. He'd write because Mildred couldn't.

When Sister Jones took sick, he and Mildred helped out. What he learned about Sister Jones caused him to do some thinking. Mary was her first name; she decided some things a long time ago and never looked back. She was eighteen and doing day work when she got saved in 1905. It was a life of faith.

It wasn't that she never had any doubts. Doubts were knocking all the time, but she never let them in. When she fasted, her body made a racket, but she took control, putting hunger in its place, showing who was boss—appetite was the slave, not her. Sometimes old Satan tried to mix her up and say there was no God, but she spotted him every time.

She lost a child, mourned, and praised God. She lost a husband and descended into the valley of death. It was long and hard, but she knew he was rejoicing in God's bosom. She let him go. Let go of despair too.

She didn't have much trouble with the lure of the world. She was a poor woman, and the attraction of the world was no match for the culture and good times from being with church folks, singing, praying, dancing, eating, and visiting.

She had a gift for bringing young people to the Lord and mentoring. They seemed to need her most when she was worn out. She learned to ignore the weariness. Afterward, she would be refreshed, renewed, rejuvenated for days. That was how the gift worked.

Mitchell didn't listen at first and held religion squarely in the female province; from his count, more women were going to heaven than men, and it made him suspicious. If you were born male and with any kind of grit, you had a leg up on hell already.

He or Mildred would prepare her dinner, and he'd usually bring it over, watch her eat, and carry the dish back. That was when she did most of her sharing.

"I had a little missionary church in the South, about thirty families. I got a young preacher to come down every other Sunday and Wednesday and I did the support work."

Mildred had worked that Saturday, and Mitchell had prepared the lunch. Sister Jones's grandmother had been a slave. He got a good feeling looking after her, and it was intriguing conversation. He nodded as she put her spoon and fork on the plate.

"Anybody ever tell you, you a fine cook for a man?"

"Comin' from you, that's a sho'nuff compliment."

"As I was sayin', now sometimes that preacher wouldn't get there for seven to ten days if he was needed in his own church. I had to take up the slack. We were havin' a heap of problems. New Christians havin' a hard time holdin' on.

"I was prayin' all the time. Felt drained, but each time, after I had done some chore, I got new strength. One time I was in my room prayin'. I had been married awhile then, and I decided to go to the livin' room to concentrate. I felt the presence of evil and looked over at the chair, and there was Satan watchin' me. I had never seen him before—most people don't even think he real. He was grinning, the handsomest man I ever seen. I was scared. Then I started praising God and commenced singin'. Then I said, 'Why don't you praisin' him wid me?' Puff! He disappeared. I think I shamed him."

Mitchell turned pale, if a colored man could turn pale. His eyes gaped, and his skin prickled. He wasn't a talker, but she could tell he had things on his mind. Mildred came sometimes, but he did most of it himself.

Months passed, and she got weaker. He wrote some letters to her relatives. When church people came, he left. It wasn't that he disliked them. They were mostly womenfolk; the few men seemed manly enough, but he wasn't built for praying and carrying on. There was some deep thinking inside that head of his, and she hoped he would let it out.

One evening, he brought the supper Mildred had prepared. When she finished, he sat for a long time.

"You know, I ain't never told anybody this, but when I was a young man, I got in a fight. James Dross came at me with a knife. It was just one of those things. Two young men both too proud to back down. He was as good a man as I was, maybe better. People were watching and our pride was on the line. I shoulda run. Something told me to, but I was a proudun too. There lay a hammer. He rushed me, and I brought him down. Knew he was dead. I got off for self-defense. Lucky for me he was colored.

"I married Mildred. She was from another town, and we moved North. She never knew, and I haven't told her to this day. Before Caleb an 'em came, I visited the grave . . . It's something that need telling."

Mitchell watched her die a few days later; she had no fear, no doubts, and no complaints. Her sons were older than him and in California. He mailed her Bible and cash from selling the furniture. It took three days to write Babe-Ruth, and he kept rearranging the words.

On Thursday, Babe-Ruth got the letter. She could feel Sister Jone's spirit and knew that it would stay.

That Friday, Babe-Ruth's shift ended, and they gathered around the punch-out clock. She was accustomed to the line now. Her once-blistered hands were callused, and she had acclimated to the rapid movement and standing and hardly sensed the sulfur and cigarette smoke saturating her clothing. She was thirty-six and had brought seven children into the world. She hadn't read the books or seen the movies that said she needed a man. When Caleb was home and was kind, her nature was fulfilled; it was a part of life, a good part. At times her nature surfaced, but it was out of place. At times the desires were strong, and she remembered Gloria. Courting would be like letting a fox loose in the chicken coop.

It was Saturday. Trees were budding, and the sun highlighted children in light jackets and tennis shoes. The ground was soft and cool. Babe-Ruth worked in the garden; she was meditating and looked around for a pot.

Caleb was a good man until he started drinking. He worked like a dog and had a lotta good in him. I was Ma'dear, but what was he? They always got me something on Mother's Day. Father's Day wasn't even noticed. You never know what happens in the navy. I was no help with those things. Didn't know what to do or say when Reuben died . . . I put the chillun first . . .

Jessica looked out at Babe-Ruth working in her garden. Saturday was personal time. She was nearer to being out of school and on her own. The teachers were considerate, and she was catching up. Her grades wouldn't be good, but she would pass everything. Going to summer school was a chance to improve and lighten her schoolwork in the fall.

Dear Glo,

I received your letter yesterday. It sounds like you're doing well. I guess the south isn't as bad as we thought. I can tell your aunt is a good woman.

Everything is fine here. I have a part-time job. The funeral director's wife across the street asked me to be a hostess during wakes and social events. She's proper and fun to be around. Ma'dear said I can keep whatever I earn for school clothes.

An exciting thing happened over the past few months. I have a lady friend. She was our social worker when we were getting government surplus foods. I was thinking of dropping out after you left, but I changed my mind. She had me read Ain't I A Woman by Harriet Tubman; it opened my eyes. I intend to use my opportunities. I'm not going to judge myself by my clothes or the way I talk. I'm improving everyday.

I know what I want. Times been wasted, but it's not too late. I'm going to be a social worker. It's a good job. Lots of poor people are high class on the inside, and with help they can advance themselves.

The kids are doing good. The boys are as mannish as ever. Ma'dear adjusted to the job, and it doesn't seem to take as much out of her like it used to. She's planning on getting a car. No, I don't have a boyfriend.

I'll be looking forward to your next letter.

Love, Jessica

She folded it and put it into the envelope. She and Lona had talked about Caleb, and Lona hardly remembered him. She had been his favorite. To Caleb, Jessica seemed to be always on Babe-Ruth's side. She resented him for making her choose and calling her scarface. She remembered the good times and his stories and the way he laughed. Then she stopped—they were doing fine without him. He had left them to starve!

More coloreds were moving in on Windell Street. The Vsekas, Vaults, Victorios, Russos, and Steins were moving to be with the Vandenbergs and Dykemas.

Cars filled Windell Street, and the rooms above the funeral parlor were lit up; the bright chandelier illuminated a table of delicacies. A grand piano filled the rooms with ragtime. Mr. Ford, head of the Elks, wore a dark suit and white bow tie and held a drink in his callused hand where a gold ring glimmered.

The room had vanilla walls and was wide, with a high ceiling and leather and patterned chairs and sofas. Pearls dangled from Mrs. Crambrook's ears (her husband was the first colored dentist in town), and larger ones lay on her breast above a blue speckled gown. Men in tuxedos and elegantly dressed ladies surrounded the punch bowl.

Dr. Lacy sipped champagne, engrossed in the Tanner paintings. Mr. Writ rattled his martini, looking younger than his sixty-five years, as Jessica glided by with a silver tray.

"Would you like an hors d'oeuvre?" Mrs. Writ had tutored Jessica herself.

When the evening was over, Jessica donned a full apron and joined Myrtle, the cook, and they swept, stacked, washed, and put things away.

"You did real good." Myrtle patted Jessica's shoulder.

Mrs. Writ bent over to inspect the rug. "You finished early tonight."

"Things go good with good help." Myrtle smiled at Jessica.

Jessica thought seven dollars was a lot for working a few hours in a dreamworld. She pocketed the cash and headed across the street. The porch light was on, and Babe-Ruth straightened the curtains.

School was out, and Babe-Ruth enjoyed the sun, the longer daylight hours, and life greening and sprouting. The general church picnic came in early July.

"Sister Jefferson, you're a credit to the church." Rev. Clemmons smiled.

"God is good." Babe-Ruth blushed. It was good sitting at the picnic in the sunshine, receiving praise, and everybody having a good time.

It was Monday the second week of summer, and Babe-Ruth slept in. Jessica was at summer school, and Ann was in charge. Junior and George were doing chores before leaving for the ballpark. They cleaned the yard and cut the grass, then moved inside to scrub floors (scrubbing was male work and done on the hands and knees after scraping with a butter knife).

The boys finished around ten and prepared to go to the ballpark. Babe-Ruth inspected. She trusted baseball and expected them back before she left for work. Practices were Mondays and Tuesdays, and games were on Thursdays. George was in the minors, but he followed Junior's team closely. He was as big as Junior and good enough, he thought, to be moved up. They had dreamed about the first day of practice (oiling their gloves and gazing through snowfall). The park came into view, and they galloped. Heaven was a baseball diamond.

"Come ta me, babe. Bring it!" SWOOOOSH! The ball was new with a wonderful sound and feel.

"Ya smokin'!"

Junior pounded his glove and squatted. Catching was a craft. Larry, the original catcher, could pitch, and the year before, the coach had switched Junior from third base. Being a catcher was the first thing Junior had studied on his own. It took grit to stop pitches in the dirt, and he observed the techniques of older boys.

Doug's family had been missionaries in Pakistan, and they moved into his grandfather's house, which was on the edge of a rapidly changing neighborhood. His father was a surgeon, and his grandfather emigrated from Holland and made his money in the furniture business. Doug was breaking in a new first baseman's glove and needed to work on his hitting, but he cracked the starting lineup. They lived in a brick Tudor in an all-white neighborhood two blocks from school. In Pakistan they were homeschooled. Each of Doug's siblings was at the top of their respective classes.

Larry, the pitcher, threw so hard that Junior had to put a sponge in his glove; Larry came over from Franklin School and quickly established himself as a fierce competitor. When that was done, he was his affable self. He pitched, also played second, and was the catcher at times. He had eight brothers and sisters, and his mother worked part-time. He had her face and eyes.

Tim lived a few houses down from Doug and always got playing time. He had red hair and freckles, and his mother was the coach. Having a lady coach was unique, but she knew her baseball and was a volunteer room mother. The boys had been throwing since the first thaw. The Madison Rockets wore T-shirts emblazoned with the name and blue caps and were the only team without uniforms.

"You mean you don't have a TV set?" Junior found it strange and figured Doug and his family were rich because his dad was a doctor.

After practice, they sprawled on the grass, playing catch on their backs.

"We read books!" Doug's cowlick bobbed over blue eyes. "Adult books too!"

Junior was curious about the inside of their brick Tudor.

"Come in, but leave the comic books outside." Doug's mother pulled him through the door; she was good looking and proper, but Junior felt comfortable. It was true they had no television, but there was music, books, checkers, and chess.

Dr. Young wasn't home. Cal stayed three hours, then stuffed his comic books back into his pocket, still wishing they had their television back.

It was the middle of summer. With Babe-Ruth at work, everyone stayed near the house. At dusk they came in, and Jessica locked up.

"Y'all gotta hear this." She took out a small brown book. "You're gonna like these readings. It's Paul Laurence Dunbar. I'm gonna read him in my speech class tomorrow."

On Caleb's side, folks loved tales. He said it was because nobody could sing. Their specialties were talking animals and ghost stories from Caleb and old Jesop.

"When de Co'n Pone's Hot" by Laurence Dunbar.

They sat at the dining room table. Jessica stood and cleared her throat. The back of a chair served as the podium.

"Dey is times in life when Nature
Seems to slip a cog an' go,
Jes' a-rattlin' down creation,
Lak an ocean's overflow . . ."

The rhythm of the words jumped out. They giggled, cackled, and stamped.

"Where did you get that?"

The room glowed, and she bowed to the applause. They passed the book, and each took a turn. Jessica rechecked the doors and put the porch light on. Her ma'dear would be home in an hour.

Jessica felt her right cheek. The scar was fading. She lay in bed thinking about speech class. She was a little afraid of the extemporaneous readings beginning in a week. Geometry was orderly. If the answer was right, they couldn't mark her down even if they didn't like her. Her typing was improving. She was fast and felt like showing off.

In summer school, kids came from different schools. How would they respond to Dunbar? She was nervous. It was like starting over. She would be a sophomore in the fall. Mrs. Tezon had come by again two days ago.

"Jessica, this is America, and in 1954 you can be anything you want to be if you have the ability and work hard. You will have to sacrifice, and you may not be able to dress like the others, but if you don't fulfill your dreams, you will have nobody to blame but yourself."

Ann rolled over and pulled the covers; Jessica pulled back and fluffed her pillow and continued staring in the darkness. *Ma'dear said I shouldn't be expecting to do no dating.* Jessica hadn't thought about it when it was said.

"If a boy want to come over and meet the family and visit, that's fine. He can get to know you that way. If he won't, he probably ain't worth knowin'." Ann pulled the covers, and Jessica wondered if Ann was really asleep and jerked them back.

Nice clothes don't make you who you are, she was thinking. *I'm not judging myself and others by clothes. I can wait to have things, to be with boys. It's time to learn and grow.* From things she admired from Babe-Ruth, Mrs. Tezon, Mrs. Clay, and her favorite teachers, she constructed her composite woman and dozed off to sleep.

The young people's picnic came in August and was attended by the young and the young at heart. Older folks loved to come and were not considered gate-crashers and enjoyed themselves; it was one of Jessica's favorite outings.

At summer's end, she had saved a hundred dollars and wouldn't accept the free books the board of education provided the poor. Standing in the long line for the books was humiliating. There would be enough left to buy undergarments and a few dresses and blouses. She was the oldest, and her ma'dear said the rest of the kids would copy her.

The church's young people's wiener roast came in September, and again older saints came. Preteens clustered in groups giggling and watched the teenagers or played games.

Once or twice a year, visitors came for the state Pentecostal convention or young people's convention. They were put up in their homes and served meals at the church. A choir was usually rehearsing in the auditorium for the competitions, and there were young ministers and officers meetings. It took a lot of work and preparation, but nobody complained. There was a lot of visiting; socializing was one of the joys of living.

Chapter 24

In 1954, Ike promised Ngo Dinh Diem more help in South Vietnam, and between putts, he signed a resolution to put "under God" in the Pledge of Allegiance. The Supreme Court struck down the "separate but equal" laws, the senate condemned Joe McCarthy, and the Giants took four straight from Cleveland in the World Series. The Republicans were in office, and the prevailing wisdom was that things would be bad for the poor.

"Junior, come in here now!"

Junior was raking and talking to a man over the fence. The stranger drifted down the alley.

"What you talking to a man in the backyard for?"

"He does imitations. Said he was in show business . . . Knows some people on TV."

"Teenage girls live here, and I'm a single woman. I don't want no men hanging around. It ain't proper."

He returned to his raking and didn't understand Babe-Ruth at first. Then it made sense. He remembered Caleb's drinking and fighting, then a man and a beautiful woman he saw in the park. He slapped her. It was strange that she kissed him before they left. Jonas, a good athlete, dropped out to get a job and marry his pregnant girlfriend. Two blocks down, a woman dowsed her boyfriend with gasoline and burned him alive. He wasn't the first she'd killed, and she never went to jail. She paid her paper bill on time. Girls were like cigarettes, something to avoid if you were going to play in the big leagues.

It was Saturday, and Babe-Ruth hadn't gone shopping and was in the living room at the front window again. She had been laid off for two weeks, and they said it might be another month before they were called back. Both boys could tell she was worried. They had been eating bread and rice.

Junior didn't believe in stealing. Both his mother and Sunday school said that it was wrong. He reasoned that if he borrowed a few grapes and ate them in the store, that wasn't really stealing. He extended the logic to creamsicles. He would lean over into the horizontal freezer and take a few bites of the delicious delights and put the cover back on and eat while he was there. Such was the extension of the logic of an eleven-year-old with a growling stomach. Two weeks before, he had earned four dollars and brought Babe-Ruth her two dollars. He put it on the table, and then she said it. "I need it all."

He had plans for his half, and they had rules. He put his in his pocket and stared at hers on the table. She took her share and walked away, and he did too, but then the thought came: *She's not asking for it for herself.* He returned and put his half on the table.

Now she had come in from the living room and her thinking window, and he could tell she was concerned.

"Junior, bring George in. Let's talk. We've run out of money. I don't expect to get back to work for a few weeks. Y'all asked me to let you sell Sunday papers on Saturday nights, and I said no. I don't like my boys out in the streets all night. How much can you earn sellin' tonight?"

"With a good night, we could earn ten or twelve dollars."

George nodded. "Some have done it."

"Y'all need to do it tonight for groceries. Stay together—be smart."

At 9:00 p.m., they disappeared down the avenue with gray newspaper bags over their shoulders, and she thought about them fighting over a tricycle and Junior running away and wondered what it would be like to be alone on the street at night as a child; she heard about the bullies who made you buy the papers back if it was sold on their corner. She dozed and fell asleep at the dining room table, resting on her arms. A siren went by, the window rattled, and she jerked. Hours passed, and she awakened with the door rattling.

"Ma'dear!"

She adjusted to the light.

"We been knocking a long time!" Junior put the fruit in the punch bowl.

"Well, you in now."

It was 4:30 a.m.

"Mr. Russo gave us a lot of fruit. Most is good too." They filled the fruit bowl in the dining room.

They had done well; she could see it in their eyes. Boys became men in the Bible at twelve, she thought, as Junior carried the rest of the fruit to the kitchen.

"Well?" George waited until he returned, and they put the money on the table. "Well?"

"Seventeen dollars and thirty-seven cents." They spoke together.

In 1954, seventeen dollars and thirty-seven bought a lot of groceries. When the shopping was done, Junior and George sat at the ends of the table. In the days that followed, they ate their potatoes fried, boiled, and baked with meat loaf, liver, or mackerel patties and margarine on their corn bread. And they were expecting fried chicken on Sunday.

It rained a lot that week. On Friday it poured. That Saturday morning, the sun came out. Mr. Yocum, the supervisor from Caleb's job, knocked. His truck was parked, and Babe-Ruth and Jessica came out and sat in front, and the rest climbed in back. He had called Babe-Ruth before he got his produce ready for the market and told her that she and the kids could pick all they could carry home. The country air and smell of ripening fruit was invigorating, and the ride took thirty minutes

"How much land you got here?" Babe-Ruth and Jessica got out. "You know, I'm a country girl."

"Five hundred acres. The pickers will be here on Monday." He pointed to the baskets. "Y'all better get yours now."

Weeks before, he had thought about Caleb's family and wondered how they were getting along. Mr. Yocum made furniture as a hobby, and his wife suggested that he bring her two end tables. He thought that if Babe-Ruth canned the fruit, it would last them all winter. At lunchtime, Mrs. Yocum served hot dogs and Kool-Aid and drove them back in her station wagon. Mr. Yocum followed with his truck loaded with fruit and George and Junior in the front with him.

"Dan says Caleb was quite the workingman." She looked over as she turned off the dirt road. "Comin' from him, that's sayin' something. Says you're a good worker too. Runs in the family. Things turn out."

They came home laughing and eating. George ate so many peaches, his lips itched. When he wiped with his forearm, it itched too. Junior ate plums. When they got home, he had a bellyful, by evening a bellyache, and that night the runs.

Now they had three fifty-pound bags of potatoes, plenty of cornmeal, and a world of fruit. The house seemed like a store.

The seasons passed swiftly. Thanksgiving was a potluck at the church. The parishioners brought turkeys with all the trimmings. What was left over was brought home for sandwiches. Before long it was snowing and Christmas and Easter and spring again. At the beginning of summer, Junior and George stretched out on the grass, describing the mouthwatering dishes of the past year. These dishes with the wonders of childhood would remain in their minds forever.

In another part of town, Maurice packed away his horn. He was living exclusively with Lillie, and it had gotten stale. It had worn on her too. He never bought groceries, just liquor, and he never bought anything he didn't use.

"Why don't you take me anywhere? All you do is sit around and drink. I work all day, and I don't get a thrill out of watching you sitting around my house."

He knew it was coming.

"Get out! Leave!"

He had other places he could go to. It was the reason he didn't take her out. Once, two of his women met, and he got injured breaking it up.

"You really think I don't know you a two-timer? I wasn't born yesterday. Hey, I'm a two-timer too. You don't really think I have a sister I go to stay with, do you?"

He turned, buttoning his shirt, as she lunged, scratching and spitting.

"Bitch!" A right cross to her jaw brought her down. She was still. Sweat dripped from his forehead. Then she stirred. He put her on the bed and put ice on her jaw. After a while, she snored.

He lay beside her with a bottle of scotch, listening to music on the radio and sipping. It was the end for them; he guessed she was all right. He took another swig, feeling a buzz, and caressed her neck and took her for the last time.

He was a hyena, and it was her dark side that lay there and took it with her jaw swollen and teeth offtrack, abhorring the stench of scotch, saliva, and sweat. He was snoring as she eased out and returned with the butcher knife over her head.

"Maurice, Maurice!" His eyes opened, and she plunged down.

Babe-Ruth drank her morning coffee and read the paper. An item caught her eye, and she frowned, then thought about the prayer meeting the night before. It was a glorious time, and she had felt her joy running over. They had rejoiced and didn't expect anything more. Amens echoed from the pews, and Rev. Clemmons' suit was soaked.

He had a special gleam when he introduced the lady. She was older and stately like Eleanor Roosevelt or Queen Elizabeth.

"Saints, I want you to meet an old friend. She's a wonderful woman, and I want you to hear her testimony." She walked to the pulpit with a Bible in her hand.

"Praise the Lord, saints!" She had a handsome face and looked down, weighing the Bible. "I was a rich girl. My father always got me everything I wanted. I was full of myself, and truthfully, I didn't care for anyone but myself.

"I attended the university and went to a lot of parties. I traveled to Europe and Asia. When I met Rev. Clemmons, I was a woman of the world. I gave him this Bible. I had no use for it then. I traveled all over doing what I could do and seeing what I could. Then I found myself looking down at my father's grave. I hadn't been there for the funeral. I realized there wasn't anyone left I cared about, not even myself.

"I drank and smoked reefers. I was a drunk like my mother. She died when I was twelve. All I could remember about her was they argued and she drank. She killed herself with alcohol. It was the same as suicide. I never knew who she really was . . . I don't know that she did. I decided to end it all. I got drunk, went into the kitchen, closed all the windows and doors, and turned on the gas.

"I was almost unconscious. But, I was given a moment. I don't know how, but it was from above. I was in the death's valley, and I could see the reverend. He was young, not old like he is now. I knew if I called out, he'd pray. Old Satan said don't give him the last laugh, but I prayed anyway.

"The next thing I knew, I was in the hospital. God changed my life. I've been changed for decades. The reverend left the Windy City. I was visiting a friend, and I asked where to go for a good service. She said Rev. Clemmons was holding a service tonight, and I was welcome.

"When I saw him, I said, 'I think you have a Bible of mine.' He didn't know me at first. Then he cried. You know, it broke him down. You know how he is. Pray for me, keep praying. Prayer works."

Babe-Ruth put the newspaper down and finished her coffee. She had found some day work and needed to bathe and get ready. She thought about the killing in the paper and whispered a prayer.

She got three days of day work. She knew God would provide; they had enough food, but there was the mortgage to pay. She couldn't pay everything on time and paid the more pressing bills first (she was glad it was summer and she didn't have to buy coal). That Friday, a stranger worked under the sink, a pair of puffy white hands and a red neck. Junior and George kept watch. The girls stayed away, and Babe-Ruth waited in the front room. He disappeared down the basement steps; after ten minutes, the spigot snorted, and water gushed out.

"That does it." He was back upstairs. George fetched Babe-Ruth. He was tall, weatherworn, and thoughtful as he wrote on his pad and wiped his hands. "That'll be twenty-one dollars, ma'am."

"Can I pay a little each week?" The boys converged at her side, with li'l Jesop on her leg.

"Lady, this job needed to be done." He looked at the boys. "I want to be paid, need to be, but don't take food from their mouths to pay me—you pay me last."

He put the bill down and grabbed his tools. They would remember it for the rest their lives—an example of what a man ought to be, something to aim for. It took days to can all the fruit, and Babe-Ruth was glad when they called her back to work.

Chapter 25

I t was the beginning of winter, and Jessica studied at the dining room table and didn't look up as Junior walked through in his BVDs; it was against Babe-Ruth's rules, but the boys did it anyway. She would be the first to graduate. Junior climbed the stairs, thinking that going to the hospital weekly to give the clerk a dollar for Jesop's birth was shameful. The clerk acted like she was better than him. He overheard Babe-Ruth begging the coal company to wait a week. He pounded on the wall going upstairs. It was disgusting being poor and being judged by his clothes.

On Saturday, Babe-Ruth pushed her stacked cart and stopped, as the butcher nodded.

"Hamburger is three pounds for a dollar—makes a good meat loaf. Three? We got some good pork steaks, thirty-nine cents a pound." He wrapped them quickly. "Neck bones?"

She put six packages in her cart and moved to the produce department. George pushed, hoping she would buy apples.

"Lo, Mrs. Jefferson." She acknowledged the tip of the hat. "Gotta sale on Idaho potatoes. Fifty pounds?"

They borrowed the grocery cart and pushed toward home. Men nodded and tipped their hats. Women spoke with respectful tones; children nodded and moved on. Not everybody liked them, but most did. It was hard to ignore a single woman with six kids, a factory job, and a neat lawn. It made them think. Opinions varied, but most acknowledged she was doing a good job. It was going be difficult, but this was America.

Mr. Harry Tyrone had a good job, and his kids were going to do better than him. Harry Jr., their middle child and only son, was Junior's age. Harry Sr. never cared for Caleb.

"Give, you better say it or you gonna eat some dirt." Junior pressed young Harry's face to the ground, applying a full nelson.

"Get off him or I'll knock you off!" Junior got up as Harry Sr. approached. "Get your ass out of here!"

Junior hustled home and told Babe-Ruth, who put on her hat, grabbed her purse, and marched back to the Tyrone house.

"I'd like to speak to your mother please." Young Harry bowed his head and eased into the kitchen.

Mrs. Tyrone came out, wiping her hands on a dishtowel. They talked, and young Harry tried listening from the kitchen, but the words were too soft. He heard his mother call his father in.

"Harry, what you threatening Mrs. Jefferson's son for? If I was her, I'd be mad myself!" He was silent and fidgeting. "You know these boys will be fighting one minute and laughing and playing the next. Why you wanna get involved and make it bigger than it is?"

"I was wrong . . . OK!" He threw up his hands.

"Mrs. Jefferson, it won't happen again. Harry's a good man. He just got to realize we dealing with children here." They hugged. "You know you doing a wonderful job. You're an example to us all."

Babe-Ruth told Junior, and that was the end of it. She said respect wasn't something you earned but something you were born with. You had to work to keep it, and you couldn't let anybody or anything take it away.

The first snowfall melted before Junior and George could reap any profits. They always covered their hands with old socks. Snow was opportunity. Shoveling Mr. Writ's walk was a neighborhood race they expected to win. It wasn't every day you could earn two dollars for an hour's work.

The second snowfall would set the tone. It was still dark, and Junior was out of bed and at the window. It was six inches high and fluffy.

"Get up, George. We got work to do."

They dressed rapidly, heading out with shovels over their shoulders. George wore three pairs of socks on his hands. It was deep but came up easily; they worked fast, relishing the triumph, knowing the job would be theirs for the winter.

A patrol car passed. Junior dumped his last shovelful as George finished the steps. Then they glided home to stoke the furnace and deliver the *Herald*.

At lunchtime, Junior rushed home to collect. "Mr. Writ, sir, I'm one of the Jefferson boys. Me and my brother shoveled your walk this morning."

"Come right on in. You and your brother do good work. How much do I owe you?"

"Three dollars, sir." Junior swallowed hard.

"Three?" Mr. Writ stared down.

"Yes, sir." Junior held his breath and looked at Mr. Writ's shoes as he gave him the money. "Thank you." Junior stumbled out and went home for lunch.

He loved tomato soup and corn bread with margarine melting inside. The phone rang, and Babe-Ruth answered and returned. He took a swallow of chocolate (the kind made from powdered milk and Hershey) and realized she was studying him.

"Junior, how much did you earn shoveling Mr. Writ's walk this morning?"

George stopped eating.

"Three dollars." Junior took a dollar and a half out of his pocket and handed it over. "Here's your half."

"That was Mr. Writ on the phone. Says he's been paying two dollars for that job for two years. It's a dollar more than anyone else would even think of paying." She could see it in his eyes. "Taking advantage of Mr. Writ's generosity is wrong." George looked down. "What you gonna do?"

"He gets the next job done for a dollar. I'll tell him on the way back to school."

They were growing up fast, and she didn't always know what to do. Maybe he should return the money now?

"What will y'all do with the money?" She was buying time for her judgment.

"We got a project," George spoke up. "All the kids need gloves, and we figured it would take seven or eight dollars to buy gloves and scarves and boots for everybody at the rummage store."

She pushed her $1.50 back across the table. "That's a good project. Start with my share and y'all don't have to share 'til the 'project' is done."

They returned to school, and she went in to nap before work. She wasn't comfortable raising boys, but at least they were acting normal (greedy was normal). She had a fear of them being sissies, and it made her think.

On Sunday morning, Junior and George watched grown-ups dig their cars out of the snow. The *Press* didn't have a Sunday paper, and the Sunday *Herald* was delivered in trucks and sold mainly on the street. They were relaxing after getting up in the dark and doing Mr. Writ's walkway for a dollar. They would be ready for church in two hours.

The weeks were cold but exhilarating. Almost-new gloves added a delightful dimension. They lay on their backs and made angels, had snowball fights, and slid on cardboard, then made statues.

"When we gonna get a Christmas tree?" George put wet mittens on the register, with his nose dripping, rubbing his hands and turning toward Babe-Ruth.

"Same as last year, Christmas Eve, when the price is a dollar."

George smiled. It would be fun to watch the girls decorate the tree and put the gifts out. He and Junior had been thinking about the mince pies and the thick icing-covered cakes; their eyes sparkled. She couldn't get them all gifts, but they had a home, and there would be plenty to eat. She knew good memories carried you through the bad times in life. She would explain to the older ones and buy secondhand toys for the others. It was always a joyous season, she assured herself. On the last Sunday before Christmas, each received a box of candy after church, a tradition, with hard candy on the bottom and chocolates shaped like rounded pyramids on top. A child, adults included, would have to be deathly ill to miss that service.

On Christmas Eve, the Salvation Army rented the Civic Auditorium for the Christmas party. The smell of children and pine and anticipation filled the air. It was a chore to brave the cold and bring them there, but the grown-ups remembered when they were young and what Christmas meant. Most were white, with a smattering of brown faces—fat, skinny, toothless, unshaven, and the poor whose pride had gone, accustomed to receiving, or who were down on their luck and swallowing their pride for the children's sake. The band played behind a long table piled high with gifts. Clowns turned summersaults, and Santa anointed them. It was a circus, with a large Christmas tree surrounded by hundreds of gifts and sacks of fruit and candy.

When entertainment was over and all the carols sung, they gathered the gifts, bags of fruit, and hundreds of turkeys donated by the grocers' association, then trudged home, prepared for morning.

On Windel Street, the smell of pies and cakes mingled with that of a six-foot Christmas tree costing a dollar, with its robust golden angel on top. Packages underneath were handmade. Ann and Jessica decorated, and the rest watched. Babe-Ruth opened the closet, moving her leopard-skin coat, exposing a used tricycle, a teddy bear, and a red truck and two shopping bags filled with nuts, fruits, and candies. Two mincemeat pies and two sweet potato pies cooled on the stovetop. The counter contained three cakes, a bowl of frosting, and scattered decorations.

It was snowing, and the street was still. It was their custom to wait until the younger ones were asleep and put the brown bags filled with fruits, nuts, and candies beside each bed with a gift. Ann and Jessica ushered the other children up as Babe-Ruth looked out, admiring the snowfall. They sipped chocolate and prepared the bags. They would wait another hour to be sure the younger children were asleep.

"Someone's knocking." Jessica put the porch light on. She saw women in red caps, and she recognized Mrs. Tezon right away.

"Merry Christmas! Come in." Babe-Ruth widened the door.

"Merry Christmas!" Mrs. Tezon hugged all three and introduced her friends. "We're a part of the Santa Claus girls." They put their boxes and bags down.

Babe-Ruth was speechless. Then they were gone. Ann rummaged, and Jessica lined up the packages. Each had a name.

On Christmas morning, Babe-Ruth rolled over, fluffed her pillow, and went back to sleep. Jessica got a sweater and a shirt; Ann, a jumper and a scarf; Junior and George, sweaters and socks; and the younger ones, an assortment of puzzles, dolls, trucks, and coloring books. It was a day they hoped would never end. At 10:00 a.m., Babe-Ruth started cooking the turkey. At night, Junior and George lay on their hands, gazing through the window at the stars.

The spirit of Christmas lingered for weeks; school was out. The New Year's Eve service would start at 9:00 p.m.; many wouldn't arrive until 10:30. The service would be stopped at midnight for prayer and to usher in the New Year. The preacher always stated the rapture hadn't come in the past year but they were expecting it in the New Year. Food was served in the cafeteria, and they socialized until 3:00 or 4:00 a.m.

In January, their aunt Jean came from Minnesota. She and their uncle Jim had moved there shortly after Caleb and Babe-Ruth came North. They wrote regularly. Uncle Jim worked on the railroad and never came, but they felt like they knew him (they knew he taught Babe-Ruth to read). Aunt Jean was childless and stayed for weeks.

Dignified and proper, she represented an inspecting authority. By a nod or a look, one could tell if she approved of their behaviors, manners, and attitudes. She meant well, and Babe-Ruth deferred to her in ways that extended the joys of the holidays.

Junior spent the morning delivering his newspapers, shoveling Mr. Writ's walk with George, and collecting for his paper route. It was warm for a winter's day, and the boys shoveled the snow from the basketball court. His wallet bulged with twenty-three dollars and change. The sun was out; if they had waited, Mr. Writ wouldn't have needed his snow shoveled at all. Ten played, and ten waited to play the winners. The winning five played on, and Junior's team won two rounds. It heated up, and he removed his jacket; his wallet was in the inside pocket, and he kept an eye on it as he played.

He was playing the third round when the thought seized him, and he rushed to his jacket. The wallet was gone—twenty-three dollars and some change, a part of which belonged to the morning *Herald*. He figured Babe-Ruth would whip him good. On the way home, he remembered stealing the quarter from the Noxzema jar when he was in the second grade.

His aunt Jean was in the kitchen, wearing a black dress and slippers and picking beans.

"Ma'dear, I had my money stolen at the park," he blurted out.

"What happened?"

He explained, and her expression changed several times. Foolish, stupid, irresponsible, she was thinking, while Aunt Jean observed.

"I hope you learned you lesson. That's your money you lost. You did Mr. Writ's shoveling this morning for nothing, and the newspaper will deduct it from your savings."

Aunt Jean was silent and approving.

"Boy, you should be thankful you didn't get it today." Aunt Jean stood up." "When we were children, things were scarce and a mistake like that would have made us starve. We almost starved anyway."

Babe-Ruth seemed not to have heard. Jessica passed through beltless in an old dress.

"Jessica, I guess you walk around looking any old way! Let's go up to your room. I looked in there, and we need to talk about some things." Aunt Jean clenched her teeth and looked over at Babe-Ruth. The women were in Jessica's room a long time. Babe-Ruth was in and out, and everybody else stayed clear. They were upset about order and some other womanly things. When Jessica came out, her eyes were red, but her hair was combed and the belt neatly fastened around her waist. It would have been a great time to tease her, and Junior and George wanted to, but the ladies were in a correcting mood.

Babe-Ruth and Aunt Jean shared different views of their childhood. Their aunt Mary was in her third marriage. Uncle Leslie passed, and her second husband, they said, was no good. Junior catalogued the events and tried understanding the conflicting accounts. Why didn't his aunts have children? Were they afraid of being poor like when they were growing up? Why didn't Uncle Jim visit them? Aunt Mary seemed troubled. Why was it his ma'dear only shared the good times and made everything seem perfect?

Aunt Jean stayed six weeks, and Jessica was happy to see her go. It wasn't that she disliked her; she didn't like being in the spotlight.

Spring was idyllic when you were a child.

"Junior, don't you see Mrs. Brooks sitting here?"

"How are you, Mrs. Brooks?"

How could he forget? It was the beginning of spring, and he was sent downtown to pay bills, and afterward he had a Cherry Coke. There was time left to return home, finish his chores, and play ball.

The street was busy, and Mrs. Brooks was in a crowd waiting for the bus, tall, proper, and looking straight ahead with two shopping bags. He tried to catch her eye, and he thought she saw him, but she stared straight ahead.

He arrived home, changed to his old clothes, and approached Babe-Ruth.

"Ma'dear, I'm finished with everything. I think I'll go play ball."

"Did you see anybody downtown?" She had a knowing stare.

"No . . . nobody I remember."

"Mrs. Brooks just called. Said you walked right past her and didn't bother to come up and speak."

"I saw her, Ma'dear, and tried to catch her eye, but she looked straight ahead."

"Why didn't you go up and say, 'After noon, how are you, Mrs. Brooks?' You know she's one of my good friends and old enough to be my mother. You never know, she might have needed help."

Some of it soaked in. Babe-Ruth had plenty of lady friends, and most were old. It was about decency and being raised right, things grown-ups put a lot of stock in. There was a set of beliefs about children that filtered down.

The few years a body lived could in no way equal the vast number to be enjoyed in heaven or suffered in hell. When a good soul died, he laid his burdens down, and in heaven life was better, with a better body and no more sorrow and sickness.

A bad soul's sorrows would be just beginning. It didn't matter how important you became or how much you got for yourself. Everyone had to answer to God! Childhood was a time of preparation. True, it was the best time spent on earth, but it was also the time to get moving in the right direction. Children weren't to be pampered but molded, their conscience and ideals shaped, putting them in control and not bossed by appetites but by oughts—what you owed your brother, yourself, God. Babe-Ruth's children were taught and at times bruised. As grown-ups, some would not accept this point of view.

"He is risen!" It was celebrated by all of Christendom.

Easter took weeks of preparation, with special pre-Easter and Easter sermons. The choir rehearsed the season's specialties. The sunrise service was at six, and the parishioners hurried home to awaken the children for Sunday school. They wore their very best, which was new or new to them—large hats and bright ties, looking sharp and on parade. After the sermon, they sang "The New Jerusalem" with the choir.

Families had Easter egg hunts and baskets of jelly beans and colorful eggs mixed with shredded paper. Ham was the main dish, and there were pies. Mincemeat was the favorite in the Jefferson household.

A few days before Easter, Babe-Ruth, Mrs. Clay, Sister Grant, and Mrs. Brooks with some of their daughters finished cleaning the kitchen. Pies and cakes cooled on the tables and stove top. The boys passed through and spoke but moved on. No sign said so, but it was for women only.

With the windows opened, the breeze moved through the rooms and up the stairs. Old and young relaxed in the front rooms, braiding after washing their hair and massaging it with coffee, treating skin with a mixture of Vaseline and lemons, trimming nails, squatting, stretching, laughing, being women.

Junior thought about the ladies taking over his home. Most of the rearing he endured came from them. Their point of view passed from generation to generation. Folks called it *motherwit*: natural good sense passed down. Others called it *understanding*. Junior had seen them come together for as long as he could remember, social creatures. It was more than socializing; wisdom was the spirit in the gathering of women.

PART FIVE

A NEW WORLD COMING

"Cast thy bread upon the water and you will find it after many days" (Ecclesiastes 11:1)

Chapter 26

Their names were in the newspapers: Stalin, McCarthy, the Rosenbergs, Mao, Franco, and Robeson. The headlines were THE DODGERS WIN THE PENNANT; ALABAMA BOYCOTT IN THE THIRD MONTH; EMMETT TILL SLAIN, FACE BATTERED BEYOND RECOGNITION.

An eighth grader from Chicago was mutilated in Mississippi for whistling at a white woman. Till's battered, deformed face was carried to the nation's coloreds on the cover of *Jet* magazine. His killers were never convicted.

Jackie Robinson's Dodgers won the first and last World Series for the New York borough, and the words "My feet is tired, but my soul is rested" resonated through the civil rights movement. Dr. Carver had said to prepare, and the chance would come.

Jessica was a junior and was for the first time getting Bs. After school, she studied and worked for Mrs. Writ and was number two boss at home. She read Du Bois, Hughes, Redding, and Dunbar.

Tom came to see Junior and George, but Jessica knew better. *I got no time for you, boy, strutting around here like somebody looking at you and you just content to be with younger boys. Excuse me! Who do you think you are?*

He was comfortable with the family, and Babe-Ruth didn't mind. She didn't believe in courting or marrying young. He had direct ways, looked you in the eye, and stayed to eat.

"Ma'dear, what's he hanging around here for? He needs to be running with boys his own age."

199

Tom had left, and they were washing dishes.

"Maybe he come to see me, big sister. You know his mama's dead."

"Oh, that's funny, Ma'dear."

Tom gave boxing lessons.

"The left jab's special. Keep it straight and in one plane. Put the back leg into it. A fellow coming in will knock himself out. Daddy said he wouldn't always be there, and I needed to know how to defend myself."

Junior left Tom talking to George; he would later realize that leaving was a mistake.

Babe-Ruth remembered Carter and Henry and kept close tabs on their friends. Tim was stocky, with a brush cut and two buckteeth. He wasn't fat but clearly never missed a meal. Larry was the best athlete and very dark and didn't need to prove his toughness. Doug, the doctor's son, wore braces, a rare item in those days. Mike was good at math and wanted to be an engineer. His father had his own barbershop.

Keith helped out at home. He was stout and brown skinned and had a drawl like his daddy, who was sickly. He built a bicycle from abandoned parts and had two paper routes and put baskets on the handlebars and behind the seat. When the first route was completed, he reloaded. He had it timed.

It was the interval when the papers were done and the morning chores completed and the grown-ups were working, a time for pilfering grapes and pears from Italian backyards. Cal and Larry hopped on their bicycles, riding into the sun and freedom.

"Shit!" Cal leaned against the wall with his hands in his pocket and a blade of grass between his teeth. "Shit!"

Larry delivered a blow to the stomach, the blade went flying, and the chase began.

At 2:00 p.m., they ate peanut butter sandwiches in Larry's kitchen.

"I'm thirsty. Guess I'll have a beer." He poured and wiped the foam from his mouth. "Ah, good!" A noise came from the front room. "Can I get you something, Ma?" They eased into the backyard.

The six had been together for years. Teachers noticed and approved.

"Isn't it nice that Doug and Cal are friends?" Junior knew what they were thinking and felt like punching Doug out. Even Babe-Ruth was pleased.

"So his dad's a doctor!" Cal frowned and left the room.

Doug's family was only borrowing the house from Doug's grandmother. In the eighth grade, coinciding with the growth of his father's medical practice, they moved to the richer part of town.

Junior didn't need Doug, he was thinking. Everybody, including the teachers, thought Doug was better than him because his father was a doctor. Doug was the best student in the entire school, but Junior could lick him in a fight and was a faster runner.

Months went by. It was snowing, and Cal untied his newspapers and transferred them to his bag. A car stopped, and Doug's mother turned the motor off and waited. Doug crossed the street; they missed one another and said so.

"We never had the chance to say goodbye." Doug seemed taller, and it had only been a few months.

"I was thinking about you and asked Mom to drive me over to see if you were on your paper route. It only took twenty-five minutes."

They talked about Doug's new neighborhood, and he said he had no special friends.

"People think I should be glad you my friend. They think you better'n me."

"Let 'em think what they want."

"Let's stay in touch." They shook. Cal watched their car disappear down the avenue. It was as pure as friendship would ever be.

In 1956, Babe-Ruth's children were in the shadows of adulthood. The winter was cold, with plenty of snow and sufficient money, with gloves and boots and enough to eat. They were special times, especially holidays. Life had a rhythm and pattern; the country was changing.

That spring, there was a tornado warning with sirens and lightning. There had been false alarms. They huddled in the basement, listening to the radio, hoping Babe-Ruth wouldn't try to come home.

Hail peppered the house. Lightning cracked, and they flinched. "Anne, hold Jesop."

"Somebody's knocking."

"It's the wind." Then Junior ran upstairs and returned with Tom, who picked Jesop up.

"Have you eaten?" Jessica skipped upstairs.

She returned with pinto beans and a hamburger. They watched him eat while he recounted his boxing feats. Hours passed. Then the radio said it was over. He stayed until Babe-Ruth arrived.

In the days that followed, Tom helped paint the porch and stayed for dinner. Afterward he winked at Junior and eased out to the porch, where he and Jessica watched the passing cars. He thought she had a pretty face and said so. He had won the state Golden Gloves title the year before and was preparing for the nationals. He planned to join the army after graduation and make a career of it, or be a diesel mechanic or a carpenter like his dad. Jessica shared why she wanted to be a social worker.

He went with them to church, but he felt uneasy. He came for dinner and didn't talk much. Jessica wondered if he even thought about anything when he was eating and realized she had liked him all along.

"Ma'dear, Tom reminds you of Daddy some?" Babe-Ruth shrugged. "He does to me."

Babe-Ruth was watchful but trusted Tom. School started, and he was studying or training and came once a week. Jessica was getting some As for the first time, and Junior and George were growing and often mistaken for her boyfriends.

"Why y'all gotta speak to everybody?" She walked between Junior and George past the liquor store.

"'Cause we ain't stuck up like you." Junior waved at Willie the wino to irritate her. "Miss Proper."

Heads turned when Babe-Ruth bought a 1954 Buick, deep maroon, with whitewall tires, a four-door sedan. Babe-Ruth didn't know what it symbolized, but it fit them fine. Some were surprised she could afford any car, let alone a Buick. Most figured they were a Chevy family, secondhand or not.

The country was not at war. They had their own home and a car, and everyone was healthy. It was good being teenagers and growing muscles, hair, and breasts under the sun.

Jessica watched Tom retreating down the street. He had won his fight. She looked at the clock as it struck midnight. She had promised to wait up. Fifteen minutes was all he stayed, saying that he had won and was fine. She touched his bruised face and put his swollen hands on her cheeks.

"Was your daddy there?" He nodded yes. "You did good?"

"It was no knockout, but yes."

She had too much school and chores to daydream. She caught up with her feelings when she wrote Gloria. She liked Tom and said so in the letter. Gloria remembered him and thought he was handsome in his way.

Tom repeated as the state's light heavyweight champion, but two months later, he lost in the finals at the nationals in Chicago. He took it well.

"Second in the country ain't bad. It was a split decision. He might have had a better night." Jessica was glad it was over.

Jessica was accepted at the junior college, and Tom couldn't wait to go into the army. She was surprised when she told Babe-Ruth that she had refused his invitation to the prom.

"Go with him, girl" was all she said. The church didn't believe in dances. It was contradictory, but it made sense.

The big night arrived. Tom wore a white tuxedo and a red-and-white cummerbund.

"Is that you, Tom?" Babe-Ruth laughed. "My, you look nice." He took a seat and crossed his legs.

"Girl, you looking good!" Jessica twirled, and Tom applauded.

The dress was light blue like a summer sky, with an open neck (Mrs. Writ's daughter wore it to her prom). It fit Jessica perfectly.

"Who, in the world, is this . . . You in the wrong house. You need to be downtown!" George entered, clapping.

"That's where I'm taking her."

Babe-Ruth would wait up. Tom's dad's car was polished. Six faces watched until it was out of sight.

The stadium was lit up for graduation. The whole family and old man Fenton were there to watch them march. It was the end of the beginning, and the next few days, Jessica hardly said a word.

Babe-Ruth was at the window, staring out and thinking. She could read and drive, she knew how to carry herself in public, and she hadn't spent a day in school. After two years in junior college, Jessica would go away to the state college (the thought was on both their minds). Thirteen years was more learning than Babe-Ruth could imagine, and she figured Jessica's head had to be be stuffed.

Ann's graduation became a memory, and time flew by after that. She figured that getting the first to graduate would set the example for those following . . . the children thought she was right.

Chapter 27

C al tossed and turned. His eyes opened. Emmett Till's mutilated face on the cover of *Jet* magazine still haunted his dreams. Only Babe-Ruth called him Junior anymore. He looked into the mirror, massaging the growth on his upper lip. He was six feet, sixteen, and still taking orders from a woman.

"Boy, you the man of the house now, and you better start acting like it."

He was bigger than her, but it didn't release him from her lectures. He gazed as the sun highlighted the leaves.

"When you gonna take out the trash without me asking you? You were more use to me when you were small."

He was different from George; Cal was stubborn, and she would make him into a man, she was thinking. They had been close, and then it all began to change. It was natural, but that didn't make it easier. He hated the sound of her voice and the distinctive clearing of her throat, which he could discern in a crowd.

"Come out here! I'll teach you to listen to your mother." He promised himself he wouldn't be whipped again. "Did you hear me?"

"I hear ya." He stood behind the bathroom door with it locked and his body resting against it.

"What did you say? You better get yourself out here and take what's coming to ya."

"No way!"

Her eyes rolled back. No child disobeyed her to her face even behind a door.

"What did you say?" Something was different, she was thinking. Maybe she didn't know what she was doing anymore. Perhaps just going to the factory and back home and church didn't tell her what was happening in the world or the neighborhood. She was right.

Keith's father died when he was sixteen. He turned his books in and met Cal as he was leaving.

"What you quitting for, man? You gotta get that diploma with me."

"I need to work full-time. Mama and the kids need me. She's working herself to death."

"If you get that diploma, you gonna be able to help more."

"Bought me a truck" was all he said. Junior remembered him making a bike from scraps and his two paper routes. Keith hadn't lived close enough to compete for Mr. Writ's shoveling job, or it would have been a challenge. Junior remembered him skidding on the gravel road, holding up an RC Cola and crashing, not wasting a drop.

Tim's family moved to Ohio in the ninth grade. Larry's parents divorced, and he moved in with his dad, stopped sports, worked after school, and had a girlfriend. He didn't hang out anymore. Fat Mike got slimmer. When he wasn't playing ball, he was at the barbershop cleaning up, shining shoes, studying, and listening to men talk.

Disgusting pimples sprouted on Cal's face. He scrubbed and applied Noxzema, but it didn't help. He brushed with baking soda and gargled with salt and water and put a quarter away each week for haircuts. Fifty cents was a lot, but Babe-Ruth's haircuts made him look like a bowl was put over his head and cut around it (it would become the fashion years later). He had four good shirts, three pairs of pants, and one very special tweed suit. He washed his underwear in the face bowl at night and let them dry in the bathroom.

During basketball season, George inherited the paper route. Naked boys filled the locker room. Louis and Mike were the stars; neither looked to play beyond high school. Cal showered and was on the bench, wiping off.

"Get off my shirt!" Louis jerked his T-shirt from under him and inspected it, then compared it to Junior's graying briefs. "Look! Stinking muthafucka wearin' dirty draws . . . Nigga, when you gonna start wearin' clean clothes?"

They rammed into the lockers, and Louis landed a right to the head. His left jab was caught in midair by the coach.

"What's going on here?" The coach pulled them up, and Louis pinched his nose. "Come here, let's have a look at your face. Louis, don't leave!"

Louis heaved Cal's shorts in the air. Some laughed.

"Coming down on Cal make you feel big?"

"You want some too?" Mike ignored Louis's fist in his face as he dressed. Nobody was a match for Louis.

Word would get around, and they will be talking tomorrow. Mike is the only one whose opinion matters. Sports are fantasy, a dream. Cal was by the window eating an apple and thinking; he thought about Babe-Ruth pretending to be drunk when screeching came from the street, and he rushed out. There was blood in the street. It wasn't li'l Jesop. Caesar was down. Cal would miss him; in his day he was king.

Cal quit sports in the middle of the season and began working at the corner grocery store, stocking and bagging groceries; he was the first colored boy they ever hired. There were plenty of people on food stamps, and he remembered the shame he felt when Babe-Ruth took government surplus. He realized the owners were Catholic when nuns carted away groceries without paying, leaving the owners smiling.

Catholicism was strange from what Cal had heard—baptizing babies, priests not marrying, adding books to the Bible, believing fish wasn't meat, and worshipping statues. Alonzo Russo was sent to Mass every Sunday and had to return with the bulletin. Kids knew he spent the quarter, skipped Mass, and picked up the newsletter inside the door. The Catholic boys that Cal knew cursed up a storm (to his understanding swearing was unchristian, and it surprised him when Babe-Ruth hollered, "Shit!"). His view of Catholicism was a distortion, but it was the way that Protestants viewed Catholics and Catholics viewed Protestants.

The store was a view of the wider world. People stole everything, many he would have never suspected. He ran down a well-dressed colored man in a gray suit and grabbed a chicken from his coat pocket.

"Excuse me, sir, you didn't pay for that."

A tall white man with a red face demanded change back for a ten when Cal had clearly seen him give the clerk a five (that was why the clerks never put the money in the cash register until the transaction was done).

"Listen, young man." The man was fortyish, light skinned, and wearing a blue turtleneck sweater. "Why don't you come up to my place. I got some things to show you."

It was a strange request; the reason occurred to Cal later. "George, you know those men who like boys? I met one the other day. If you had seen him, you'da never guessed."

Babe-Ruth was counting on sports and Scouting to help her raise them. They couldn't continue Scouting because the summer camps were too costly. They were bigger than her and smelled like men and ate like horses. She wasn't sure, but she thought the beatings she had applied had been salutary. She had no strategy, but she learned along the way. Yes, they were like mules, but she saw early that just beating George wouldn't work. He was born a man, so she changed up. She knew he loved her and wanted to help out.

"Don't do anything to bring shame on us. All we got is honesty and hour honor and if you bring shame we got nothing!" She could tell it was sinking in. "Now you smart. If you stay out of trouble and get good grades, I'm gonna be proud. And when I'm out there working, it gives me a purpose . . . a reason to do it."

When Cal quit sports, much of his rivalry with George stopped. George was bigger and a college football prospect. Two years before, shirtless, they had been looking into the refrigerator, when both reached for the last piece of chicken.

"I touched it first." Junior took a bite, but George ripped it away and retreated, chewing and smiling. It went on, blocking, jabbing, taunting. Cal always won, but George no longer withered. George rammed him into the refrigerator and fled (nobody licked his big brother!). Afterward, there were unwritten rules.

"If I hear you been drinking beer with those guys, I'll have to tell. That stuff no good—you know what it did to Daddy. Ma'dear been through too much already."

George resented the intrusion but appreciated Cal keeping a secret. One beer didn't make you a drunkard or wife beater. George drank on occasion when it was put in his hand, but he wouldn't buy it anymore.

Babe-Ruth couldn't conceal that George was her favorite. She liked his toughness and adaptability and reasoned it was the way a man should be. Cal thought so too; he never said so, but George was his model for valor.

It was Saturday, and Dennis and little Jesop squatted in the alley next to a vacant lot, shooting marbles.

"Why don't you have a daddy?" Dennis rose up after shooting and missing the Cat Eye. He was good but realized he had met his match in Jesop.

"Lotta kids don't have a daddy. Butch and Frazier got no daddies." Jesop knew losing had put Dennis into a pissing fit.

"Did your daddy run off or did your mama never get married?" Dennis snarled as Jesop knocked the Cat Eye from the circle.

"My daddy's God . . . Jesus Christ is my daddy. He's the best daddy there is. My mama told me so."

It caught Dennis off guard. He went to Sunday school enough to know that pursuing the intended put-down bordered on sacrilege, so he eased off. It was trying getting whipped, so he used another approach.

"Y'all must be pretty poor."

"Got two sisters in college—is that poor enough for you?" Jesop blew on the Cat Eye. "This poor boy can whip you at marbles, baseball, and basketball too. How does that make you feel? Abraham Lincoln was poor."

Dennis sulked for a moment; then he said it and knew there would be a fight.

"Grabs!"

There was no way Jesop was going to lose his newly acquired Cat Eye and the rest of his winnings in a grabbing free-for-all. He gave Dennis a good whipping, and Dennis stayed out of sight for days.

Little Jesop couldn't remember missing a meal. There were four years between him and George. Little Jesop never wore hand-me-downs. He studied the picture of Caleb in his sailor suit and thought he didn't even seem like a real father and looked a little older than Cal.

Old Jesop's picture mesmerized him. Many of the old men in the neighborhood had a similar look, but he was his namesake. He didn't like Babe-Ruth bossing him around, but it was better than her swinging at him and then getting the same treatment from his brothers. They roughed him up anyway. Babe-Ruth was a little easier on him than she had been on them, and it was their way of evening things up.

His eyes reminded you of Babe-Ruth. He seemed to be born using his brain and caught on quickly. He had a few chores, and his brothers' bullying kept him from being too comfortable.

He visited his aunt Jean in Minnesota for a month and was glad to be back home.

"Man, I'm glad to be back. If you think Ma'dear's bossy, you gotta live with Aunt Jean and Uncle James. They tell you when to breathe."

It was better at home even if it meant he had to attend church on Sunday.

"Well, they ain't got children, and you get their undivided attention. You survived." Cal and George thought it was funny.

Little Jesop enjoyed books, mainly adventure stories: *Robinson Crusoe* and *The Great Axe Bretwalda*, a Viking tale. He absorbed the tales Junior learned from Caleb, and he tried them on friends. Somebody said they weren't Jefferson tales and they had read some in a book.

In 1960, Cassius Clay was an unknown from Louisville until he won a gold medal in the Olympic games. That same year, Cal was a senior and would be the third to graduate. Ann was finishing her second year of nurse's training, and Jessica was in her last year at the state university. Babe-Ruth had raised them to be Christians, and Cal began attending church on his own. Most of the boys at church weren't athletes, but he now thought there was more to life than sports. Church people respected their family, people got along, and there were plenty of girls and things to eat. He would look back on this time and realize that something that had been twisted inside began untwisting. Life was home, school, the grocery store, and church. Every Monday, he watched the *Sing Along with Mitch* show and called Leslie Uggams "my woman."

Studying filled a void—he had dropped sports, lost friends. Jessica and Ann were at school. He kept track of baseball. The Birmingham Black Barons played several exhibition games, and he even saw Satchel Paige walking across the street and wondered how old he was and knew he was still pitching. He studied at the dining room table like Jessica had. It was quiet, with good lighting. He studied two hours at a time, then took a fifteen-minute break. When Babe-Ruth came home, she always looked tired. He decided that when he was grown, if he couldn't help her, he never wanted to see her again.

Babe-Ruth fasted Wednesdays and took only liquids and said it made her stronger and closer to God. He tried it, and it taught him things. When he wasn't determined, he was famished. When he was determined, he soared. The mind and the appetite were distinct faculties, and the mind ruled. There were so many kinds of people and so many things going on in different parts of the country that he felt ignorant; it was the right sense. He figured he didn't have to be smart if he did what was right and worked hard.

In summer school, he took economics and government, his first intellectual experience other than baseball, which had caused him to think deeply and differently. The economics teacher, Mr. Davis, talked about the Russian five-year plan and its debacles and Vance Packard's *The Hidden Persuaders*, *The Status Seekers*, and *The Waste Makers*. Mr. Vanderlen was in the state senate and taught the politics of government: "The constitution of this nation is a hope, a prayer for our better selves!" and "To be president of the United States you must be white, you must be male, you must be protestant!" Cal was stunned. It was 1960.

He read Dickens, *Stride Toward Freedom*, *On Being Negro in America*, *Ain't I a Woman* (Jessica's old copy), and *Promises to Keep* by Dr. Tom Dooley and started writing poems. His favorite television shows were *Sing Along with Mitch* (featuring his woman), *Dr. Kildare*, and *Ben Casey*. Cal remembered the young doctor who pumped rat poison out of his stomach, and he thought he and Doug's father were a cut above the men he had met. Why not be a professional man who wouldn't have to smile at some white boss to feed his family? Thoughts of Emmett Till came to his mind. The South was a hellish and perplexing place. He couldn't stand the sound of a Southern white's drawl and reasoned that most of the white people in the South were bad—those that did bad things like killing Emmett Till and those that were silent.

As was the tradition for Jefferson seniors, he kept all his earnings and needed every cent, and he bought his own books as Jessica had. Applying to the university was an added expense. He wouldn't go to state but to the university, and he'd stay there for medical school. So what if they didn't take many colored students and he was poor. They were the best.

Babe-Ruth had trouble remembering their names and called George's and Junior's names interchangeably. It was Saturday morning, and Cal sat on a stump in the backyard, holding the letter Babe-Ruth had brought out in the long official-appearing envelope: "We are sorry to inform you that you have not been accepted to the university." It was several paragraphs long, but "you have not been accepted" was all he read.

She knew something was wrong and took it out of his grip and showed it to George. The back door slammed, and George headed for the stump.

"Junior, when you got serious about school and stopped sports, it was just in time because I was gonna be the leader here. I have never seen anybody change like you did. That's not the only university around. You can be anything you want!"

Cal remembered being paired with Joey Jackson at camp for the Friday night fights. He was twelve and had just watched George pummel Tough Tookey. When the match with Joey Jackson was announced, Cal wanted to run and would have, but the look in George's eyes said, "Shame me and you're not my big brother anymore." Joey had bullied Cal for years. The bell sounded, and he whipped Joey Jackson for George.

Cal tried to be a good example, and George became a catcher too and caught for the varsity. Catching was manly—too dirty and painful for most boys who had fathers. It became a Jefferson tradition.

Babe-Ruth watched through the kitchen door as George handed Cal the letter back. An hour passed, and Cal, crumpled letter in hand, sat motionless on the stump. She was at the front window like she always was when she didn't have what it took. She used to worry they would be sissies or that he might be crazy. She gazed down at the street, sharing her thoughts with God; two boys chased bowleys (big marbles), and a dog stopped to piss.

Suddenly, Cal knew!

"You gonna make some of that chili, Ma?" She didn't hear until he spoke louder. "Please make some chili, Ma." She got busy. The man knew what he wanted for dinner.

On Monday, a second letter came. Cal wasn't home, and Babe-Ruth couldn't resist opening it.

Dear Mr. Jefferson,

Please disregard the previous letter. Congratulations, you have been accepted to the freshman class.

Chapter 28

Caleb's full head of hair now had gray strands. Working at the factory and farming suited him. He dropped the bags of groceries off at Geraldine's and sat for a spell. Her mother had died, and he had fathered two more kids. He paid the bills and worked on their shanty and did whatever needed doing. He stayed for about an hour, then got into his pickup and headed for his trailer. At home he put Polish sausage in a black skillet and heated the coffee. Then he relaxed and read the paper. It was the time of day he enjoyed. He didn't drink liquor anymore and didn't miss it.

When the man came to register colored voters, he was one of the first. He had voted regularly in the North, and it wasn't a right to give up. The white folks in the county saw it coming and tried to make it peaceful. White men were campaigning for his vote. He kept track of baseball, especially the colored players. Willie Mays was his favorite. Occasionally he stopped to watch the high school boys. His three dogs watched the trailer and were better company, he thought, than some humans.

It took several years, but he began writing Mildred and Mitchell. Mitchell was having sick spells, and Mildred was worried. Mitchell did the writing. She felt Caleb was in the wrong but didn't say so. He wondered if Babe-Ruth's last child was a boy. He didn't ask directly, and Mitchell didn't say.

Young Reuben had a brother and sister. When Caleb needed to, he took the strap to them. If they got on his nerves, he went to the peace of his trailer.

One Friday, he stopped by to bring groceries, and young Jimmy Pickard was hanging around. He fetched his gun and came back.

"If you're lookin' for trouble, you in the right place!"

Jimmy Pickard backed up and lit out running and reported him to the sheriff.

The sheriff had known Caleb a long time. "You put the fear of death in JP. There ain't a need to be carrying no gun."

"I wasn't gonna do him no harm. I pays the bills here, and I wanted him to know if he was messin' with me and mine, he need to reckon with me."

That was the end of it. Geraldine was a good-looking woman, simple, but pretty, and Caleb guessed she liked the attention.

"If you let anybody around here, just tell him to start payin' the bills, and I won't be back."

"Caleb, I don't know what got on his mind. He be started comin' around. I glad you ran him off. You know he got a wife and chillun."

Caleb put money on the table and left. He figured fair was fair.

Back in Michigan, on Saturdays Babe-Ruth did day work. All of the children except little Jesop were out of the house, and her life had drastically changed.

"Stop working now, Ruth, and have some lunch." Mrs. Prowser looked younger than fifty-five. She wanted Babe-Ruth to come more often. "I like to look good when I'm on my husband's arm. It's good for his business. It's not like I'm Jacqueline Kennedy, but in my way." She blushed, looking over her teacup.

"Shucks, you look nice dressed up or not." Babe-Ruth wasn't a flatterer, but she could see Mrs. Prowser relished it. "I like that Jackie, but as for being a human being, I'm as good as her myself."

Mrs. Prowser's mouth dropped, and she could have fallen out of her chair. Babe-Ruth shared the story when Junior and George were home, and they laughed until their sides hurt.

Some things were hard for her to understand. The new storefront church down the street called themselves Black Muslims. She had never heard of such a thing. Young people were marching in the streets, growing long hair, and calling themselves black instead of colored. *Colored* had always been a nice word, and *black*, like *darky*, seemed derogatory. In time she would see it their way.

People were being killed for their opinions. The black newspapers said the boys in the neighborhood were being killed in Vietnam at a greater rate than the whites. When she read their names, she remembered some of their faces. There was much that needed changing, and she realized she didn't understand everything.

"Mr. Fenton, won't you come in." She sensed heaviness as he took off his hat.

"That war done killed my boy . . . Tom's dead."

She put her hand in his and took his hat and cried, then went into the kitchen and returned with coffee.

Jesop came down from upstairs and realized something was wrong. "Hello, Mr. Fenton."

Babe-Ruth put photographs of Tom on Mr. Fenton's lap and turned the lamp on. He stayed a long time and didn't talk and took some photographs when he left.

Tom's death made the days gray and the winter long. She hadn't become accustomed to thinking about her own life. Jessica had found a social work job in Detroit. Babe-Ruth wished it was closer to home. Detroit was too big for Babe-Ruth's liking, but Jessica was grown. Jessica stopped writing, and when she came home, she was distant and didn't share details about her life.

A year had passed since Tom's death. Babe-Ruth peered out her window. *That child is hurting, and I understand that. God took Tom. That's all there is. She needs to get over this thing. She don't have understanding.*

The red, yellow, and blues glass squares bordering the window had seen her think, pray, and grow old. *Jessica's working and stopped attending church, living in that big city. She seems like she's fleeing, trying to get away from the past. It's hard to understand young people. She looks good and that burn on her face is gone. She's grown and acts like it.*

Ann always wanted to be a nurse. It's a gift. She could do anything to comfort a person. She wanted to wear that uniform and one of those hats. She gonna be good with the kids.

The street below was busy for a Sunday afternoon.

Junior stopped going to church. Hard to understand why. He was doing well in school. The Lord blessed him and he's ungrateful. He don't talk much. That university's changing him—heathens, saying God is dead. Blasphemous!

George left his football scholarship to go into the marines. With the colored boys dying like they are, he should have more sense. He's trying to put me in my grave, ungrateful puppy! He was always full of fight. I guess it has something to do with being a man. Caleb went because he was drafted!

Lona's a freshman at state and doing well with her scholarship. She was always quiet. It is difficult to know how she's doing. She never been any trouble.

She noticed the traffic in the street and a dog limping. *Jesop is coming along well enough. He has his friends and is obedient. We went to church this morning, and it was like sitting with a grown man. He's a blend of his brothers—full of fight like George, but a thinker like Cal. They write each other. I'm not on top of things with him like I was for them. He was having trouble with a teacher, and Cal dealt with it. It seemed to make a difference. Said he's going to city college.*

She got up from the window; they were in God's hands now.

Her life now was work and the church. She began to teach Sunday school for little girls, and she had a gift for it. They seemed engrossed in the Bible stories.

She wondered if she could do more. Rev. Clemmons gave her other work, and she got hooked. She went to night school Tuesday and Thursday (they were not church nights). Typing was her first task, and she combined it with a desire to spell and use the period, question mark, and comma properly. She typed sixty words a minute and received a B.

Then it was on to history, English, and government. Math was hard, but she endured. It would take several years and a lot of Tuesdays and Thursdays, but she finally received her GED (high school equivalency diploma). She worked part-time as a receptionist at the neighborhood Afro-American Center. There was no fanfare as the children's achievements drowned out any personal pride, but she wasn't being left behind.

Her curiosity about the world was being satisfied. She would take the bus and ride to see the city developing. Her dress had changed gradually; styles on posters and in magazines and on television affected her choices. She had observed the propriety and grace of the rich for whom she worked; she would be churchy and stylish. Some of her teachers had opposing points of view, and she realized either might be right. The truth was not always easy to see, and the light of knowledge was sometimes threatening and seemed to contradict some of her long-held notions. She knew she wasn't ignorant, and she was understanding the voyages of her children.

She gave Cal some advice when he left for the university: "Don't let anybody pull you down, and don't be messing with any gal you wouldn't marry."

She kept herself busy, and the years flowed by. She saw her children changing and called it the influence of the world (meaning not the church).

"What you gonna do, son, now that you graduated?"

It was summer, four years had passed, and Cal needed to earn fifteen hundred dollars. He was at the table with her and Jesop, finishing dinner as she poured three cups of coffee.

"Didn't I tell you? I've been accepted to medical school." She vaguely remembered him mentioning it and didn't know what benefit his bachelor's degree would bring. It meant more schooling at that godless university. Where would he get the money?

"When does it start?" Jesop put down his cup. His brother would be a doctor. That, he thought, was black power. Babe-Ruth was silent. It was difficult to evaluate Cal's education when he didn't go to church anymore.

Cal got a summer job at Learjet as a security guard and read a lot of books: Pasteur's *Experiments* and Schweitzer's *Out of My Life and Thought*, *Reverence for Life*, and *The Quest of the Historical Jesus*. Babe-Ruth enjoyed having him home. It was different now that he was grown. She shared something, and he didn't know what to make of it.

It had been difficult to sleep, and she tossed and turned, worrying about George in Vietnam. The next morning, the worry was thick, oppressive. It was a feeling she never had when Caleb was in the navy. Maybe it was because he was on a ship. Perhaps it was because of Tom's death. She needed to get away from the gloom, and she headed for Chicago to visit her second cousin Edna (Cal was hearing about Edna for the first time).

They had stayed in touch over the years but hadn't seen each other since childhood. With the children grown, Babe-Ruth had the luxury to come and go as she pleased and still make ends meet. She liked trains. The countryside was greening; it was like running away.

Edna wanted out of the South and couldn't wait to grow up and go North; that was over thirty years ago. Her husband was dead, and she lived in a nice apartment. They stayed up late discussing relatives and events.

Babe-Ruth's worry seemed to fade. But when she lay in bed, she could feel that George was in danger, out there in Vietnam being the man, and something was about to snuff his life out. Finally, she dozed. In the tranquility of sleep, she heard a distant scream, like Edna trying to wake her, but she slept on. She awoke in the morning as light as a feather and knew George would be safe for the rest of the war.

Edna left work and came home early.

"Girl, how you feeling?"

"Fine, I'm feeling good . . . Did you come into my room last night?"

"I certainly did . . . After you went to sleep, I got up and checked the doors. When I passed your room, something was shining in there. That's when I started screaming. It was all over you—an angel? . . . If there's such a thing!

It was like a child's tale. Cal wiped his eyes; he cried easily and didn't take his crying seriously. The God he didn't believe in loved his mother. It was a kindness he appreciated even as he rejected the story altogether.

Cal was the only daddy little Jesop ever had. Babe-Ruth called him several times about Jesop's behavior at school. Jesop was the spokesman for the black students, and some of his confrontations with the teachers bordered on sass. She just threw up her hands.

"I can't do it anymore. Y'all done wore me out. Come see about your brother."

Cal borrowed a car and came home and talked to the teachers and then to Jesop. Because Jesop believed he was in the right didn't mean he had the right to stop showing respect to people more than twice his age. There was a way to do things, and the point was made. Cal felt like Mr. Solum correcting him. Cal stuttered as a boy and was impressed with Jesop being a spokesman for the Black Student Union. If there was a function for a big brother, Babe-Ruth was calling him to do his part, and he recruited George.

When Jesop was ready to transfer to the university, he called Cal and George, who was on leave, into the room.

"I'm leaving in a few weeks. I got a few needs I was wondering if y'all might help me with."

"Sure, shoot." George looked over at Cal.

"I'm gonna be needing a stereo set."

There was silence, and George grinned. So did Cal. They roared, digesting it. Jesop had their same mama, but he was middle class.

"Well"—George got up slowly—"the next time you have some 'needs,' gimme a call. You know what I mean, like you starving or don't have money for books."

Jesop called Cal frequently; much of the conversation was about money and women.

"Did you call home? I know you're glad to be away, but it's important. It makes her feel good."

"Did you know she tried to spank me when I was sixteen. Then she tried to coldcock me, tried to hit me as hard as she could. I caught her fist in the air, and she looked at me like 'How dare you grab you mama's fist when she is trying to knock your head off!' I just left. She got in her Buick and came after me and pulled up alongside. 'Get in!' I kept walking. I was too big to be whipped."

Cal shook his head, not letting on that it had been a rite of passage. "She's used to being in charge."

Chapter 29

B abe-Ruth never quite digested that Junior was in medical school. Every time she thought about it, she thanked the Lord. Anatomy was difficult for Cal's digestion too, and it made him feel like a memory machine.

"A parrot could pass this course." Professor Woodson had written the book and was looking over Cal's shoulder. "Lots of memorization, sir." He didn't know what else to say.

Rote memory was threatening. Effortlessly he memorized numbers on passing trucks and felt his deductive powers withering. What was he becoming? He dressed and headed to the hospital with Babe-Ruth's letter in his book bag. The corridors smelled of medicines. Men in housecoats roamed, some in wheelchairs. Most smoked cigarettes. He retrieved Babe-Ruth's letter from his backpack; his white coat would come in clinical rotations in a year.

"Visit the VA hospital and pay Mr. Solum your respect."

Thinking of Old Smokey (Mr. Solum) was like entering the old neighborhood. The old soldier had time on his hands and shared his adventures of the Depression and the First World War. After the war, there was no work, men were on the road, and he wandered looking for a job or a meal. Times got better, and he became a porter. His wife died young and childless. Cal remembered his style. He'd tap his pipe between sentences, packing between chapters, expecting him to wait. The stories mingled with the smell of old black men, pipe tobacco, and the neighborhood where he knew every soul and each fantasy-filled nook and cranny.

He stopped at the desk and took the elevator to the third floor and opened the door. Everything was white but for a thin dark face within a shroud. Mr. Solum was almost unrecognizable, sitting up in bed with the sheet around him, like a guru, with the white intern beside him.

There was stillness in the air as the young doctor took his blood pressure. Old Smokey had been there two weeks and was losing weight.

This old nigga stinks and is wasting my time. The thought was on the face of the young doctor as he paused to look at the old man sternly staring back. *He ain't worth nothin'. He's ignorant and proud, and I don't see anything he got to be proud of.*

"Are you finished yet?" *Young boy, education don't make you no man.* Mr. Solum's jaws tightened. He was thinking, *Just 'cause you done scrubbed your neck and washed your face, you still a rednecked cracker with no rearing.*

It was the season for an old man to think, wrap things up, and cross the river in peace, yet they battled silently.

"Junior? Is that you, Junior?" Light entered the old man's eyes. He smiled as Cal extended his hand.

"Morning, Mr. Solum. Ma'dear said you were here." Mr. Solum's voice brought back memories; the young doctor eased out. "How ya feelin'?"

"None too well." He paused, opening the sheet, revealing his bony chest. "Po' looking, eh? Gettin' ready to punch outta here. How's yo ma'dear?"

"The same." They reared back cackling, sharing an understanding between men.

"How's school?" Cal could see it hurt him to talk. "You still gone be a doctor, son?"

It was different from when they were man and boy. The handshake had not been strong. Cal recalled their fishing trip. They sat in the boat watching their lines, with the sun on the water and Old Smokey commenting on Cal's deficiencies and attributes: the neglected lawn work, the unpainted garage, and the way he rightfully respected his elders. It was a lecture, but it didn't seem like it at the time.

At other times, Cal was running to the store to buy chewing tobacco to earn a nickel or dime. It was funny how deliberate Old Smokey was, counting and paying up. Cal thought it took more time to collect than to fetch the tobacco, but he didn't dare say so. Seeing him now, thin and speaking in pain, Cal remembered him as he was, a man of grace and dignity.

"I got cancer all over. They been keepin' me pumped with morphine. I guess you know something about that. When it wears off, it feels like a million ants eatin' at me. Man, I done lived. I don't want no more of this, son." The young doctor returned, holding a syringe. "Come here! Come right on over here! I don't want no more of that stuff, son. I want you to meet my boy. He's up here studyin' to be a doctor too—just like you! . . . Just like you!"

Cal was pensive going home and thought about Babe-Ruth whipping him with the ironing cord until he bleed. She cried and didn't know what to do. Another time, she was on the phone begging a creditor. If he couldn't help her, he never wanted to see her again.

He doubted that any of his ancestors ever contemplated suicide and chuckled. All the old people—like his ma'dear, Brother and Sister Crawford, Old Smokey, and Mrs. Clay—were education light, but dignity and integrity heavy. Cal reasoned he had lost something.

Wayfaring men drank wine from cold glasses
Talked of past lasses and things,
Laughed at past tasks
Gulping its last
Sipping and soaking their throats with its sting
During the night forlorn
Thus slugged throats gave them the courage to go
Provided wings not to know.

He would write it down when he got home. He walked back thinking of steak and beer, of being in love, and undistinguished survivors humming and talking to the Lord.

Mr. Solum died that night. Babe-Ruth called, and he was thoughtful while she prayed. Old Smokey made you appreciate things; he was a fine and gentle man.

Things were changing at a shocking pace. Babe-Ruth sensed it but was unaware of most of the details. The sit-in movement gained momentum in the South and became a harbinger of things to come. The birth control pill hit the market and opened a "can of worms." Kennedy outshined Nixon in the first television debate and won by a narrow margin. The missile race escalated, George and other American sons went to Vietnam, and the Bay of Pigs Invasion was a disaster.

Chubby Checker introduced the twist the same year, Roger Maris hit 61 homers, and America went into space. The following year, the Cuban missile crisis put the world on the brink of war. Kennedy spoke at the Berlin Wall and later said there were no "white only" signs in foxholes.

Martin Luther King Jr. said he had a dream. Kennedy was gunned down in Texas, and Malcolm X said the chicken had come home to roost. A new president with a Texas twang pledged a great society, the United States went on the offensive in Vietnam, and Malcolm X was silenced by assassins' bullets.

The Vatican Council began its historic meeting the year Watts exploded in chaos. Antiwar protest swept the country the year Masters and Johnson published *Human Sexual Response*. In 1966, race riots inflamed Atlanta and Chicago, and black power split the civil rights movement.

The Packers won their first Super Bowl in1967. Muhammad Ali was stripped of his title for resisting the draft, and the race riot in Detroit was declared the worst in U.S. history. Flower children flocked to San Francisco and would later march on the Pentagon.

In 1968, Martin Luther King Jr.'s assassination was followed by Robert Kennedy's. The entire world watched the Democratic National Convention as Mayor Daley and the protestors faced off. Nixon beat McCarthy, and black gloves were raised in protest on the podium at the Olympics in Mexico City.

The My Lai Massacre was revealed, and antiwar rallies escalated. Nixon's Vietnamization gradually put the war back in the hands of the South Vietnamese. Agnew blamed the criticism on an "effete corps of impudent snobs." And finally, the United States put a man on the moon.

Cal kept in touch with Babe-Ruth and with old friends. Mike and Doug wrote back. When he wrote Doug, he thought about Babe-Ruth and thought she would have approved.

Dear Doug,

It was good hearing from you. It is strange that we both are studying medicine. I think your father had something to do with it. For my part it wasn't something he said, but the man. How is the admiral and your lovely mother? I will always cherish the way they treated me. It wasn't always clear, but I was deeply affected by my visits to your house and the music, chess, and the genuine acceptance.

There is so much happening it's hard to keep up. You seemed estranged from your dad, but it's probably natural. It must be difficult following someone who is the best thoracic surgeon in the world. Don't worry, you'll find your niche. For me, every step I take is a step further than any one in my family has ever gone. Ma'dear has no idea. Some of the pressure comes from knowing I owe over twenty thousand dollars, and it will be more before I can start paying it back.

I admit I was jealous when you told me you spent the summer after freshman year in Africa. I would love to study tropical medicine. Maybe I will someday.

We're still single—who would have believed it, especially you. I've met some interesting prospects, but there isn't time and too much to learn. I plan to master medicine, improve my Spanish, and see the world. What's your excuse?

I feel torn between Internal Medicine and Psychiatry. I like the deduction over the agony of wrestling with mental pain. I have seen people lose control, some were friends.

Enough said. I expect a letter.

Cal

He tucked the letter in his backpack. The years had slipped away. There would be a time to understand it all better. Perhaps that's what being old was for.

For Cal and George, Babe-Ruth's old house seemed a constant in a changing world. After tossing his marine coat over the chair, George sat cross-legged, satisfied that it hadn't changed.

"I need a job so I can make me some money."

"I'll be finished in eight weeks. I'm going to Spain for some rest and relaxation before the internship starts."

"I been away fighting for this country, and I ain't got shit. You don't have to worry, you a doctor!"

"It won't be easy. I'm down over twenty thousand, and I have an internship and three years of residency. I'll will need twice that to hang out a shingle."

"Right." George noticed Cal's oxford cloth shirts on the dresser and pointed. "Nice."

"Take as many as you want."

"I was the sarg—God!" George sat down, admiring the freshly starched shirts. "I picked the patrols, determined the point man. When the gooks opened fire, if the man got his head blown off, I put him there!"

"Sounds horrible." *Is he bragging or confessing?*

"Vietnamese were getting rich in Saigon. This nigga's putting his ass on the line, and they're drinking and hustling Americans."

Hey! You volunteered. You were born a man. You wanted to fight! Cal didn't say it.

"I know you been to hell. Are we having a problem here?"

"No, no. I'm mad as hell! Glad you're benefiting from the system we been defending. Fuckin' students call us baby killers, and the brothers are being killed at a higher rate. You learn to hate. I tried to take care of the brothers, but my white soldiers got mamas too!

"A man leads by taking care of his men. We weren't fighting to end all wars or to make the world safe for democracy. If a man thought we were, he sure as hell hadn't been in Nam long. If you're supposed to engage the Vietcong to target our big guns, you decide if you gonna risk lives for information already confirmed."

"Look at these good-looking men." Babe-Ruth brought coffee in. "It does my heart good to see you together. I prayed, and God brought you back."

"God didn't bring me no damn where! I brought myself back!" George's coffee spilled as he stood up. "God didn't do a damn thing! Some ladies' sons are over there fertilizing the ground. What did God do for them? You worked yourself to the bone raising six kids. God didn't do that—you did!"

225

"God is good!" She wiped the spill. It was a hard world; she knew that. The silence thickened as she remembered them as boys.

George drove Cal downtown along the route they delivered newspapers when they were boys. "Thanks for driving me."

"Take the coat. Got two. Your campus SDSers like military clothes 'n' shit." Cal laughed. And George laughed back.

"I ain't the marrying kind," Cal had written to Lena. "You might as well go on to Detroit and get a job. Don't be waiting around for me."

She took him at his word. Nine months had passed. He thought he meant it too. It had been a year of hard study, and internship was going to be hell. He was going to Spain before the drudgery. Three weeks wasn't much, but it would be an adventure, time outside the country, and good for his Spanish.

Then he wrote her again:

Dear Lena,

I'm going to Spain. Why don't we get married and go together?

Love,
Cal

He realized he wasn't likely to find someone very soon like Lena. She saw him like he was, and she was too good for him. A fool, even as big a fool as he was, should know good fortune when he saw it.

The justice of the peace married them. Lena had her passport in order, and they were off to Spain. They spent the first week in Madrid, the old and the new, Museo del Prado, La Puerta del Sol, bullfights. But it was being together without a schedule that counted. They traveled across to Barcelona and up to Montserrat, the mountain in the clouds with the Blessed Black Virgin, where honeymooners flocked. Then it was back down to Seville and a night train to Salamanca. Salamanca was the home of Miguel de Unamuno, who died around 1936. Through his writings, he had introduced Cal to Cervantes, whose view of the world and reality helped shape Cal's own. It was the world inside that shaped the world outside—the *adentro* from which hope and beauty emanated, where truth and justice reigned in their purest forms.

They arrived back with enough time to settle into the apartment provided by the hospital. Lena met the doctors' wives and began looking for a job.

Only George knew about the marriage. It was Cal's first weekend back, and they walked through the old neighborhood to Babe-Ruth's house.

"Ma'dear, this is Mrs. Jefferson!"

"Well . . ." Babe-Ruth smiled and looked her over. "Welcome to the family! You coulda told somebody—you such a man!" Babe-Ruth thought she looked like a good one, and she had a lot of questions.

The women talked, and Cal checked the refrigerator and eased out. There were places he hadn't seen for a while. Mr. Writ whizzed by in his hearse, and Cal felt like a kid again; he wondered if Mr. Writ still gave the best trick or treats. The two-room grocery store was unchanged, although not as well stocked. He took his time gathering what he thought Babe-Ruth needed. The owner's eyes lit up when he saw him. Cal remembered him as a fair man and wondered if the nuns still came and poached. He walked back with two bags of groceries. Men lingered in front of the nearby beer store with paper bags wrapped around bottles.

"Hey, Cal! Is that you?" Louis had changed.

"Louis?"

Scars tattooed Louis's face and notched his left eyebrow; another twisted his lip. His front teeth gleamed, with some missing on the sides, but he still had a handsome face. They seemed to be thinking similar thoughts.

"The same . . . Why you bigger than me now. And you a doctor? Remember . . ." Louis hesitated. "When I kicked your ass?" It slipped out, and he wanted to take it back.

"I do indeed. It was one of the most humiliating days of my life." Caleb pulled his shirt up and showed him the rim of his under shorts. "Clean enough for you?"

"We was kids and I was wrong." Louis smiled and offered a swig and took one himself.

"What you been up to?"

"I boxed awhile. Was the National Golden Gloves champion. Had a few pro fights. Got drunk one night and came home and found my girl with somebody. Almost killed them. He shot me in the belly. Was my own gun." He raised his shirt, showing his scar and gray shorts. "I wasn't myself after that." And he made a fist. "I had a good pair."

Fighting was in his blood. His dad and brother had been ranked.

"How's Leroy?"

"Dead."

Cal was thoughtful going home. Some houses were vacant lots, and others were changed and run-down. The funeral home was still elegant. He thought about Louis and put away the groceries. Their meeting seemed to have happened before.

"I guess you like to see this house full of food." Babe-Ruth and Lena seemed to get on; he would bring her back soon.

Internship was learning and surviving with his patients. He felt dumb, and he wasn't alone. He hardly saw Lena the first months, and they left notes to keep in touch. Lena did substitute teaching and telephoned Babe-Ruth often.

Months went by, and Cal was returning from the state capital and his licensing exam. He drove slowly and was halfway back to the hospital and thinking about the past week when he felt a rumbling from a flat tire. He steered to the gas station nearby and observed the red streak going up the attendant's arm and wandered into the drugstore next to a coffee shop. Babe-Ruth embarrassed him when she introduced him as "my son, the doctor." He slipped the purchase into his pocket and opened the restaurant door.

He thought about his fishing trips with Old Smokey and the old men who would sit and laugh at him doing yard work. "Junior, when I see you working, I get an itch right here." Old Smokey would point to the tip of his toe and set them roaring. They were older, but friends. They thought the younger generation was slower, lazy, and irresponsible. He laughed. Every generation thought that way about the oncoming one.

Babe-Ruth was a singular experience, he thought—difficult! He had cleaned the basement and was preparing to go out.

"Good job, Junior, nice job . . . Why did I have to tell you to do it?" She couldn't be pleased, and he would no longer try. He would do the right thing and let it rest. It somehow made their relationship better and cleaner, but she still preached and lectured.

"Hold your heads up. You as good as anybody. If you don't respect nothing, you can't amount to nothing." She made these statements by the score:

"I can't stand laziness—won't put up with it! I ain't raisin' no tramps.

"Right is right, and right don't wrong nobody.

"You ain't gonna kill me, boy!

"If I can't raise you, I'll find somebody that will."

The threat of reform school seemed real. She rarely showed a weak side in those days. Nothing bordered on rebellion—they wouldn't have had a chance!

"Shit." He was sipping his coffee and chuckled. She was as constant as the moon. If there was a heaven, she'd get there. But who wanted to live forever anywhere?

He pulled down his cap, finished the coffee, and headed back to the garage. He didn't trust mechanics.

"What's the damage?"

The attendant took the bill from the clipboard. "That'll be fifteen dollars."

He put the money down with a white tube.

"Use this ointment on your arm three times a day. You have a skin infection that's starting to spread." He wrote a prescription on the attendant's side of the bill. "What's your name? Have any allergies? You need some antibiotic in your bloodstream. The infection is getting out of control. If you don't treat it, you're gonna have a fever."

The man rolled up his sleeve more, surveying his arm.

"A doctor eh? What'd the medicine cost?"

"A few dollars—forget it."

"The wife's been tellin' me my arm needed doctoring—guess I'm stubborn. Let's call it even." He returned the payment and winked.

Cal was back on the road and passed an accident and slowed for the next several miles. Cars were piled up, and there were ambulances; he was tempted, but he could see they had it in hand.

Then it was back to patient care and eighty-hour workweeks, eating, sleeping, and writing Lena notes. When he had a two-day weekend, they visited Babe-Ruth again. Lena enjoyed walking and talking.

This time, they took a different route. "This was the American Laundry." The huge doors opened. It was half the size of a football field and stocked with dump trucks. A man with a pencil on his ear hurried toward the mailbox, carrying a clipboard.

"Keith?" Cal stared as the man came forward.

"Cal, Cal Jefferson. You a doctor? . . . I ain't done too bad myself. Remember when I quit school and bought me a truck? Well, them thirty beauties is mine."

Cal cackled, and they reshook. "This is Keith. We've been friends since we were ten."

"What kinda doctor are you?"

"Internal medicine: diagnosis and treating with medicines. I hope you never need me."

"Me too." Keith didn't show his age. "Have you kept track of Mike, Tim, or Douglas?"

"Mike's an engineer, started his own company and got a contract with Ford. A small operation, but with possibilities."

"If it's on you, it's got possibilities."

"Douglas is a doctor too, not a surgeon like his dad. He's an artist, a painter, and getting national recognition. I don't know if he'll practice medicine long."

They had lunch with Babe-Ruth. Cal was pensive going home.

Weeks passed, Lena was teaching, and he visited Babe-Ruth to get out of the hospital and get some home cooking.

"How's school?" Cal was eating chicken and biscuits and looking out at the backyard. Jesop watched from the doorway, surprised he had been detected. "You gotta get up a lot earlier and enter a lot quieter to sneak up on big bro."

"I'm finishing the college bit. Gonna head up to medical school."

"So, you aren't telling you've been accepted until you're starting? That's original."

Jesop was in town for the weekend. George worked with neighborhood boys at the youth center and was taking advantage of the GI Bill. The job gave him plenty of time to study, he was settled, and the studies came easy. They consulted about family matters; it was like sharing their earnings when they were boys.

Chapter 30

It cost more to set up a practice than it did to go to college for eight years. Cal owed over fifty thousand dollars in 1974, and Lena had their first child, George. "Take care of medicine, and it will take care of you." It was the departing words of his mentor, Dr. Schmidt, and it was simple enough to be true.

In his first week, he saw a lot of old women, and it reminded him of Babe-Ruth and her lady friends. Months passed, and the practice was picking up. After lunch, he looked into the waiting room at an elderly lady that was dressed up like she was going to church. He thought of something Rev. Clemmons said: "A person works hard all week. When they come to church, they expect something."

"Mrs. Jackson, we been trying to get your pressure down for months, and nothing seems to work." She was long, stern, independent, gripping her purse at the top as it stood like a steeple on her lap. "What's bothering you?"

"I'm a strong woman. I can take care of myself and don't need nobody readin' my mind." He didn't answer. After a long pause, she began talking. "When John died, I raised that boy by myself. I'm a typist, and I do a good job. Used to always like going to work. I don't sleep well lately."

"How's your son doing?" She frowned and blinked, and moisture welled up in her eyes.

"He got divorced and living with me now for these last eight months. Just eatin' and sleepin', laid off, not really looking for work."

"Why don't you make him pay something, or kick him out?" Her face relaxed. Then she sighed.

"You think a mother would do that?"

"A good one would, one that had the backbone to raise him by herself instead of going on welfare. She would make him pitch in out of pride." She laughed, then cried and sighed. Her face seemed broader. "Let me take your pressure again." She wiped tears away as he retook it. "One thirty over eighty. I think you need to stop letting him take advantage of you and lower your blood pressure and raise his."

It was taking the time and giving a portion of himself that mattered, being the patient's very own confidant. He felt like Rev. Clemmons.

George was teaching high school, and Jesop was determined to be a surgeon.

"I want y'all to look after your sisters."

They had heard it *ad nauseam.* It was evening, and George and Cal were on the phone.

"Did you say she got a black eye? I'll kill that—"

"If you do, whose gonna raise his kids?" Cal reasoned. "We talked. He gonna be all right. I told him we didn't want any bloodshed. He understood. Let them work it out. She hit him with a stick. He said he was defending himself. His head's swollen."

Another time: "Lona is thinking about getting a divorce. That man treats her and the kids well. She gotta grow up." Cal nodded to the phone as George finished.

"Ma'dear shoulda had all boys, and she'd have had it made. Jessica got a fine man. I wish Tom had lived though."

Babe-Ruth kept them informed. She never said what they should do and left it up to them. She believed that brothers caring for their sisters was a special thing.

Jesop liked things black-and-white, thus surgery. "If a belly stays tender for six hours, it needs opening. Listening, comforting, or giving medicines won't get it done—they need the blade!"

"I suppose a good surgeon need to have an attitude like yours." The three were together, and Cal stretched his legs at George's after dinner. "It's always good to get a complete history and do an exam first."

Cal was photographing his little brother, the future surgeon, with his mind, remembering when Jesop was a newborn and they surrounded him, kissing his rump.

"The first thing I'm gonna do when I pay my loans off is get a Mercedes. Gotta have the right coach!"

Cal thought it was fun to see him so pompous. There would be trouble enough to bend his neck; it was good for him to start out a little cocky.

The year was 1978, and Cal had some unfinished business. Babe-Ruth felt uneasy about his desire to locate his father, Caleb. Cal didn't know why she was worried and didn't care. He was a man, and it was business, and he needed closure.

There was no plane going directly there and no train until seven in the morning. He had found Caleb in Lilbourn, Cal's birthplace. He hadn't seen him for over twenty-five years and remembered him as a big man with pearly teeth, with a large gap in front, and frightening. Now it would be at eye level, man-to-man. He flew to Cape Girardeau and took a bus. The bus moved through the countryside. The bus was old, and the ride was bumpy. Caleb would be a stranger, and Cal wondered if he knew he and Jesop were doctors and how well Jessica had done, and how did it make him feel that they made it without him?

The bus stopped at a closed gas station on the country road. A dark figure emerged from the shadows.

"Daddy? Daddy?"

"Junior? Is that you, Junior? It was too dark to see faces. Let me tote your suitcase, son." Cal followed him to his pickup. "When I got that letter, I cried. Never thought you wanted to see me again."

They moved through the country with windows down and headlights cutting through the mist. Caleb's belly touched the steering wheel, and he was balding, with white sideburns, and strong like Cal remembered him.

"This is it." The mobile home beside a large tree was fenced. Two dogs hitched to a pole barked. In back was a tractor and farmland. "Come in and rest your feet."

Three rifles hung on the far wall. Two guns were dismantled on the table, next to a box of shells. Caleb removed a blanket from the cushioned chair.

"I guess you can tell ain't no woman here." He put the suitcase away and returned. "Hungry? What can I get ya? Eggs? Whatever you want, I probably got." He opened the refrigerator, and then opened a cupboard, displaying liquor. "If you want a drink, I can fix one. Don't drink myself, but I keeps it for guests."

"I'll just have a glass of water." Caleb was still imposing; work was good for a man, Cal thought.

"So, you a doctor?" Cal nodded thinking Lena must have told him. "Yo ma'dear didn't talk me down, did she?"

"No, she didn't."

"I can tell. I can tell by the how looking at me, trying to see who I am." He packed his pipe. "She's a fine woman, your ma'dear."

"She always said you were a hard worker and a good man until you started drinking."

"She's right." He lit the pipe and crossed his legs. "When I came down here, the alcohol had a holda me, and I drank myself silly . . . A wonder I didn't die. During the week I worked, and on the weekends I drank. I don't know why. I liked working so I worked on the weekends. I ended up drinking less."

"You pulled yourself out."

"I was a young bull . . . Used to run wild with the women. I was full of steam and meanness. After a while, I just worked. Work, I understood. I'm old now. Don't need a woman and no liquor. Be workin' 'til I drop . . . Your ma'dear was something. She put up with a lot with me. I was a crazy man. You know she taught me to read?" Cal nodded. "I had to leave. I woulda ended up destroyin' y'all, especially you and Jessica." He blew his nose.

"How big is this farm?"

"'Bout two thousand acres. I just works it. I have a factory job too and don't work no overtime. The overtime goes into this place. I got some seasonal workers. Have a big summer crop, and I just grow wheat in the winter. Farm belongs to young Tom Jefferson, old colonel's grandson. We share the profits. He an engineer. I own ten acres. He's been wanting to sell the whole place." The wind blew hard, and he looked out. "Beginning to rain. Hope it don't get muddy. Want to show you the crops and your grandpa Jesop's, my mother's, and Louis's graves, and the oak we married under."

It was too muddy in the morning, so they went to town. He bought groceries and stopped by Geraldine's. A young girl, Elena, called him *Pa.* She was sixteen.

"I worry about that 'un. Her brothers done gone North and she's stuck here. Done dropped out of school. I don't know. She may be in a family way—I can't worry. Gotta take care of number one."

"That's one way of looking at it." Cal thought he hadn't heard. The next day, Cal boarded the bus for Cape Girardeau. The airport had an unpaved landing field, and the Ozark Air Lines plane's wings were unpainted. He was glad that it would be a short flight home.

Cal told George. They hadn't fought for over thirty years and wouldn't start now.

George had his own thoughts. *The bastard left with six mouths to feed—he wasn't flesh and blood, not the way I see it. He left a lot of bellies growling and ragged kids to be ridiculed. If there is a god, he'd go to hell. He'd die someday, and if they don't bury him in his backyard, there would be some kind of funeral. I'd attend, unless I was eating, sleeping, or thinking. I'd pay my respects, if I could find the time.*

Why in the hell Cal went looking for the bastard, I'll never know. I'd like to get him in my sights like in Nam . . . He'd die slow.

To little Jesop, Caleb was the photo of a young sailor. How could you hate someone from a photograph?

Cal remembered, "Stumps and trees grow on land. Education makes the man." Education was no panacea. He had pondered it growing up. Most of his black friends didn't respect their dads, but he had had Rev. Clemmons, Old Smokey, and his chief of medicine, Dr. Schmidt.

Cal named his first son George. Babe-Ruth approved because they all knew he was the favorite. It was the right name; he sensed the warrior in him. His practice was busy, but he made time, and he and George were a pair. Cal had read the memoirs of a famous surgeon. In the surgeon's final year of high school, he put something unique under his photograph in the yearbook. It was next to such high-sounding quotes of classmates as "Step-by-step I climb the heights, reach for the stars, don't look back until you are where you want to be."

The future renowned surgeon wrote, "I will be home for dinner on time." The dictum resurfaced as a formula. Lena was pregnant every other year, and there was a lot to do and pay for. They built a brick Tudor inspired by Doug's old house. The front-room window was a tribute to Babe-Ruth's front window. They had chessboards and all kinds of music, but he allowed comic books and television. Cal came to dinner on time; sometimes the dinner and kids were brought to the hospital for a picnic.

"Why did your daddy leave Grandma Jefferson, Daddy?"

Caleb's picture in his navy suit was on the dresser. The question had been answered before, but as George grew, he needed more answers.

"It was a long time ago. Life was difficult and many men hit the road. Your grandpa was a farm boy turned sailor. Then he began to drink. Drinking can make you less than you are. You worried about something, son?" Perhaps George was worrying that something would happen to Cal, who frequently discussed death and illnesses.

George was tough like his namesake, and they were both mama's boys. He was the oldest, and Lena found ways of treating him special without causing jealousy. He loved banana pudding. He'd clean the bowl. George had his uncle's name but his father's brain and was curious about everything. They visited the museum so often, the attendant knew him by name. He was fascinated by marine life, anything that moved in and about water.

"Dad, did you know there are twenty thousand different kinds of fish?"

"Really?"

"The bigger fish eat the littler ones down to the smallest, like the shrimp, which eat plankton, and the zooplanktons eat phytoplanktons, which are plants. They call it the food chain."

"Say what?"

Cal introduced him to fishing as Old Smokey had done with him. They fished for hours, eating soda crackers and bologna and talking.

The museum had a large skeleton of a whale stretched across the first-floor ceiling, extending the length of the building. They got books, but he never seemed to learn enough. Pictures of whales lined the walls of George's bedroom. Cal began reading to keep pace.

Cal got him a copy of *Moby-Dick*. It was enough reading for an educated adult, but George never tired, relentlessly reading night after night. He closed the book with a bang, called Cal at the hospital to report his achievement, and started it over again.

He had a round face, a wide forehead, square jaws, and eyes that sparkled when he was thinking. His nose was like old Jesop's, flat and wide, and his nostrils flared when he was excited. There was no gap between his teeth, an oddity because it was present in his siblings.

He had Lena's gentleness, but he changed when he was competing or in a brawl. Then he was cold and fierce. A few figured a doctor's kid would be easy pickings, but they were surprised and passed the information along.

His three siblings—all boys, Jim, Randy, and Douglas—copied him to the letter; Cal spent a lot of time making him a good one to copy.

"Don't give me that, George. They did it because they saw you doing it. Anytime that happens, I'm gonna take care of you first."

His twelfth birthday was special. Father and son would go salmon fishing. George was big enough to wade in instead of working from the shore. He unwrapped his wading suit after they cut the cake, and he didn't take it off 'til he went to bed.

It was a bright sunny day and like a circus, with all the splashing, fishermen, and nets. They caught so many, they had to buy more dry ice and would have enough to give away. Nature had them firmly in its grasp and wonder when the river ran into George's suit, and the drop-off pulled him under.

"Help!" Cal dove in after him, filling up his suit too. Others rushed in, but they could only reach Cal. It was like a dream with the bright sun and splashing and men screaming. It took twenty minutes to recover George's body.

Lena didn't like it when they were late. She knew Cal was right: "If you raised them with get-up-and-go, there is always some danger." The moon was out. They usually called when they were late. She was at the window when Cal arrived alone.

She hated God and hated Cal too. Babe-Ruth cooked, cleaned, and sat with them. Lena stayed in bed and wanted to die and would have if it would have changed anything. She had three other boys, but she felt life was hopeless.

She wouldn't speak and was up all hours of the night, walking around, mumbling, and losing weight. Babe-Ruth didn't say much and stayed often and slept on the couch. It was a day and a breath at a time. Months went by, and Babe-Ruth began taking her to rummage sales. Lena wore old clothes like Babe-Ruth did.

"When the kids were growing up, I made the rounds. Never did have to buy new clothes. Couldn't afford to anyway. When they got bigger and started working, they wanted everything new and bought it for themselves. I don't think it hurt them none."

She went to church with Babe-Ruth. She hadn't gone for months. A year went by, and she made a banana pudding. Lena joined the Santa Claus girls. She gave rummage sales and after a few years was elected president. Babe-Ruth never missed a meeting. They loved working together and earned thousands of dollars for the Santa Claus girls.

Chapter 31

Babe-Ruth had fifteen grandchildren, and they were all about to sit down for Thanksgiving dinner. Children played kick ball in the alley, and cars lined the street bumper to bumper. It was the same old house with the big front-room window and motley-colored rugs on the floor. The dining room table had her best tablecloth; a golden turkey was on one end, and a sweet-smelling ham was cooking in the oven. There was a separate table for the smaller children. The shelves held pecan and pumpkin pies and two white frosted cakes. They alternated looking into the pot of greens. Noise came from the men in the front room and the children in the yard.

Babe-Ruth was thanking the Lord: *Two are doctors. George teaches school and coaches basketball. Jessica's a social worker, Lona a secretary, and Ann a nurse. They married decent people, and nobody had trouble with the law. Jesop got married to a white girl, Jenny, and she treats him well and it don't bother me so much as it did at first. She is here and is just one of us. Most don't go to church.* She was about to call them in to say grace when the phone rang, and she pulled up a chair and talked awhile.

"It's time to eat, Ma'dear. You gotta get off the phone." Jessica turned to Ann. "She always had a lot of lady friends, usually about ten to fifteen years older. I'm surprised they alive." Jessica tapped her on the shoulder. Babe-Ruth didn't act like she heard.

"Now, you have a nice Thanksgiving, and you be sure to call again . . . That's your father wishing me a happy Thanksgiving."

"What he calling you for? He's got his nerve!"

"Watch your mouth, girl. He still your father. He's tried to get in touch with each of you. If y'all don't have anything to do with him, that's your business." She poured the steaming greens into the dish. "He calls me regula'. Used to be my husband, you know, and old folks likes to talk."

Jessica told everybody, and they gathered around as Babe-Ruth put the dishes out.

"What y'all looking at me?" she returned. "He told me about the conversation with Junior and the ones he tried to have with the rest of you. When Junior found him, I had ill feelings. I was afraid that after I stuck with y'all, y'all was gonna forget me. I was resentful, and I ain't felt so much like a sinner since I found the Lord. I got down and asked God to take my jealousy and bitterness away and clean my heart." She folded her apron over a chair. "Then, I felt good and clean. The Lord gave me a new heart. I been feeling good ever since . . . We just talk about growing old and relatives and things. I think he gets lonely and me and him is friends, not like husband and wife, but we share things. He's enjoying y'all's lives through me." She carried the steaming ham in. "Food's gonna get cold. Come in and thank God for this dinner he provided."

Babe-Ruth felt good having the whole family together. That night, she had a dream:

It was the end of a long journey. She straightened the curtains, noticing some dust on the windowsill. Her life was now the church and home. Maybe she would do some volunteering at the grade school. She paused and looked out. It was not a rarity in the past to see a horse pulling a cart of vegetables or a milk wagon. The change was deeper, but she didn't know why. The sun felt good on her forehead where her wrinkles had deepened, and her brown eyes with their gray halo gave her countenance a stately glow.

It seemed like yesterday. She looked around the room. The house was empty. She had brought them through as a family and taught them what she knew. After dinner, they'd sit around reading comics that would be passed from the oldest to the youngest, enjoying life and one another. Now they were on their own.

She settled in her chair for what seemed like the last time. It was the end of time, and the Lord God Almighty was judging the earth. On his right was the great book of deeds; an angel turned the pages, and edicts went forth. Over his right was a crowd. She saw herself with Jessica, Ann, Cal, Louis, George, Lona, and Jesop. Young Tom was there beside his daddy. So was Mr. Solum, Mrs. Clay, Sister Grant, Sister and Brother Crawford, and old Jesop, and faces resembling Caleb's and others.

She meditated on the dream and kneeled, releasing it to heaven as a prayer.

In 2005, Cal got news that their father, Caleb, had died. His oldest daughter and Cal's half sister, Elena, had called. He called Babe-Ruth and all of his brothers and sisters. Some seemed indifferent, but he really didn't know what was going on inside their heads. Little Jesop didn't react at all as far as Cal could tell. Years before, Jessica and her husband had met with Caleb in Cape Girardeau. After dinner, she asked him why he abandoned them and why he used to call her scarface. He broke down and cried. Cal spent a lot of time on the phone with Elena and sent money to help with the arrangements.

"What kind of man was Daddy?" He was getting to know Elena. She was working in St. Louis and had come down to take care of Caleb's affairs. He was getting acquainted with his half-sister.

"He always acted like y'all were better than us, like his Northern family was better."

"What was he like?"

"He was a good worker . . . mean . . . Are you coming to the funeral?"

"No."

"Can't come?"

"No, I can."

He still didn't know why he hadn't gone. Perhaps he never would.

It was 2010, and they were meeting at the church to celebrate Babe-Ruth's ninetieth birthday. It was snowing. He drove around the neighborhood and wondered if the local boys still shoveled snow for Mr. Writ, who, Cal reasoned, was close to a hundred.

The church's social hall was full, there was plenty to eat, and no one was in a hurry. She had touched many lives. Some shared secrets known only to them and her. She was quiet and thinking:

So many things have changed these many years. It is hard to believe. I remember the first car I saw and then airplanes and then they put a man on the moon. A black man president. I never would have expected it. He intelligent likes my boys, only younger. I taught them to blame themselves for their failures and not somebody you can't control. I almost always voted Democrat except for Ford. He was a nice man. I never told anybody that I ever voted for him. The Democrats think being real smart is all you need to be a good president . . . It ain't so. The Republicans think you only need to have a certain point of view, and that ain't so either. I don't know the world anymore. Everything's fast and change so often. Our country is blessed of God . . . If we don't appreciate it, we a stupid people.

George wished he had a whiskey. He was remembering being bitten by a dog; he was playing baseball, and Babe-Ruth came right unto the field. He barely got his catcher's equipment off before she took him to get a shot. Afterward, she trotted him to the dog's owner to deliver the bill.

Another time, he had a scalp infection because the bootleg barber didn't have proper sterilizing equipment. He remembered the inflamed growth plate and having to wear a cast for a month and the time she had the school principal change him from Mrs. Whitehead's third-grade class to Mr. Hauley's. It worked, and he liked school after that.

Cal was reminiscing too: *She delivered our newspapers so we could attend summer camp.* He thought about the time he was with a group of kids that broke the printer's window during a snowball fight. Each family had to pay $20, and it was 1954. She whipped him good for that, and a week later, she remembered it again and whipped him again. It was double jeopardy—something he swore never to do.

A few years ago, he had paid her credit card debt, which she used to keep up her house. The interest was so much that the monthly allowance he gave completely absorbed it. He paid it off and reduced her allowance. She promised not to use her credit card again. She went back on her word (she was in her early eighties), and when he confronted her, she replied, "I'm only human!" He had never used the I'm-only-human excuse when she chastised him as a boy. *The saint is claiming to be only human!* He remembered her challenge:

"You the oldest boy and I expect you to show it. If this family gonna be something and stick together, somebody gotta care about everybody . . . That gonna be you."

Driving back was easy; Lena slept in the back. Snowing increased, and Cal checked through the mirror and turned on the windshield wipers, keeping his eyes on the white lines, remembering the revelation on the stump when he was eighteen and thinking about Babe-Ruth's amazing life:

"God put us here for a purpose. We a light on a hill to show that with his help, a single woman could raise six kids and raise them right, and we'll have something left over to give."

His mind roamed, and he thought about his trip to New Jersey to give Dr. Willett's paper on "The Ethics of Medicine in an Undeveloped Country." He was returning to Atlantic City for the first time in more than forty years and was itching to see the old neighborhood. His uncle Mitchell and aunt Mildred were dead, and he wouldn't see anyone he knew. What prodded his mind was a game, and it emerged as a passion.

Scummy was somehow mingled with his childhood imagination and was played with brightly colored bottle caps. The best were found on whiskey bottles and shot like marbles between numbers and lines. He had forgotten most of the details, but the winner received the loser's tops in tribute.

He had become unsure over the years if it was his imagination or a real game. Babe-Ruth didn't remember it, and neither did his siblings. Perhaps it was a fantasy, along with angels, the revelation on the stump, miraculous healing, and shining rooms. When he met someone from New Jersey or nearby Philadelphia, he would ask if they played it, and no one had. He realized that Scummy might only be played by small black boys in a single neighborhood in the entire universe. And he was there.

Gambling had changed the jewel of the Jersey shore. The hotels were bigger and better. Mainly blacks worked the hotels when he was a boy. The thought came as he tipped a young white man who brought his luggage in.

Cal visited the old neighborhood. It was more run-down than he remembered. The row houses were gone. He looked down Indiana Avenue, and the old brick grade school was still standing. The grocery store that had been on the corner was now a vacant lot, the building on the opposite corner was sealed, and the sign with red paint pouring over a globe was gone.

"Hey, son, what's your name?" The small youngster walking toward him looked up.

"John, name's John." He was fat cheeked and bright eyed.

"John, did you ever play a game called Scummy . . . in the school yard?" The air thickened with anticipation.

"Oh, yes, sir, we play it all the time." He reached into his pocket and took out some brightly colored tops.

"Let me see." Cal weighed them in his palm, then reached into his pocket and handed him a dollar. "May I have some of these?"

"Take them all." The lad smirked, pocketing the money. Cal watched him advance down the street.

The old school was like he remembered it, but run-down. The floors creaked as he walked to the principal's office. It was empty, and after a few minutes, a young man entered.

"May I help you?"

"I'm wondering. I went to school here many years ago. Do the boys still play Scummy in the school yard?"

The young principal smiled like he was being asked if there was a sun or a moon. "Why sure. Can I do anything else for you?" Cal shook his head, pleased. "They play it all the time."

Cal moved down the avenue, caressing the tops. It was all as real as he was.

Epilogue

The generations of the Jeffersons were these. George secured the colonel's farm. It was over two hundred years old and one of the oldest in Missouri. Then and now, if you asked for Boss Jefferson, you got him. He was a lawyer and the son of Babe—Ruth's youngest son, Jesop, and the second to move back South as many blacks had begun to do. In addition to practicing law, he was a farmer with over two thousand acres, including a legendary oak, and ten acres of forest. He reasoned his grandmother was great, and that was the reason they had given her that nickname.

George II attended West Point and was an officer in the Iraq War. He was begotten by George (who served in Vietnam), the brother of Cal Jr. and little Jesop, both of whom became physicians. Caleb married Babe-Ruth when she was fourteen, and he served in World War II. Caleb's daddy, Jesop, never knew his father and took on the Jefferson name.

Light in Winter

(A Mama's Prayer)

In the 1930s, Caleb and Babe-Ruth and their growing family migrate to New Jersey to live with his sister and her husband to find work and taste modern living for the first time.

After Pearl Harbor, he is drafted into the navy, then returns from the Pacific a drinker and a changed man to find that Babe-Ruth has found religion. Relatives and neighbors buffer their discord until they move to Michigan and face their differences alone.

The Michigan neighborhood is racially mixed, and she prepares them for work and school, and they settle in. He works hard, and in spite of their troubles, they purchase a house, making him proud. Things go well for awhile, and he returns home drunk and fires his service revolver over Junior's head to frighten Babe-Ruth. A week later, he is drunk again and beating her when Junior eats rat poison to stop him.

Junior's suicide attempt, the shooting, and an almost-fatal explosion at work make Caleb reconsider his life. He talks to the preacher and is baptized and is in the throes of decision when he suddenly abandons them. Babe-Ruth is destitute and pregnant with her sixth child but will not accept welfare (ADC) and weans the boy to find work and guide them through a tumultuous and changing America.

Short Autobiography

This is the first novel for O. Henderson Jr. His other works include essays, editorials, an unpublished children's book, and a collection of poems. He is a retired physician and volunteers in the USA and Nicaragua with Hope Clinic and Hoper Clinic International. He lives in Ann Arbor, Michigan.